A Date with Danger

A Date with Danger

A Novel

KARI IROZ

Covenant Communications, Inc.

Cover image *Lost in Blues* by 101 Dalmations, *Night City* by Peshkova, *Salt Lake City, Utah, USA* by Chris Hepburn.

Cover design copyright © 2016 by Covenant Communications, Inc.
Published by Covenant Communications, Inc.
American Fork, Utah

Printed in the United States of America
First Printing: June 2016

22 21 20 19 18 17 16   10 9 8 7 6 5 4 3 2 1

ISBN 978-1-62108-933-9

For my family. You built my road here.

For my Zach. Every love story I write pales compared to ours.

For my girls, Mina and Talia.
You're my greatest dreams come true.

And for all the Mormon girls who think you're nothing special.
Your adventure is coming.

Acknowledgments

IF I THANKED EVERYONE WHO has made this happen, the list would be longer than the book itself. Forgive me in advance for not thanking by name all those who've helped me on this journey.

First, I must thank my mom and dad. My greatest supporters from day one, you've spent thirty years believing I could do it. Thank you for keeping faith in me even when I had none. This never would've happened without you. Thank you for also teaching me the truths that have anchored my life. I know Heavenly Father because of you.

Thank you to my siblings and scores of nieces and nephews. You've helped me become who I am. You were my first readership, and your love and support sustain me. Sisters, I sure hope Damon meets with your approval.

Thank you to my husband, Zach. You healed me. You strengthen my faith. You make me better. You've put your own dreams away for so many years to fulfill mine. You've slaved over every book with me and are my unabashed groupie. Thank you for the husband, the father, and the man of God you are.

Thank you to my beautiful daughters, Mina and Talia. The world is so much brighter with you in it. Being your mom is my greatest honor. I hope someday to make you proud.

Thank you to dear friends who will see themselves in these characters and our misadventures in this story. You've been such a support and an inspiration. I love you all!

Thank you to beloved teachers and professors who have tried so hard to make something of me. Carpy, I finally got here!

Thank you to my editor, Stacey, for holding my hand on this road and finally bringing my words to the page.

And thank you to my Father in Heaven, who has given me everything and carried me all my life. I will try to deserve it.

1

Kill me now.

Seriously, if I have to stay at this wedding reception five minutes more, I'm going to bludgeon myself with a glass centerpiece.

Cause of death? Well, the centerpiece, obviously. Compounded by exposure to inappropriate questions ("Why aren't *you* married yet, Jacklyn?"), constant critique from the jealous singles ("Did you see the colors? Orange, pink, and yellow is *so* last year."), and an overdose of cake—because binging on junk food is the Mormon equivalent of getting drunk, the only way to survive these receptions.

It's inevitable. The second any single Mormon girl opens one of those fancy taupe envelopes with the hearts and roses postage stamp, she thinks, *Yup. I'm going to get cake-faced.*

In fact, if the average, single Mormon girl is anything like me, she probably gets started early by mooning over the invitation with a tub of ice cream. She picks out the cookie dough chunks and cries, "Look how cute this engagement picture is. See how he hugs her while she sits on a fence? I could sit on a feeeeeence . . ."

But we show up anyway. Gluttons for punishment? Maybe. Perhaps we see it as painful but necessary motivation, a reminder that we have to work hard to get here: the winner's circle, the reception hall (or the church gym depending on your budget).

And it *is* hard work to make it here. Gone are the days when you could just be your sweet self and expect that in due time you'd be picked out of the lineup by some cute RM.

These days LDS women seem to outnumber the men so drastically the competition is as fierce as getting into the Ivy League, maybe worse.

At least when you apply to Harvard you get to send in a résumé, list your credentials. As a single woman you have to walk around *as* your résumé. It's like you've got to be five seven, size two, blonde, beautiful, Relief Society president, state soccer champ in high school, play the harp and the piano, dabble in modern dance, speak three languages, be employed at a shelter for blind orphans, and have your bachelor's degree in homemaking before you merit a second glance.

Do I sound bitter? I guess I am a little. Probably because my personal dossier reads nothing like what's expected. My dating résumé would look something like this: Jacklyn Wyatt ("Jack" to everyone but my mother), twenty-five years old (which is roughly 103 in Mormon years), five five, size N/A, brunette, choir director's assistant in my ward, no language skills (unless you count ordering at Taco Bell), working the sales counter at Forever 21 (or Forever Minimum Wage, as I call it), studying literature with no graduation date in sight, and perhaps the worst homemaker on the planet (ingredients run from me in fear).

So you can see, my prospects are grim. When I recently turned the big two-five, it was like tattooing *spinster* on my forehead. I've never had much luck with guys in the past except for my lasting romance with Mr. Darcy from *Pride and Prejudice*. If only he knew about it— and was a real person—we'd be very happy together.

The other reason for the cake binge is because I've become resigned to the fact that this square of sugary denial is my date for the evening. It wouldn't be such a blow if I hadn't fallen victim to the idea that maybe a wedding reception would be a good place to meet guys. We all do it; it's part of why we go. Despite our loathing of the event, we think, *But maybe it's the place I'll finally meet* him. So we curl our hair in that loose "I wasn't even trying" way and wear our most strategic lavender dress that makes us look simultaneously classy and *fun.* Then we breeze in, trying to appear effortless and glowing.

That glow carries us down the reception line, shaking hands with total strangers and clocking the groomsmens' ring fingers. It wanes a bit at the gift table, where we deposit our regifted toaster, and gets thin at the guest book, where we debate whether we have it in us to put an exclamation point on "So happy for you!" And the glow finally sputters out as we stagger to the refreshment table.

Which brings me here—a corner table off the dance floor sucking the candy coating off the Jordan Almonds and glaring at the dancing couples. And eating cake. Sometimes, no lie, I turn up just for the cake. Because I'm a poor student and it's free cake.

Tonight the cake isn't quite lifting my spirits like it usually does. The atmosphere is nice enough. It's uncharacteristically warm for a spring evening in Utah. The reception is a backyard affair with ivy and roses climbing trellises along the fence line. Candles float in the swimming pool, casting rising and ebbing shadows across the faces of the guests. There are white lights strewn in the trees and pink and yellow petals dappling the stone walkway. With a man on your arm, this stupid place would be downright magical.

On the dance floor the bride and groom are swaying, lost in each other's eyes. I watch them—his hand on her cheek, a tangle of black and white in gown and tuxedo—and lick the frosting flower off my dessert. *Oh, that's good.* Real roses should taste like that.

"—dress is so predictable," says one of the girls at my table. I didn't know her name or any of the others. We all sort of landed here like we were beckoned by Sad Single Girl beacons. Despite their general consensus that this reception "lacks imagination," the girls look as miserable as I feel. Their curls are going flat, their heels have been cast aside, and one girl keeps sniffling noisily into a cocktail napkin. We're a pathetic lot.

"Cap sleeves, really?" the fashionista continues. "I mean, would you wear that dress?"

It's a minute before I realize their bleary, mascara-smudged eyes are all on me. "Me?" I ask. The critic nods, and I surreptitiously spit an almond into a napkin before answering. "Tough call. Cap sleeves are overdone, but really, what's the alternative?"

There are nods all around.

"I'd kill to wear strapless," one girl mutters.

"Garments limit the options," I agree. They continue nodding, and after a moment I add, "But really, why should I have an opinion? Sure, maybe *I* like the tulle skirt look better, but should I even think about it? It's probably safer not to have an opinion. I should throw out my shoe box full of color swatches and dress ideas I've cut out of magazines because really that's just setting myself up for disappointment. You know? In case it never happens for me, it's probably better not to . . . hope."

They all stare at me for several seconds. Then the sniffler bursts into tears.

"Well," I say, gathering my keys and purse as the others halfheartedly try to console her, "I guess my work here is done." Muttering an apology, I slip my heels on and totter toward the dance floor. *Made someone cry. Fine work, Jack.*

Candace, the blushing bride, and I were in choir together in high school, and I feel like I should say good-bye—even though she's too blind with bliss to notice.

Halfway there I'm intercepted by a short woman wearing a cloud of perfume that nearly gags me. "Jack, dear!" she gushes and embraces me, nails digging into my arms. "How are you enjoying the party?"

"I'm fine, Sister Daniels," I say. It's Candace's aunt, who I met a couple times at concerts. "And you?"

"Oh, it's lovely." She glances around dreamily and then clasps my hands in her overly soft palms. "I do so hope to see you married, dear. Why haven't you?"

The dreaded question. Honestly, how do they expect you to answer this question? Like you have some control over it? Like you receive an annual form in the mail: *Would you like to be married this year? Mark the box: Yes or No.*

I sift through the usual answers: a) Just focusing on school. b) I want to be really ready so we can start a family *right away.* c) Waiting for the Spirit to tell me it's time. But for some reason, tonight I'm tired of pretending. "I don't know," I answer with a smile. "I guess something's wrong with me." I cross my fingers. "Maybe next year!"

Sister Daniels looks so gobsmacked I feel a little bad, but when I step back to retreat, I topple into the person behind me. A steadying hand on my elbow keeps me from falling, but both my ankles turn, and I stagger, trying to regain my balance.

"Sorry," I say, still leaning on the catcher as I bend to retrieve my shoe. "I, uh . . ." I look up and momentarily lose my words. "I didn't mean to—"

The guy still holding my elbow is looking at me so intently I nearly draw back. It's not a look of attraction, just extreme focus—like he recognizes me. I don't know him, but I'm still a little stunned. Not by his looks exactly, he's not that much of a looker. He's cute enough, with a strong jawline and features and dark eyes. His hair is dirty blond and a little unruly but not in a brooding, disheveled way. More in an "I've got no time for product" way. He's only a head taller than me and not super muscular. There's something about him that makes me not mind leaning on him. As I scrutinize him, he raises both eyebrows in question.

"Sorry," I stammer and shove on my shoe. "I've got two feet."

His mouth twitches. "Isn't it two *left* feet?"

My cheeks blaze at the blunder. "Yes, that's the saying, but I'm unsteady enough with them exactly as they are."

His lips twitch again and crack at the edge in an almost-smile. "I see. Well." He lets go of me. "All right now?"

I nod even though the toes on my right foot are bent under. "Sure, sure."

"Okay then." He nods and turns, headed for the refreshment table. I watch him dither for a moment, select a plate, and sprinkle on a few peanuts before he glances back in my direction. I swivel toward the exit, fighting not to limp with my foot curled wrong inside the shoe.

No good-bye to Candace, I realize when I reach my car. But it's too late now. I wouldn't go back in there for the whole cake, no matter how good the roses were. I unlock my rusting car, step out of my shoes and toss them in the backseat, and slide behind the wheel. There's a blister on my left ankle, frosting on my skirt, and the slimy decoated Jordan Almonds I was hoarding in a napkin have spilled inside my purse. "Another successful evening in good old Provo, Utah," I grumble and start the engine.

It's only eight forty-five, so there's still time to salvage the night. In my book, that means Chinese food and an old movie. Something classic to reinforce the illusion there are still gentlemen in the world.

I snake my way through downtown Provo, where the storefronts lining the main avenue are already beginning to darken. Despite being a college town, most places in Provo close at roughly nine o'clock. Any late-night entertainment must be found in the dining hall of fast food franchises or at the dollar movie theater. Established around Brigham Young University, Provo is a hodgepodge of the old and the new. The ancient malt shop where my own parents courted over a banana split is now neighbor to modern crazes like Café Rio and JCW's. Beautiful relics of architecture like the Provo tabernacle stand between an Abercrombie here and a Fitch there, but these symbols of progress operate within a sheltered setting. The familiar ridgeline of mountains encircling the valley reinforces the feeling that there is no world beyond this place, at least no world I've ever met.

Leaving Provo behind in mere minutes, I enter Orem, Provo's younger sister. Also a college town, Orem is centered on Utah Valley University. My own mom didn't hear a word I said about UVU's excellent English program or the growing school. She was in mourning about having to attend football games in a new color. When I told her UVU didn't yet have a competitive football team, I learned the definition of the scriptural "wailing and gnashing of teeth."

This time of night, the Panda Express parking lot is sparsely populated. The strong, hot aroma of spices greets me as I open the door, and for a moment I revel in it. That is the smell of happiness. In my case it's also the smell of being single.

I bend to examine the dishes behind the glass case, but I always get the same thing. "Yes, chow mein, please," I say. Creature of habit. Before the Blockbuster next door went out of business, every Friday night found me here—orange chicken and a chick flick. My wild, wild party life.

Just as I'm pointing at the orange chicken, I notice a blond head near the far door. A guy is standing beside the garbage can with the collar of his dark jacket popped around his face. He's typing on his phone and is turned slightly away from me, but I'm almost sure it's the same guy from the reception.

I straighten, trying to get a better look, but he stays turned away, focused on his device. Isn't that the same guy? *I could swear . . .*

"What entrée?" The girl behind the counter is talking to me.

"Uh, double orange chicken, please." I smile apologetically and finish my order, the hair prickling along the back of my neck. When I get my cup and move toward the soda machine, he's gone. No sign of him beyond the window in the parking lot either.

"Excuse me." I approach the counter again, and the dark-haired woman behind the register looks up. "Did, uh . . ." Now that I've started into this I feel ridiculous. "The guy who was just standing here by the garbage can, did he order anything?"

The woman, whose name tag reads *Lupe,* narrows her eyes. "Yes?" she asks, her voice slightly accented. "He order."

"Can you . . ." I laugh self-consciously. "It sounds so strange, I know, but can you by any chance tell me what he looked like?"

She blinks at me. "Beijing beef."

"No, I mean"—I motion toward my own face—"what he looked like? Did he have like, dark eyes and blond hair? A pretty, uh, strong jawline? You know, like the kind from classic literature?"

She blinks again. "Cream cheese rangoon. Three."

"No, I—never mind." I smile awkwardly and turn away, embarrassed by my own weirdness. So what if the reception guy was here? Is he not allowed to get Chinese food too? Panda is a popular place.

Walking back to my car, order in hand, I check my phone. Two texts from my older sister Jen, the first an hour and a half ago: *Do you have my blue cardigan??* Then fifteen minutes later: *I know you have my cardigan, filthy sweater thief.* And an angry-face emoticon.

Three voice mails from Mom. She knows about the wedding and no doubt wants a status report. My mom is an amazing, kind, giving woman of faith. Her vocabulary is also strangely limited to the phrase "When are you getting married?" With my two sisters happily wed, Mom's entire world revolves around hustling me to the altar.

And before you say, "Oh, my mom's just as bad," hold your tongue. No matter how bad you think your mom is, mine takes the cake. And by that I mean she literally *takes the cake.* She steals wedding cake from receptions. Of course, she would strongly object to the word "steal." Her version is that she "borrows a few extra pieces" for research.

What research, you ask? Her research for my reception. Oh, wait, I'm not even dating anyone, let alone engaged! But don't try telling her that. She just waves it off with a little smile and head wag like this is an insignificant detail and then checks on the pot roast. And her *Jacklyn's Wedding: Fingers Crossed!* Pinterest page is a bit much.

Not that I mean to paint her as a cliché, but she is one. Clichés get that way because they're the extreme of something. Mom is the extreme.

I click into the voice mails, listen for about four minutes to her cheery, "So how were the flowers? What fabric were the bridesmaid dresses? Did they have dinner mints?" before hanging up and dialing her directly.

After two rings she picks up and trills, "Details! Details!"

"Hello, Mom," I say, but she's already talking over me.

"How was the wedding? Was Candace beautiful? How did she do her hair?"

"It was lovely," I say wearily, knowing we'll get nowhere until the questioning is over. For all her sweetness, Mom would be a great police interrogator. I can just imagine a bright light and her sugary voice demanding, "Was it taffeta or silk? *Taffeta or silk?!*"

"Candace was beautiful. Her dress had cap sleeves, which caused quite a stir at the lonely hearts table."

"And did you . . . meet anyone there?"

"Not so much." *Except for a brooding stranger who may now be following me.* "There weren't that many guys there."

Mom clicks her tongue. "Where are all the young men these days? Why do they no longer attend weddings?"

Probably because they know we're all on the hunt. "No idea."

"Oh, well." I can hear the rhythmic *thwump* of her kneading dough like she does every Saturday night. Conversations with Mom are always underscored by the sound of some chore—the snip of pruning shears as she trims roses, the slap of folding laundry. It's like a homemaker's quiet symphony. "Your cousin Gina's reception is in May. If you meet someone there, that would still leave enough time for a summer wedding."

Again, this is my wedding she's talking about. You know, the one to my nonexistent fiancé? I don't mention that May is only four months from the end of summer—and I haven't even met the guy yet. She's operating on Mormon Standard Time, which can conceivably mark a mere eight weeks from "Hi, I'm Lemuel" to "See you at the altar." Happens all the time.

Just not to me. I'd rather try out a guy for longer than it takes to break in a pair of jeans.

"Are you coming to dinner tomorrow?" she asks, the percussion of her kneading continuing.

"Of course." I always attend Sunday dinner with my family. It gives them a chance for a physical inspection to be sure I'm nourished and not yet covered in piercings. "What're we having?"

"Roast." She gives a little chuckle. It's a family joke, as ... . eaten pot roast every Sunday since I was a fetus. "Big surprise, I know."

"Can I bring anything?" I ask.

"Hmm, maybe some rolls. No, wait. I've got all this dough, and I'll have plenty left over after the bread. Maybe a vegetable. No, wait. The beans from my garden are ripe; we better use them. Maybe . . . a dessert? Although, I still have some of that custard thing I took to choir. Well, just surprise me."

"Okay." I stifle a laugh. We have this same conversation every Saturday night. She never actually gives me a food assignment. Half the time I take a handful of old candy bars that my sisters and I sneak before the meal. "I gotta go. I'm driving home, and I just picked up dinner."

"Jacklyn, it's not good to eat a big meal this late." Mom's voice is low like we're discussing a national secret. "It will wreak havoc on your . . . *digestion*." She's always embarrassed by words that have anything to do with bodily functions. Even something as mild as *digestion*. "Really, you shouldn't eat after seven p.m."

I don't mention the half a pizza I had at eleven last night. Or that I ate the rest at two a.m. when I couldn't sleep. "I'll remember that," I say. "See you tomorrow, Mom. Love you."

"Love you. Rest up for church!"

It's nearly nine fifteen by the time I pull into the lot of my apartment complex and tramp up the stairs to the second floor. I always live on the second floor or higher because Dad insists it's safer—something I regret from the first time I have to lug groceries up the stairs. Sometimes I'd prefer an intruder over eight trips from the Laundromat.

Groping for the light switch as I open the door, I haul the food sack in and drop it on the kitchen table atop a biology book. The kitchen, directly to the right of the entryway, serves as more of a library and junk food dispensary. The table is littered with textbooks, paperback novels, and my typewriter. I like to write first drafts of papers on it. The sound of the keys is like something out of an old movie. The countertops are similarly strewn with literary anthropologies, cereal boxes, and empty paper sacks from fast-food places. Most of the time if I'm at the stove, I'm using the cooktop to balance a book while I wait for my corn dogs to heat in the microwave.

To the left of the door is the living room, dedicated to comfort. The squashy red couch and love seat are pointed toward the TV and piled with beaded throw pillows and plush blankets. Here is where I eat, study, write, and engage in my favorite pastime: lounging with Cary Grant and Jimmy Stewart. Sometimes James Dean if he's in a tolerable mood. Both sides of the TV are stacked high with videotapes and DVD boxes. Orchids in every color spill from pots. Even though I'm an indoor creature, I love orchids, plants, and camping. I'd live in a tree house provided there were corn dogs and a working VCR.

Dropping my keys in a bowl near the door, I head toward the only bedroom, past framed snapshots of my family that line the hall. There's my oldest sister, Delia, laughing with her kids; Jen's wedding portrait; my brothers playing football; and my parents' old engagement snapshot. To me, family photos make a space. It's not home without their faces around.

My sister Jen calls my bedroom a "Hindi explosion." A deep-purple canopy shrouds the small bed obscured by tasseled pillows. Gilded lanterns hang from the ceiling, and ceramic elephants perch on the dresser and crammed bookshelf. "Seriously, it's like India threw up in here," Jen had said. But it was probably as close to world travel as I'd ever get.

I shrug into a pair of striped pajama pants and a T-shirt and stuff the lavender dress into the back of the closet. I'm not trying to be cute anymore.

At least not for a while.

Back in the living room, I have just settled in to watch Cary Grant run for his life on *North by Northwest* when a shadow catches my peripheral vision. I turn toward the window, suddenly chilled despite the quilt around my shoulders. The gauzy red curtains are more decorative than functional and don't entirely block the view from outside. Backlit by the porch light across the hall, someone has passed directly in front of my window.

Heart thumping unevenly, I cross to the window and cautiously push back the curtain to peer out. The apartment across from mine looks dark. The girl who lives there—Amber or something—is a graveyard-shift waitress and doesn't usually get home until the middle of the night. Ours are the last doors in the hallway, which means no one would come this way unless their destination was my place or hers.

Unless they were lost. Maybe they got down here and realized they had the wrong apartment. But the rest of the corridor is equally empty. Whoever it was had to clear out of here fast.

Maybe I imagined it. Or it could've been a trick of light bouncing off the TV. But in that fleeting moment, the shadow had looked exactly like a person's silhouette.

And it if was, where did they go?

As I stare into the hallway, I have the sudden impression that someone could be in shadow at the end of the corridor, watching and silent.

Shivering, I step back from the window and push the gauze curtain back in place. I return to my movie.

But not before getting a butcher knife from the kitchen.

2

I'M STILL ALIVE IN THE morning, owing, no doubt, to the bookshelf and armoire I pushed in front of the door and the knife I kept on my nightstand.

And the can of hairspray. Just as backup. There's a possibility I overreacted. A little paranoia is inevitable when you live alone.

I've got to stop watching *CSI* before bed.

I drag myself to the bathroom and halfheartedly get ready for nine a.m. church—the worst time slot. It takes about eight pieces of clothing to make one modest church outfit: a shirt, a cardigan, a skirt, and another skirt since the first skirt isn't long enough but the second is partly sheer. It's seriously impossible to dress simply these days. It's either a muumuu or a bikini. And there are days when I'm tempted by the muumuu. It would be easier.

The church building is roughly a forty-five-second drive from my house, so I dawdle as usual and walk out at 9:03. Parking is impossible. The spot I find is halfway back to my apartment, and I huff into the chapel at 9:09 during the last strains of the sacrament hymn.

I slide onto a bench next to my old roommate Bridget, sing the last two notes, and try to pretend like I've been there all along. Bridget gives me a sidelong glance of mock disapproval and a little smile before we close our eyes for the prayer.

While the sacrament is being passed around, I open my scriptures and try to concentrate on my current chapter. But my gaze keeps roving about the chapel. Being in a Utah singles ward is like a weekly beauty pageant. Seriously, there are pretty girls everywhere. Glamorous blondes, demure brunettes, even the occasional redhead. I almost don't blame the guys for not knowing where to start.

I do, however, blame them for only asking out the same half dozen girls while the rest of us wait around. When I see the contestant from Pleasant Grove with her perfect teeth and her platform to "make the world a better place with brownies," I kind of get it. Referring to a numerical system of hotness, Bridget likes to say, "The problem here is that any guy, even like a 4 or a 6, can have an 11. Any guy!" I'd rather not know my number.

My eyes linger briefly on "Ring Row": the bench along the back lined with glassy-eyed, hand-holding engaged couples who found each other and no longer need to sit closer to the front where they can be noticed.

Then, there in the back left corner, is the guy. I mean *the guy*—the blond from the wedding reception that I stepped on, the one I thought I saw buying Rangoons—*that* guy.

He's sitting calmly near the door in an immaculate suit and gray tie, one ankle crossed over the opposite knee, hands knit in his lap and looking totally at home.

My stomach lurches up to my teeth.

"Bridget," I hiss, poking her in the ribs.

She looks up from the *Ensign* app on her phone and mouths, "What?"

I point subtly over my shoulder at the guy, adamantly looking toward the ceiling as I do so. Bridget follows my finger and raises her eyebrows with interest.

"Cute," she whispers.

"I know he's cute," I mutter fiercely. "That's not what I mean. What's he doing here?"

Bridget's gaze narrows. "I'm going to say . . . attending church?"

I roll my eyes. "Have you ever seen him before?"

"No."

Someone on the bench in front of us hisses, "Shush!" and I lower my voice even further before asking, "Don't you find that a little suspicious?"

She shrugs. "Maybe he's new."

The shusher glares, and I glower back. That's the problem with singles wards; they're so *quiet*. In a family ward, there are so many babies crying and kids howling you could set off a bomb and the speaker would go right on talking.

New in the ward. That's a possibility. With all the marriages, the turnover here is fairly high. It's like a new group every week. But what are the odds I'd see the same guy at a reception Saturday night and then at church the next morning?

Okay. In Utah Valley it's possible. But it *feels* suspicious. Like when a guy insists that helping with his laundry and eating Lucky Charms is "totally a date." You just know you're being played.

Need more recon. I open a hymn book and sink down behind it, trying to watch him surreptitiously. He doesn't have a set of scriptures with him. Since the invasion of the smart phone, lots of people read their reference books digitally. Or they pretend to so they can text in church. If he has a phone, it's put away, but he could just be pondering.

Like you should be doing. Not playing detective.

With a stab of guilt I open my scripture set and give him a final glance when I notice the sacrament tray moving down his aisle. When the guy to his right offers him the tray, he lifts his flat palm and gives a tiny shake of the head, declining it.

There could be a lot of reasons for declining the sacrament, chief among them not feeling worthy to take it. One of the three times in my life I slipped a swear word, I declined the sacrament for two weeks. Which may have been a bit excessive, but I've got a guilty conscience the size of Texas.

Or maybe he's not a member. That's entirely plausible. *But if he's not, then what's he doing here?*

Bridget has noticed me staring again. "Do you know him?" she whispers.

This isn't the time or the place to go into it. What would I say? No, I don't know him, but I think he may be stalking me? Instead I just shake my head and try to read.

I stoically ignore the stranger for the rest of the meeting. But after the closing prayer as we all rise from our seats, I turn, scooping my purse off the bench. As he gets to his feet, he makes eye contact with me—just for an instant—before striding out of the chapel.

3

"Freak out much?" Bridget asks.

The regular block of church meetings has concluded, and we're at the Munch and Mingle in the gymnasium: an excuse to eat store-bought lasagna and do more socializing or, in my case, lingering by the dessert table.

Since I have family dinner soon, I'm not eating, but I munch on a brownie while Bridget butters a roll and surveys me with expectation. "Want to explain yourself?"

"I don't even know where to start," I say, picking nuts out of the brownie into a discard pile.

"Well, you saw that guy and wigged out." She gives a dazzling smile. "Overcome by his raw masculinity?"

Bridget is one of those infuriating people who happens to be beautiful and genuine at the same time. With naturally platinum hair nearly to her waist and green eyes as big as a cartoon woodland creature, she can stop guys in their tracks. Literally. Once when we were walking through an intersection, a guy on a bike saw her and pedaled into a truck. She'd be married ten times over if she weren't so hard to catch. We'd lived together two years of college before the spirit of adventure whisked her off to Africa to go on safari. She's tried everything from Sherpa to mechanic but is too much a dreamer to settle down. If I didn't love her like a sister, I'd hate her for being so fabulous.

"It's embarrassing," I say, balling the nuts up in a napkin.

"I once saw you pee your pants," she reminds me. "How is this worse?"

I half-shrug. "I saw him last night at that reception that you refused to attend with me."

She snorts. "Attend a wedding I'm not obligated to go to? What am I, suicidal?"

"Then I thought I saw him at Panda after."

Bridget looks up from her roll, eyes narrowed. "You went to Panda without me?"

"No pain, no Panda—those are the rules. Then he shows up here today . . ."

"So in Utah you saw the same Mormon guy at a wedding *and* church?" She gives a fake gasp. "Conspiracy!"

"Yeah, yeah." I wave her off. "But then there was this creepy shadow outside my apartment. I don't know."

A thin guy approaches the table, hands thrust into his pockets. "Hey," he says, his awed gaze on Bridget.

She flashes him a brilliant smile and answers, "Hi!" He responds by turning tail and sprinting out of the gym. Bridget sighs. "Poor guy."

"Just another dude whose therapy you should pay for." I sound glib, but this is a fairly common occurrence. She often drives men to paralysis.

"So," she fiddles with the end of a long curl, "where were we? Oh! The creepy shadow outside your window."

"Never mind." I cup my face in my palms. "I'm losing it."

"Or just overworked." Bridget snags the corner of my brownie. "Have you been sleeping at all with finals coming up?"

"More than I should. I've still got three papers to write."

She nods thoughtfully. "You think maybe you're trying to deflect your stress by focusing on that guy instead of your work?" Bridget's current area of study is psychology, and she's taken to it with the same passion she took to opera last semester and archaeology the semester before that.

"Why, thank you, Dr. Bridget. It's all clear now." I place my feet in her lap and lean back like I'm reclining on a couch. "I think it all started with the bed-wetting . . ."

She pushes my feet off her knee. "I'm serious. Try and take a break." Her eyes light up, and she claps. "Shopping!"

I know we sound like typical girls, but our affinity for shopping is not typical. We're serious about it. We could go pro if only the Olympics would recognize it as a sport. It requires training, stamina, and you have to carb up beforehand or risk dropping off in the second round. How is that not a sport?

"Maybe later this week." I finish the brownie and, mouth still full, ask, "Want to come to dinner?"

"Nah. Going tunnel singing."

"You could weather the sea of children and still have time."

"Got to give myself a facial first. I found the best scrub. It makes your skin feel like new."

This time the guy edging toward our table like he's about to address Congress is squat and sweating profusely. About six feet away he gives a shy wave and says, "Hi there. I'm Eli."

Genuinely friendly to a fault, Bridget replies, "Hey, Eli. I'm Bridget. Care to join us?"

Eli's shirtfront drenches with sweat. He begins to shake so violently that I'm starting to worry he's having a seizure before he runs for the exit. He and the first guy will probably have side-by-side asthma attacks in the hall.

"Wow," Bridget says, brow knit with concern. "Should we check on him?"

"I'll do a drive-by as I leave. He'll never recognize me. Next to you I'm utterly invisible."

"Shut up," she says good-naturedly and points at me. "Girls' night."

"Girls' night, soon," I agree and wave on my way out. As I suspected, both brave souls are still recovering in the hall, but neither has passed out. I stride by with a quick, "Maybe next week, guys."

Nothing unusual happens before I get to my parents' house for dinner. As I step out of the car to retrieve my plate of cookies from the backseat, I glance up and down the street. It looks like a normal, quiet Sunday afternoon. Not many kids playing. Most are inside with their families eating, doing their acceptable Sabbath activities. The green, manicured lawns are empty, the homes hushed. I see Sister Martin across the street sitting at the piano in her front room and faintly hear the strains of Chopin. Everything normal here.

Yet paranoia persists.

Shaking my head, I pick a path up the sloped driveway. The house has familiar beige paint and a black-tile roof with tall windows and flower boxes. Mom's rose bushes are just budding in white and yellow.

Dad's old Buick perches in one corner of the driveway like a giant dog that has gone to sleep and rusted there. Dad always talks about restoring it, but if he ever actually moved it, all the neighbors would get lost—it's a local landmark. For a moment I breathe in the familiarity of roses, car grease, and potting soil before ringing the doorbell.

The bell is met by a chorus of muffled shrieks and a stampede of little feet rushing up the hall. After a quick argument ("I wanna open it!" "No, it's *my* turn!"), the door squeaks open and two small faces appear around the jamb.

"Jack!" cries Daisy and launches into my arms. "We've been waiting for you!"

"Have you?" I ask. Jeremy Jr. has already wound himself around my ankles, and I struggle over the threshold with both of them. Once inside I'm clobbered by about ten more pairs of arms and legs and tiny faces crying, "Where've you been? What's in your purse? Do you have candy for us?"

"Take it!" I tell them, relinquishing my meager plate of cookies. "Take it—just spare me! I'd taste awful." Half of them move off with the plate and instantly tear open the tinfoil. My Oreos will be gone in approximately twenty seconds. The other half of the kids remain attached to me, all talking at once.

"I got a new pony animal with pink hair—" Daisy is telling me.

"There's a new boy in my class named Matthew—" says Jeremy.

"I has fingers!" tiny Anna declares, splaying her hands for me to examine.

"—and it has a sparkly tail—"

"—um, he has four dogs. I mean, not four but three dogs, and the big one had puppies—"

"Mama paint my fingers!" Anna's digits are right up in my face now as she shows me her purple polish.

This is one of the things I love about kids. They're full of so much exuberance it just pours out of them. "They are so pretty!" I tell Anna, then to Daisy and Matthew in order, "What's your pony's name? And that's awesome, dude. What kinds of puppies did it have?"

"Okay, let her breathe a bit." My sister Delia is ambling out of the kitchen with a stack of bowls and utensils in the crook of her arm. "Help finish setting the table. Jeremy, take the forks, and no stabbing anyone. Daisy, set out the bowls. Thank you." She hands off the dishes, then plops Anna on her hip.

Her daughter is a miniature of her—caramel curls and dainty features with huge brown eyes. Delia's one of those wonder moms who teaches Primary and bandages a scraped knee while simultaneously baking fresh bread and looking completely unruffled by the whole thing. I can barely keep track of all her kids as she has roughly twenty of them. Or maybe it's only six.

"How was the reception last night?" she asks, giving me a side hug and fixing Anna's crooked sock.

"Disaster." Stripping off my jacket, I hang it on a peg and hook my purse handle over it. "I don't know why I even bother going to those things."

"The food?" Jen has followed her out of the kitchen, her pregnant belly preceding her into the room. She embraces me around the bump and chomps on a dinner roll. "That's why I'd go. Then again, these days I'd go just about anywhere for food."

"How much longer?" I ask, touching her belly in the hopes of catching a kick.

"Five weeks. I can't wait that long." She leans on Delia and takes off her shoes. "How have you done this *six times?*"

"The first is the hardest."

"Really?"

Delia smiles. "Not so much, but let's pretend for now."

A younger version of Delia, Jen has the same snapping brown eyes, and her chestnut hair is cut in a pixie. Naturally slender, she's *all belly*. From behind she doesn't even look pregnant, and then she turns around and *bam!*

"Don't worry," I say. "This baby will probably be graduating college before I give it a cousin."

They cock their heads in twin looks of sympathy. "Don't be silly," Delia says. "You have plenty of time to find the right guy."

"Any guy would suffice at this point. Ooh!" I point at her wedges. "Love the shoes!"

Our conversation turns to trivial things—though to us great shoes will never be considered trivial—and we slowly migrate to the kitchen, where Mom is smuggling custard to the grandkids.

"Mom!" Jen laughs. "What do you always say about spoiling their appetite?"

Mom waves her off. "That's for a mom to say. Rules for grandmothers are different. Hi!" Smelling of flour and sage and warm bread, she comes around the island to hug me. For a moment I close my eyes, inhaling her and the warmth of the cozy kitchen. No matter how old I get, coming home always feels the same.

"Munch and Mingle?" she asks when she pulls back. "Successful?"

By that she means did I meet any guys and fall madly in love over the mixed salad. Her eyes, copies of my sisters' and lined with wrinkles, are full of such hope I can't bring myself to completely crush it.

"Maybe," I hedge, scooping a gob of mashed potato on my finger to my mouth. "There were a few nice guys." *Of course they were proposing marriage to Bridget, not me.*

"Really? Oh!" She bustles back around the island to take the roast from the oven. "A summer wedding would be so lovely!"

Jen rolls her eyes, and Delia pats my shoulder.

It's best to distract her. "Can I help with anything, Mom?"

"No. Everything's just now ready. Take these things into the dining room." She hands off a dish to each of us. I take the bowl of potatoes and sample another bite en route. At the head of the table, I push aside Dad's newspaper to kiss his cheek and take a seat to his left. He gives me a warm smile and returns to the news. Reserved and gentle, I've never known Dad to raise his voice or waver in anything. Always there's that calm smile. It makes me never want to disappoint him.

Jeremy Sr., Delia's husband, wrangles the last two kids to the table—one over each shoulder—and deposits them in their seats. Dad sets his paper aside and folds his hands, signaling us all to bow our heads for the prayer.

"Father in Heaven," Dad begins, his voice reverent. "We thank Thee this day for Thy incredible bounty and blessings. We thank Thee for the gospel in our lives; for our ever-expanding family; and for Thy Son, who has given us everything. Please bless us all with Thy spirit, and bestow Thy protection upon Steven. Help him to feel our love."

Peeking beneath my lashes, I reach out and clasp Jen's hand. She squeezes back, but I see her chin quiver slightly. Steven is her husband, serving his second tour in Afghanistan. Every day we pray he makes it back to see their baby girl.

"Bless this food which Thou hast given, and know of our great gratitude and love. In the name of our beloved Savior and Redeemer we pray, even Jesus Christ, Amen."

"Amen," we all echo. Jen releases my hand and is smiling as we open our eyes, her brave face on.

Over roast and potatoes, Mom (who we sometimes fondly call FIN for "Family Information Network") gives a detailed update on family members from our four brothers scattered across the states to the most distant cousins I've never heard of. I swear the woman knows everything about everyone. She really is an asset that law enforcement is neglecting.

". . . told me that Lucy is pregnant again."

"Who?" Jen asks.

"Cousin Lucy! Her ninth, apparently."

"That's a lot of kids," Jeremy Sr. says.

"You two could catch up," Mom suggests with a chuckle.

Jeremy smiles as his namesake son slaps a carrot against his dad's face. "I think we're all set."

"Helloooo!" a voice trills from the front door. "Knock, knock!"

My heart plummets.

"Come on in, Muriel!" Mom calls. "We're at the table."

"I'm not strong enough for this today," I mutter to Jen.

"What do they say in church?" she murmurs back. "Your affliction shall be but a small moment?"

Muriel strides into the dining room. There's something like Mom in her big eyes and broad, smiling mouth. But she's taller, broader, imposing, even in her proper church dress and pantyhose. Her brown bouffant adds at least a foot to her already daunting stature, and her long red fingernails are like talons. At least that's what I thought when I was a kid. That she might just pluck me up like a vulture.

I wasn't wrong.

"Well, hi!" she says, spreading her syrupy smile over the assembly. "This all looks delicious." She purses her lips slightly. "I see you couldn't wait for me to arrive."

"You said you'd be late," Mom says, motioning to the empty seat. Perhaps it's just Mom's naturally sweet nature or the effect of growing up under the constant scrutiny of a sister like Muriel, but my aunt's sugar-coated insults, grating to everyone else in the family, seem to roll off Mom as though she doesn't realize she's being insulted. I'm glad for her. At least one of us is safe.

"Well, I'm sure it won't be too cold. Roast is still tolerable at room temperature, I suppose." Muriel moves down the line of the table squeezing the cheeks of each child in turn (they shrink back from her talons the way I used to) and deposits herself in the only empty seat at the table.

Directly across from me.

I wish I were back at the wedding reception.

"Roast again, eh, Linda?" Muriel asks, reaching for the meat platter. "How very original."

"You don't fuss with a classic," Dad says and winks at Mom, who giggles into her napkin.

While Muriel loads her plate, I hurriedly clean mine, hoping that maybe I can finish, claim a headache or something, and skip out early. Or at least I could hide in the bathroom for a while—

"Do take time to chew your food, Jacklyn." Muriel licks gravy from her fingers and looks up at me. "It's rude to eat so sloppily in the company of others."

"Rude, yes," I say, but I'm not talking about myself.

She clearly doesn't catch my sarcasm. "It's well known that eating too quickly can lead to weight gain." Her eyes rake over me. "You have put on some in the last year."

You know that relative who exists only to remind you exactly how worthless you are? That's my dear auntie Muriel.

"Well, I eat to cope with the loneliness. Being without a boyfriend and all." I smile. "Perhaps you'd like to talk about that now."

"I don't like to glory in other people's suffering," she says, her face devoid of humor. "But perhaps if you took better care of yourself, that wouldn't be the case."

I nod and load my plate with seconds.

For the next half hour, I personify gluttony in an attempt to drown out the catalog of my shortcomings. Muriel drives the conversation, stopping off here and there to scold others, but she always steers her way back to Jack. For some reason I'm her favorite. Lucky me.

Muriel's husband, Uncle Bert, died when he was only forty-five. They said it was a heart attack. But I once heard Dad, who has never before or since insulted anyone, tell Mom that Bert must have gotten tired of hearing what a quitter he was and finally agreed. Mom, drinking a glass of juice at the time, choked and reprimanded him without being able to fully conceal her smile.

Bert and Muriel had five kids who all happen to live at least a state away. So she works as a florist to pass the time and spends her Sundays with us. Yay.

"And it's well known that girls over the age of twenty-three are not getting married," Muriel is saying, daintily scraping gravy residue off her plate. She always uses the phrase *it's well known* when she's stating an opinion for which she has absolutely no foundation. "Our missionaries are coming home serious about finding a companion, and most of them do that by the time they're twenty-two or twenty-three. Single girls above that age have very little hope of finding someone." She gives me a tight smile. "*Of course* there's still hope for you, Jack."

I nod and continue shoveling in corn.

Muriel's watching me. "Although, if you still want a chance at a man, you may want to slow down."

"I have to go." I'm standing, napkin still tucked into the top of my skirt, before I even realize I meant to get up. There's so much corn in my mouth I have to really chew before anyone can understand me. "I have . . . tunnel singing. Yes. There's singing, and"—I do a square motion with my hands—"a tunnel."

"Now?" Mom asks. "We still have dessert."

"And games!" puts in Daisy.

"Yes, but there will be men there," I say, backing toward the door with a fork still clutched in my hand. "And clearly I need to get on that. Not getting any younger or thinner, apparently."

"Don't be silly." Mom comes around the table to me. "You're staying, and you can sing in a tunnel later. Help me with dessert."

No better arguments come to me as she leads the way to the kitchen and places the custard pie in front of me. "You cut that while I get the cherries."

Selecting a large knife from the wood block on the counter, I hear Muriel say from the dining room, "You sure Jack should be helping you with that, Linda? You know how she gets around pie."

I pantomime stabbing myself with the knife and thump my forehead down on the countertop.

4

No creepy stalker follows me home. Although, after dessert and several rounds of charades with Muriel condemning the technique of my mime abilities, I almost wish someone *would* murder me.

I manage to slip away early enough for tunnel singing but drag myself home instead. A mountain of homework stares at me from the coffee table, but I can never bring myself to do school work on Sundays. All my growing-up years, Mom and Dad didn't allow it. Even when I would beg, "But I have hours yet to finish this project due first thing Monday!" they would calmly reply, "All right. Do you want me to wake you up at midnight or five a.m.?" At the time I couldn't understand why they wouldn't make a single exception to their honoring-the-Sabbath rule.

Now I get it. By the time I got to college, it was just habit. And no matter how ill-prepared I am for a test or how far behind I am on a paper, leaving Sunday for the Lord ensures that I'll get it done. I've never failed, no matter how little I knew Saturday night, when I waited until first thing Monday to finish cramming. One of those things your parents say, "You'll thank me later," just happens to be true. Darned if they weren't always right.

Sunday passes into Monday with a Jane Austen novel, and then it's back to the grind. Mondays I only have one class in the morning, and then I'm off to the mall for an afternoon shift.

Working retail is one of those college things, overrated and painful but part of the experience. At my age so many have graduated and moved into their professions or are already bouncing babies on their knee. And here I am folding tank tops for the thousandth time so I can just refold them as soon as some teenybopper paws through the pile and then abandons it because "They don't have my size!"

I'd like to accidentally smack them with a sales sign.

Music thunders through the speakers, and the dazzling lights bore into my skull, giving me a headache in five minutes flat. I know I'm supposed to be young and hip, but it is really loud in here. I asked my manager, Tanya, about it once, and she replied, "It's to give, like, a club atmosphere to the place. So the customers feel like they're already partying in our clothes." Then she trotted off on her four-inch heels to greet more teenyboppers coming in.

Currently I'm on "go-back" duty, which is hustling the rejects from the fitting room back to their sections on the floor. I know the layout pretty well, but with new shipments and changing floor arrangements, it's almost impossible to keep track of where every single item of clothing actually goes. So half the time I guess and just hope it's close to where it's supposed to be. Besides the guesswork, go-backs aren't a bad gig. Especially as it gives me a chance to scope out the new shipment and decide what items I'll be trading my paycheck for this week. Sometimes I feel like they should just skip drafting me a paycheck at all and let me work for clothes. Cut out the middle man.

"Excuse me?"

I've been admiring a black cocktail jacket and suddenly realize someone's talking to me. "Hmm, yes?" I whirl around guiltily and almost hide the jacket before remembering I'm allowed to hold it.

"Do you work here?" The pinched voice belongs to a girl with a pinched face, enormously teased hair, and a posse of poshly dressed, disdainful-looking teenagers behind her.

"Yes." I smile. "How can I help you?"

She thrusts a sequined party dress toward me. "Do you have any more of these?"

I take the dress and look it over with a very scrutinizing expression, buying time as I rack my brain for where this stupid dress came from. *Wait—wait! I know this one.* It's on display to the left of the accessories.

"Yes, if you'll follow me." I cross through menswear to the right with them all trooping behind like an anorexic parade. When we arrive, I motion to the display. "Here we are."

The girl flicks through too fast to really be looking at sizes and then scowls. "Do you have any smaller than this?"

Her posse folds their arms at once like they've practiced this. Synchronized snobbing.

"Smaller?" I push to the back of the rack and select the smallest dress. "Here you go. Extra small."

She tsks loudly. "I already *have* extra small in my hand." She shakes the sequins in my face, and her posse tisks in a round. "What I *mean* is do you have anything *smaller than this?*"

I'm nodding slowly. "Smaller than extra small?"

She pops her gum in a way that says, *Obviously.*

"I'm afraid not." I replace the dress on the rack. "I'd try Gymboree a few stores down. They should have what you need."

It takes her several seconds to realize she's been insulted. She makes a noise of disgust, flips her long hair over one shoulder, whipping me in the face, and stalks off. Her posse flings their hair each in turn and follows, strutting out with the exact same amount of swagger.

I've got to give them credit. That's a well-honed routine. I sigh and straighten a scarf display, reprimanding myself. That was a rude thing to say. Sometimes my mouth runs off on its own. It's one of the flaws I'm constantly repenting for. Besides, as an employee I'm supposed to live and die by the mantra "The customer is always right." At least she didn't tattle to my manager on her way out.

"Hey." Rhea—a smiling brunette with a nose stud—is just coming on shift, taking her purse and jacket toward the break room. "How long you been on?"

"Only"—I check my watch—"forty-two minutes. Time stops in here."

She laughs. "At least we're on the rest of the shift together. Want to get an Orange Julius on lunch break?"

"We'll never get our break together. Tanya's on a tear. Speaking of—" Our manager is headed our way on her towering heels, and I hurry toward the rack I left in the black-and-white section. "Gotta get back to go-backs."

"Clever." Rhea heads off to the break room, and I return to my task, trying to look busy.

I'm trudging toward the fitting rooms for more clothes when I spot a guy in the menswear section. Not really unusual for there to be a guy in menswear. What is unusual is his apparel. He's wearing a suit. Our guy clothes cater more to the hipster crowd with graphic tees and sweaters. This guy is wearing a tailored black suit, a crisp white button-up, and a dark tie. He's idly riffling through a rack of clothes I could never picture him wearing, but his gaze isn't on the merchandise. It's wandering around the store.

Weird.

Maybe he's just trying out a new look. I return to my work, trying to find where in the world this stupid little skirt originated, but my eyes keep swiveling back to Suit Guy. Now he's at a rack of fedoras, picking them up at random and putting them back. Many customers shop with no intent to buy. I myself shop when I'm too broke to even afford a button, just for the pure joy of looking. But he's not really looking. He's just sort of handling things and watching everyone else.

His gaze suddenly drifts to me, and we make eye contact.

Panicked, I duck behind the rack and wait several seconds, my heart pounding. Then I slowly part two jackets to peek. He's still looking my direction.

After nearly a minute, he turns back to the fedoras. Staying crouched, I creep through racks and around displays, trying to be inconspicuous. A pair of girls laughing over boots notices me as I crawl by, and they stop to stare. "Hello," I say with a broad smile as I crawl along. "Are you finding everything all right?" They just nod mutely.

A display table across from menswear is draped with maxi dresses that hang down in front, the perfect hideout. I slide under the over-hanging skirts and lie on my stomach to peer out beneath the hems.

Suit Guy has moved on to men's jackets but isn't even pretending to look anymore. He's just standing there, his gaze moving back and forth, and I swear he's looking for me. After a moment he's joined by another man in a twin dark suit.

There are two of them.

The second guy turns, and he's wearing dark sunglasses. Inside.

They're the Men in Black!

Oh, my gosh. What if there's an alien in the store? I don't really believe in that stuff, but it would sure take the boredom out of go-backs.

They converse for a moment, looking very serious, and then both turn my way. Though I know they can't see me, I shrink back into my hideout. As long as I stay here—

"Jack?"

I jerk, startled, and whack my head on the underside of the table, rattling my teeth together.

Tanya, my manager, is gaping down at me. "What are you doing down there?"

Massaging my throbbing scalp, I manage, "Just, uh, go-backs. Isn't this, uh . . ." I hold out the little skirt still clutched in my hand, "where this goes?"

Only now do I notice the store's district manager standing behind her.

Tanya is smiling in a terrifying way, her teeth bared like a jackal. "Come out from under there," she hisses through clenched incisors, and when I hesitate, she takes my arm and drags me out onto the floor like an overturned beetle.

Oh no. They've spotted me. The Men in Black have spotted me. They're striding across the store.

"Tanya!" I gasp. "You don't understand. You've got to call the authorities or something—"

Two pairs of shiny black shoes have stopped beside me. "Jacklyn Wyatt?" one man asks, his voice impossibly deep.

"No," I say at once.

"Yes," Tanya contradicts me.

"Yes?" asks one of the Suits.

"Yes," Tanya insists.

He points at her. "You're Jacklyn Wyatt?"

"Yes!" I exclaim.

"No!"

The Suit is scowling now. "You're *not* Jacklyn Wyatt?"

"No, I'm not!" Tanya insists and thrusts a finger down at me. "*She* is!"

Both grim faces turn down toward me.

"Hello," I say feebly from my back, giving a little wave.

"Miss Wyatt"—the one in shades flashes some kind of badge—"we need you to come with us."

5

I'VE BEEN ABDUCTED.

I've been *abducted!*

And you know what? No one seems to care! Now I understand how these things happen in movies. I always thought, *Oh, come on! Nobody saw them kidnap that girl?*

But it's true. The Suits march straight through the mall with me pinned between them—which must've looked suspicious enough—but I also frantically whisper, "I'm being abducted. I'm being abducted!" to everyone we pass. And the only people who actually looked at me acted like I was nuts.

When I get dismembered, it's on them.

We even passed one of those regenerative skin kiosks, and when the worker approached and asked, "Do you have a minute?" I responded, "No, I don't have a minute, I'm being abducted!" She looked completely unfazed and instead approached a customer strolling behind us while the Suits marched me on.

As we near the exit, I realize I should yell, shout, make a scene. If I attract attention and cry for help, surely mall security or someone will intervene. But what if one of them has a gun in his pocket pointed at me as we walk? What if they've fit the entire mall with hidden dynamite or something and are just waiting for me to resist before they blow the place up?

I could kick them in the shins and make a run for it. I definitely know this mall better than they do, and I could get lost in the middle of a clothing rack somewhere and not come out until next week. That is, unless they're planning to explode things if I don't cooperate. Or they might take someone else hostage.

Is that what's happening here? Am I a hostage?

Why could they possibly want me? My brain wildly reels through any possible reason they could want me. I'm flat broke, and my parents do okay but could never pay a ransom or anything. Maybe I saw something I wasn't supposed to see and don't even know it. Like at work I happened to glimpse a random stream of numbers which, if plugged into a key pad on an island directly at the center of the equator, blows up the core of the earth or something.

Yeah. Because that kind of information would be lying around the paperwork at the local Forever 21.

Or maybe they think I'm someone else! Yes, it's a case of mistaken identity.

Except they called me by name.

Maybe it's some kind of revenge thing. For a wild moment I wonder if the little army of teenyboppers has anything to do with this. It just goes to show, you should never provoke someone that skinny because they're bound to be hungry and mad.

We pass the security desk, and my mouth opens to cry for help, but no words come out. Moments later we've passed, and Shades is opening the exit door to lead me through.

The sunshine warms my hair, and as we march through the parking lot, I observe for a moment what a nice day it is.

A perfect day to get kidnapped.

They steer me to a dark SUV parked in the handicap spot right at the front of the lot, and the other guy unlocks the doors with a remote. I parked my own car on this side of the mall. Employees have to park at the very far side in the white spots, but maybe I could break away, run to my rust bucket—

Outrun two huge linebackers and manage to unlock the car before they catch me? Sure.

Shades is already ushering me inside and closing the door behind me like a nice gentleman kidnapper. At least they teach manners in Criminal School.

The second the door closes, I tug on the handle but it's locked. I slide over to the other door. Locked too. By then both men are climbing into their own seats in the front, and with a barely discernible rumble, the car comes to life and we're backing out of the space.

It all happened so fast.

Tanya saw them take me, but I doubt she did anything about it. She probably thinks it's appropriate punishment for someone who shirks their responsibilities and hides under display tables. In fact, she probably sent them to teach me a lesson about employee work ethics.

The driver turns right out onto University Parkway. And a minute later (traffic is far too light for this time of day—further proof of the conspiracy), they take the exit right onto the freeway headed toward Salt Lake City.

You're never supposed to actually get in the car with a kidnapper. Didn't I hear that in school somewhere? You're supposed to make a stand and force them to action before you get in because the statistics for survival drop rapidly once you change locations. If you get in the car, chances are pretty good you're not coming back alive.

So I've already done the number-one thing you're not supposed to do.

Palms sweating, gut tying itself in knots, I riffle through the mental catalog of all the crime thrillers I've seen in my life, searching for a solution. Several scenarios come to mind:

A. Jerk the steering wheel so the car crashes and you can run away.

I've seen this done on lots of movies, and the bad guy always gets banged up worse than the hero so the hero can disappear into the darkened forest with a head start. Downside: We're on the freeway going about seventy-five miles an hour. A crash at this speed would probably not help much, and there's no darkened forest to retreat to anyway.

B. Kick out a taillight and wave your hand so drivers behind see that you're in distress and they call in the license plate.

Downside: I'm not in the trunk, for starters. I could try kicking out the window, but I'm wearing worthless little ballet flats and the glass would turn my legs to mush. Besides, if I'm waving from a window, people won't think I'm in distress, they'll just think I'm being friendly. Fat lot of good that will do.

C. Send a smoke signal of Morse code.

Downside: I don't have any smoke. Or know Morse code.

D. Steal a cell phone off one of the guys and hotwire it to phone a random stranger, who then follows my clues to find us and rescue me.

Downside: I have no idea how to hotwire a cell phone. And if I got hold of a cell phone, I wouldn't hot-wire it, I would just call for help.

E. Fake a seizure and get them to pull the car over.

I could maybe manage that. Especially if I had some kind of tablets to put in my mouth to fake foaming at the mouth. Downside: No tablets, and very little shoulder here on the freeway to pull over. And even if they do pull over and I manage to get away, there's nowhere to run but straight into traffic.

F. Keep sitting here, wait until we get where we're going, and then hope to formulate a plan of escape.

Yeah, I think I'll go with F. Mostly because I don't have another option.

I grate my damp palms back and forth across my jeans compulsively, but the sweat just seems to keep coming. Maybe I have one of those glandular disorders that cause excessive sweating.

Or maybe I'm just scared out of my mind.

We're passing American Fork already, speeding toward Salt Lake at what seems to be a superhuman rate. Where could we possibly be going? I imagine all the places between here and wherever that could serve as a tiny hole in which to stuff a body.

Maybe I should do what victims do sometimes and try to identify my killers on my person somehow. Then at least in death I can point the finger at the thieves who robbed me of life. I could use blood or something to write their names on my stomach, where they won't think to look. The problem is I don't know either of their names. I can't just write "The Men in Black." That wouldn't narrow the suspect pool very far. Besides, blood makes me nauseated. Even if I could cut myself, I'd pass out before I could write anything.

I'm the most worthless kidnap victim ever.

How many times have I watched movies where fussy girls get abducted and they just cry and go along with it? I always thought, *Why don't you do something, dummy? Be proactive! Hit him with a board! Jump out of the car!* But now that it's me, I'm plastered to the seat with fear.

We're coming up on Lehi now. Beyond there's Thanksgiving Point and then Salt Lake City about thirty miles out. If they wanted to take me into the wilderness, they could easily do so once they pass the Point of the Mountain. My mouth is bone-dry at the thought.

Neither one has spoken a word since we left the store. They're absolutely silent in the front, staring straight ahead. Maybe it's a psychological tactic to put me on edge before we get where we're going. It's working.

I could ask, I think. *I could just ask where we're going.*

Something about actually interacting terrifies me. Their silence, though unnerving, isn't definite. They haven't confirmed the thousand atrocities swimming around in my brain, but if I ask where we're going, they may respond with, "To meet your new children, wifey dear." Or "To keep company with the worms and the maggots." And if they say something like that, my already tenuous composure will crack and send me spiraling into complete horror. Maybe it's better if I don't know.

But we're passing the Point of the Mountain now, and suddenly I can't bear the silence. "Where are we going?" I ask. My voice is so small I have to clear my throat and repeat the question.

Shades glances back at me and says, "We're not at liberty to say, ma'am."

Ma'am? That's unusual for a kidnapper. Now I'm back to the Men in Black theory. Before I can stop myself, I blurt, "You guys know I'm not an alien, right?" Shades turns to look at me, his expression stony, and then stares out the front again. I lean back into the seat, blotting my palms and trying to keep a rein on my breathing.

Please, Father in Heaven, I find myself praying. *Please let this be okay.*

At the speed of light, we've reached Salt Lake. I'm surprised when they take the Fifth South exit and follow the traffic surging into downtown. What is there in downtown Salt Lake? A murder lair? A secret government UFO facility? Some kind of brothel?

Coldness grips my stomach. They could be selling me into human trafficking. I saw a documentary on it once. They could be taking me downtown to some kind of auction where I'll get purchased by a foreign gentleman for a thousand rupees or whatever currency the foreigner uses.

"They just need to speak with you," Shades says as the driver guides the car onto a side street.

They? I get bold and ask, "Who are they?" He doesn't answer me.

After a few minutes we reach an area of town that looks mostly deserted. Here brick buildings have fallen into disrepair, their faces marred by layer upon layer of graffiti. The driver navigates the car to a squat, gray building with rows of identical windows, and we stop in front of the steel wall of a closed garage. He pushes a button on the dash, and the garage door lifts to give us entry. Shadow swallows the car as we enter the garage.

We pass no ticket machine or toll booth on the way in, and I notice as we travel down the row looking for a free space that all the cars are exactly the same. All black and navy blue SUVs. What kind of place has the exact same car parked in every space?

Now I'm hearing the *X-Files* theme in my head.

Our car slips into a vacant space near a stairwell. Shades comes around to my door to open it. He doesn't put a hand on me or try to restrain me as I get out, and I realize that this is my opportunity to run. But I've seen the movies. Chases in parking garages never end well. So I wait as he shuts my door and his buddy arrives, the two of them flanking me again. Shades motions a hand toward a bank of elevators, and I start to walk. They keep exact pace with me, not touching me but clearly an alert escort, ready to react at any moment.

When we reach the elevators, the other guy pulls some kind of key card from his jacket and swipes it over an electrical reader beside the elevator door, the type of device that unlocks the pool at my apartment complex—but I'm guessing this card probably has a much higher level of clearance.

Shades flashed a badge back at the store, I suddenly remember. In the haze of terror, I'd forgotten, but he did show some kind of official identification. Maybe the elevator doors will open and Mulder and Scully will be waiting for us.

Sadly, the elevator cab is empty when it arrives, and I step inside obediently. They remain at my sides and press a button for the fourth floor. There are only five floors and two parking levels. No secret underground chamber that runs forty floors below the surface. Surely the *X-Files* people wouldn't be housed in some regular, five-story building. Would they?

No plucky elevator music accompanies our ascent, and I'm half tempted to make some bad joke. I have a habit of using humor to defuse awkward situations. But the closer we get to our destination, the more my mouth fills with bile. I can hardly swallow over it.

On the fourth floor, the doors swoosh open and reveal a rather drab office space. On the left sit endless rows of open cubicles. Suited, severe-looking men and women type away at computers, consult files, and converse on landlines. To the right, a glass wall encloses a chain of personal offices. Here, too, professionally attired men and women are on phones and at computers. Periodically one stands before a bulletin board or at an incongruous piece of equipment, but there's nothing instantly identifiable about what people are doing here. No shackled women clustered in dirty cages or glowing aquariums encasing alien remains. So I guess human trafficking and Area 51 are both out.

We proceed up the hallway, though by now my legs are more jelly than solid. Some look up as we pass, their faces impassive and humorless. I think of appealing to one of these people for help, but they don't seem alarmed or even surprised by my arrival. I'm guessing they're all on the same team here.

Halfway across the floor, another corridor curves off to the right, and Shades points, indicating that I should take that branch. This hallway is even barer. Gray paint, closed doors on either side. A few doors down, both men stop. One of them opens the door and leads me inside.

There's nothing here but a metal table and two metal chairs. And a mirror, which is probably two-way like they have in police stations. I take a few steps into the room and hear the door close behind me before I realize they've left.

And locked me inside.

6

KIDNAPPED. BROUGHT TO SOME KIND of strange facility. Locked in an interrogation room.

Not my best Monday.

I spend the better part of half an hour banging on the two-way mirror, demanding someone talk to me, to tell me where I am, to let me out. No one comes or responds, but I can imagine them on the other side of the mirror, watching.

After a while I circle the metal table like a restless animal, chewing obsessively on my thumbnail. Panic has made my knees weak, but I'm scared to sit down. The chairs frighten me, mostly because I've seen what happens in interrogation rooms. They always start by sitting you down and strapping you to the chair. Then come the questions and the beating and the ripping out your teeth.

I'm not built for torture. I'll crack like an egg.

Finally, when I can pace no more, I plunk resignedly into one of the chairs and put my forehead down on the cool metal. *Please, Father, please,* I'm praying again. *Please get me out of whatever this is.*

I hear the hinges of the door squeaking open and jerk my head up.

The guy struts in.

"You!" I gasp, jumping up from my seat.

He ambles to the table and holds out his hand. "Damon Wade."

"Of course *you're* here!" I cry, ignoring his hand. "It's a conspiracy—I was right! And I'm not paranoid, by the way. I've been abducted, and *you're* part of it!"

"You haven't been abducted," he says calmly. "Please, sit."

"I was taken from my place of work by Hostile 1 and 2, dragged here, held in a room against my will, and you want me to *sit*?"

"It's all easily explained."

"Then explain it! Because so far," I shout at the window, "no one will even tell me where I am!"

He sits. "You're in a secure facility."

"Secure facility," I snort. "What are you, FBI?"

He doesn't flinch. "Yes."

That takes the wind right out of me. For several seconds I just blink at him and then manage, "Oh."

Gaze steady on mine, he wordlessly indicates the chair, and I sink despondently into it.

He straightens his tie. "As I was trying to say while you were ranting, I'm Agent Damon Wade, and you're at an FBI field office."

"This has got to be some kind of prank. Did Jen do this?" I have sudden inspiration and jump to my feet again. "Is she *this mad* about the blue cardigan? For crying out loud, she got it at a thrift store!"

His mouth twitches. "Not a prank."

"Then a hallucination? Some kind of fever dream? I thought that orange chicken tasted a little fishy. Well, not fishy like fish. Fishy like . . . suspicious."

Damon cocks his head. "Do you ever stop talking?"

"Panic makes me ramble." The adrenaline fueled by my fear is starting to die down, making the shakes in my hands worse. I take a deep breath and clench my fingers together to stop the trembling. "By the way, if you are the good guys, you should all be *shot* for handling this like you did. You scared the crap out of me. I thought I was going to die!"

"No need for panic. If you'd just . . ." He motions for me to sit, and when I deliberate he presses, "You do know how, don't you? You bend your knees and kind of sink down."

I glare at him and perch on the edge of the seat. The cold of the metal seeps through my jeans.

He folds his hands. "You've been brought here because we need your help."

"My help?" I chuckle nervously. "You sure you have the right girl?"

Damon flips open a file on the table between us. "Jacklyn Wyatt, aka Jack." His gaze flicks up to me. "Interesting. I wouldn't take you for the masculine name type." Looking back to the file, he continues. "Born September 18, 1989. Attended elementary, junior high, and high school in Pleasant Grove, Utah. College at Utah Valley University. Studying English literature. Employed at Forever 21 in the University Mall."

"My record of mediocrity." I nod.

"Shops for necessities at Walmart. Often buys eggs, ice cream, and sour-cream-and-onion potato chips. Watches a lot of old movies. Favors Hitchcock and classic murder mysteries. Frequents the Orem Library more often than the library on campus, probably because the Orem facility rents out movies. Frequents the dollar theater once a week or so. Always has lunch in the university cafeteria and reads Elizabeth Peters." He looks up.

I'm thrown. "How do you know all that?"

He closes the file. "I've been watching you for a while."

"Creepy," I say.

"Necessary," he counters.

"Why?"

"I needed to know what kind of person you are."

I lean back. "And?"

Damon shrugs. "Predictable. Nonthreatening. You seem fairly reliable, if a little dull."

"Is insulting the prisoner a normal thing with abduction?"

"You passed a cursory inspection, which is why I approached you."

"Yeah. If you're actually FBI, you're the most non-ninja agent ever. I totally saw you."

"Saturday," he nods. "What about two weeks before?"

I wet my lips. "No, I did not see you then."

"Saturday and yesterday you were supposed to see me. I needed to know how you react when threatened." He looks up. "You stayed calm."

"Not exactly." I tuck hair behind my ear. "I put furniture in front of the door."

He makes a small sound that might be a laugh. "Regardless, you didn't run to the police."

"Fat lot of good it would have done me. So you *were* at the Chinese place?"

"Yes."

"And outside my apartment? You were the sinister shadow?"

"Wasn't exactly going for sinister, but I was there."

"And why me? Why do you need me?"

"Do you know a Natalie Paul?"

"No. I don't think so."

He opens another file and pushes a photo across the table to me. "She's a student at the University of Utah, and she disappeared five weeks ago."

The girl in the photograph is blonde, trim, and laughing, posing against a tree trunk. "Disappeared?" I say. "How—where?"

"Just gone from her apartment. The last person to see her was the cashier who rang her up at Albertson's. She bought bananas and butter. Somewhere between there and home, she disappeared." He slides another photo to me—a silver car in a parking spot. "Her car was in its assigned space at the complex, and there were no signs of a break-in there or at her apartment. There has been no ransom note, no communication at all. Her parents—both teachers—live comfortably but aren't rich by any means. Natalie lived on student loans, so money doesn't seem to be a motive. Near as we can tell, she had no enemies, no one who would want to hurt her."

"Maybe she ran away—"

He nods, indicating this has been covered. "She was two semesters away from graduating and had been accepted to medical school. She had a lot of family in the area and was well-connected in the community. There was nothing missing from her place. All her clothes were still there, and we found a few hundred dollars cash in the sock drawer. Her purse was there, her car—nothing to indicate she'd run away."

"That's definitely weird."

"In five weeks, we've had only one lead."

"What?"

"Natalie had recently begun online dating. From her profile, we have a list of suspects based on the men who contacted her."

"Good for you." I nod slowly. "What's this got to do with me?"

"We need you to help us vet the suspects."

I chuckle. "How could I help with that?"

Damon hesitates. "Are you currently a member of Eter-knit-ty Online Dating?"

Realization dawns. "Oh no," I say. "Oh no, no, no, no. I'm not—no."

He consults my file. "You joined about four months ago—"

"No, I didn't join. *I* did not join. My sister Jen signed me up, created my profile, everything."

"But it's still your name on the profile."

"I haven't touched it since she signed me up. I haven't even looked to see who contacted me." I pause. "Okay, that's not true. I did look once. But I got spooked after this gardener guy asked me to be the mother of his prize squash."

Damon's eyebrows rise. "Well, there are all types out there. We've narrowed it down to eight suspects, all men who contacted Natalie through Eter-knit-ty." He produces a stack of e-mails. "Six of those eight men have also contacted you."

A chill scales my spine as I flip through the e-mails—greetings, offers for lunch or dinner. "You're saying one of these guys made Natalie disappear?"

"It's a possibility. But we need a closer look at them. That's where you come in."

"Me?" A hysterical laugh bursts out of me. "W-what are you talking about? I'm not a spy or whatever; I'm a regular girl."

"A regular girl is exactly what we need to get close to these guys. We need to know more about them."

"Then do your creepy stalker thing like you did with me."

"We've been watching them for weeks, but there's only so much you can learn from surveillance."

"Then . . . check out their histories."

"Done." He tosses a fat sheet of papers towards me. "Six of them are Mormon, all claim to be religious. Five of them are Eagle Scouts and returned missionaries. All are employed, nothing more serious on their records than speeding and a little high school vandalism. No red flags. Phone records have no commonalities with Natalie's except the few who phoned to set up dates. At this point we need contact, which leaves us with you."

I flounder. "There's got to be someone else."

"The most our suspect list was lined up with another girl was three—three who've e-mailed her. If you contact the two who haven't e-mailed you, they might respond. But she would have to win over six others. We don't have the time."

"Then"—I snap my fingers—"use one of your female agents! I see it on shows all the time."

"Again, no time. If we set up a new profile now, she'd be nowhere with these guys. The clock is ticking on this. Natalie's been missing five weeks. That's a century on the kidnapping time line. We have no evidence of foul play, which, to the Bureau, means no case. I've been granted a very small window in which to investigate. And if it *is* one of these men, their ability to contact all these unknowing women is cause for concern. It may happen again."

"Then use my name—have one of your agents pretend to be me."

"Your sister plastered your profile with pictures of you. Believe me, Miss Wyatt. We've run every scenario. You're the only option."

"So you want me to jump right in with some guy who may be a kidnapper or worse?"

"Your entire job would be gathering intel."

"I'm not trained for something like that!"

"You don't have to be," he insists. "All we really need to see is how these guys react to women: who gets attached too quickly, who shows warning signs when he doesn't know he's being watched."

"And by too attached," I bluster, "you mean what guy would be so enchanted he'd taxidermy me for his mantel."

Damon cracks a minuscule smile. "The threat to you would be minimal."

"See there? I'm concerned by the word *minimal* and how it's not the word *zero*."

"You'll be protected at all times, and your protective watch will double during the dates."

"*Dates?*" I echo. "Wait, wait—you said gather intel like answer an e-mail, not go physically to meet them in person like *in the field.*"

He chuckles low. "See? You already have the jargon down. You're perfect."

"No. I was iffy just at the thought of *writing* these guys. Actually going on a date is way too much."

Damon leans forward. "I can promise that you'll be protected. You'll be under federal watch twenty-four hours a day."

"There's no guarantee with that. Cops can be dirty, or the guy comes dressed like a delivery boy and blows away the security team."

"Jack." He pauses. "Can I call you Jack?"

"You've already called me dull," I muse. "Jack's an improvement."

His eyes twitch. "We're not dealing with a professional here. If Natalie was taken by one of these men, he's not a hit man or a trained killer. He's just a guy who got desperate and lucky. And it won't happen again."

"You can't be sure Natalie was his first. He could've done this before. And you know as well as I do that the best serial killers are the charming, groomed ones." I list on my fingers: "Ted Bundy . . ." I tap that finger against the table, thinking. "There's got to be some more . . ."

"True," Damon concedes. "Sometimes the most twisted men are the ones you'd never suspect. That may very well be what we're dealing with here. But if it *is* one of the website guys, we're on to him. And we *will* protect you."

"What if there's a mole? What if it's someone in the FBI?" I'm struck with sudden inspiration. "It could be you. Oh, that would be the best twist!" I laugh and then grow sober. "Only, I hope it's not since we're alone together."

"You can trust me."

"Ho, ho. That's exactly what the killer would say."

"Then you'll have to take my word for it."

"I don't have to take anything. Even if I was equipped for something like this, I honestly don't have time. I have school, my job."

"You can take a few weeks off," he presses. "We'll be sure your job is waiting for you. And I've been authorized to offer compensation for your help. A modest sum but still twice what you're making retail."

Twice. Not a fortune by any means, but I could stop eating Top Ramen for half my meals.

"It's tempting," I admit. "But I'm still too busy. And besides that, it scares the crap out of me. This kind of thing is all cool when I'm watching it on a movie, but in real life I'm a giant chicken and willing to admit it."

"The fact that you can admit it proves your courage."

"Yeah, I've got self-deprecation down, but put me in a dark alley with Mr. Stabby and I'm useless. I can't even play tag because I hate being chased. I just curl up and cover my head."

Damon leans toward me, his expression earnest. He's got brown eyes, I notice. You don't see many blonds with brown eyes. "Jack," he says. "I know you have reservations. That's normal. But we need you."

"But I—"

"Please," he interrupts. "Hear me out. Like I said, the clock's ticking on this. Ordinarily the FBI wouldn't even touch this case. There's reason to suspect kidnapping, but it involves an adult, and there's no indication that she's been taken across state lines. I act as a liaison between the FBI and state police when the Bureau has interest in a local case. The only reason I've been cleared to create this task force is because the state police have no leads and the operation I've proposed costs very little. If I don't have you, I don't have an operation.

"I want to find Natalie if we can, and I don't want this to happen to anyone else. You're our very best chance for getting this done. This guy might run, and we'll have lost our window. If that happens, we'll probably never find him or discover what happened to her."

He taps lightly on Natalie's picture. Reluctantly I pick it up again and study her face. She's beautiful and carefree. The smile goes all the way to her eyes. I feel a sudden tightness in my chest. "Did you say she has family?" I ask.

"Yes. And they deserve to know what happened to her, whatever the answer is."

My eyes prickle with unexpected tears, and I push the picture away. "I don't—"

"Please." Damon touches my hand briefly, his voice gentler now. "You're right that I can't guarantee your protection, but I promise to personally do everything in my power to keep you safe."

I blink rapidly, beginning to waver.

Damon swallows. "Please."

I'm imagining my own parents. What would it do to them if I was missing or Jen or Delia? If my sister had been taken, wouldn't I want the person who could help to say yes?

I lean back, slowly blowing out my breath. "What the heck? I go on lousy dates all the time. Might as well get paid."

7

I'VE AGREED TO GO UNDERCOVER for the FBI.

I'm like a female James Bond!

Diet Coke. Shaken, not stirred.

". . . any sort of personal information that might give us a better feel for them psychologically."

I'm sitting in a briefing room with Damon and Agent Jane Clemens—a woman with a severe brown bun and the unsmiling face to match. She's showing me files for each of the eight suspects and giving me a rundown on what I'm supposed to be accomplishing on these dates.

Despite feeling sick at what I've agreed to, I have the urge to take a quick selfie on my phone. It would be great for my scrapbook: *Me being briefed for my first big case!* I could decorate the page with little magnifying-glass stickers.

"Some of these guys may require looking at a second time," Clemens is saying. *Jane* is far too fluffy a name for her. Even her own parents probably call her by her last name. "So you want to connect with them enough to get asked out a second time. That's very important. Along with finding out personal information, securing a second date is your primary objective."

"So, like a regular date," I venture.

Damon gives a small cough, and Clemens purses her lips. "Indeed. Although the cursory first-date chitchat will not suffice. We won't glean much useful information from learning his favorite color and his major."

"I don't know how often you've dated Mormon boys," I say. "But I pretty much try to have an earth-shattering spiritual and emotional experience right out of the gate. It's the only way to stand out. Believe me, I've been training for this kind of thing my entire adult life."

"Let's hope so," Clemens continues. "We're taking a serious risk putting you in this situation. If you can't get what we need or you blow your cover, you won't just have wasted precious time, you may have let a kidnapper walk."

"It's good to start with low expectations," I say, nettled. "Really helps with morale."

She crosses her arms and perches on the edge of the table. "This is no joke, Miss Wyatt. It's not some fun little anecdote to tweet your friends about. There is a woman missing. By agreeing to this, you're agreeing to take her life into your hands. Are you prepared for that kind of responsibility?"

I glower at her. "I wouldn't be here if I wasn't."

"Good. I have personal doubts about the validity of this exercise, but as long as you're costing the Bureau money, I'll see to it that you're effective."

"You don't think this mission is a good idea?"

Clemens straightens her suit. "My personal opinion is that Natalie Paul walked away from her life. I find it careless to waste resources on a grown woman who's probably on a beach somewhere."

"She was on her way to becoming a doctor," I say.

"Exactly. So she's been pushed to excel her whole life, and she was locked into a future that guaranteed more of the same. More than one person has taken the option to just pick up and start over when faced with that kind of pressure."

"Then why is the mission happening?"

She glances toward Damon without actually looking at him. "Agent Wade has made the argument that if there's a predator selecting his victims via this website, the case falls under the realm of cybercrime. Which is something we are interested in."

Clemens stands again and points a remote at a projector screen, changing the image to another guy. Heavyset with dark hair and a puppy-dog face. "Skyler Randolf," she says. "He's one who has yet to contact you. We will take the liberty of e-mailing him on your account and see if he responds."

"You'll do that?" I ask. "Shouldn't I?"

"Skilled as you claim to be at the art of dating, we have people trained to make connections with other people. It's best to leave it to them."

"All due respect, but these guys didn't reach out to every girl on the site. Besides Natalie, more of them responded to me than to anyone else. Sure, Jen made my profile, but she used facts about me. There must be something similar about me and Natalie that these guys are drawn to."

Clemens muses, "Natalie was premed and an athlete. You work retail. I see very little similarity."

Ignoring the insult, I say, "Guys usually have a type. So if one of them fixated on Natalie, the person with the best chance of getting a comparable connection is me."

"I think she may be right on this," Damon breaks in from where he's lounging against the table, consulting a file. "If we're going to trust her with this, we need to trust her with all of it."

Clemens briskly straightens her suit again. "Fine." She clicks onto a new picture. "This is the other suspect you need to contact. Ralph Timen. He's in advertising at an agency in Salt Lake."

And waaay out of my league, I think. Ralph is dark haired, dark eyed, and has the kind of dazzling smile that belongs on a bus ad. I'm suddenly rethinking my insistence to write the e-mail myself. Maybe a professional flirter should do it—someone who can be witty or compose poetry or something.

But I just nod and say, "No problem."

Clemens drops the fat file into my lap. "Here's the extended dossier on each of the eight suspects. Get familiar with them and their backgrounds."

I pick up the file, as thick as a textbook. Truth is, these days I've perfected a method of reading as little as possible and still be able to write a paper. It's the only way I've survived the thousand-page-a-week reading quota. With this much information on top of my schoolwork, I'm already in over my head.

But again I just say, "No problem." I tuck the file into my overstuffed bag, bending the corners slightly to make it fit.

Clemens is talking again. "The one piece of evidence that indicates there may have been premeditated action is the letter."

"What letter?"

She points the remote at the screen, and my blood goes cold. A paper has appeared with scraps of words from magazines. In disjointed, borrowed letters it reads:

I could be your great adventure.

"This was found in a desk drawer in Natalie's apartment along with the torn envelope it came in. We believe it may have been sent by whoever took her. If, in fact, she was taken."

Hands shaking, I hug my bag to my chest and glare at Damon. "Well, I can see why you left this out when you were selling me on doing this."

"I didn't sell you," he counters. "Just told you the facts."

"But you conveniently left out the stalker note! This is a whole different thing!—It's like 'Puts the lotion on its skin' crap—which is from a movie I've never seen, but I think the reference is accurate." Panic is making me babble again. I take a breath. "With something this creepy at her house, what makes you think it was one of the Internet guys?"

"The word choice." Clemens changes the screen to an e-mail. "Natalie sent the same response to every man who contacted her through Eter-knit-ty. She closed the e-mail with the phrase 'I'm looking for a little adventure.'"

"Could be coincidence."

"Absolutely. But it could also be evidence." Clemens surveys me. "Does this mean you're out?"

"Well, I—I don't know," I stammer. "This all just got super real."

"The sooner you accept the full reality, the better," Clemens says. "I don't believe Natalie was taken, but if she was, the one who took her is a very dangerous man. You're putting yourself on the radar of a hostile individual by doing this. There's no way around that."

I nod slowly, my trembling hands making the buckles on my bag rattle.

"Now," she continues, "can you handle it or not?"

My gaze flicks to Damon settled so casually on the edge of the table, and some wild spite boils up in my stomach. I clench my jaw and say, "I can handle it."

"Good." Clemens brushes back an invisible flyaway. "I'll leave you with Agent Wade. He'll be your handler during this exercise."

"Oh, good," I mutter.

"Remember," Clemens says, crossing to the door, "Agent Wade has only been granted a ten-day window in which to conduct this exercise, and if you fail, there's not another chance. So don't screw up." The click of her heels is like gunfire as she goes into the hall.

"She should be a motivational speaker," I say.

"She's tightly wound," Damon agrees, standing. "The job will do that to you."

"So . . ." I give an uneasy smile. "You're my handler?"

"I'm in charge of the exercise. The task force I've assembled is made up of both agents and state police, and running that kind of task force is what I do. Plus they thought I could understand the culture."

"Culture?"

"LDS culture."

"LD—oh!" I'm surprised. "You're—"

"I was," he says. "I was raised in the Church."

I can't help pressing, "And now?"

"Not active." He nods once as if that's all to be said about it.

"All right, then." I tap a rhythm on the table, not sure how to fill the awkward silence.

"So . . ." He interlaces his fingers and sits on the edge of the table right in front of me—a little too close. "Operating procedures."

I sit up straighter, feeling a tiny pulse of excitement. "Yes?"

"As Clemens stated, I only have ten days to prove there's some connection between the dating site and Natalie's disappearance. So we want to get this thing rolling as soon as possible. We'll have you start e-mailing these guys and set up dates right away. As early as this evening, if you can."

"Tonight? That's fast."

"Well, time's not on our side. If you can even arrange for two or three dates in a day, that's better. The faster we do it, the faster we find Natalie. Arrange to meet them only at the sanctioned locations we'll give you. Never agree to be picked up. You will be driven to the location, and I'll position myself close by so I'm never out of earshot. Another agent will be on the entrance and one on the exit so there's no way for you to be hustled out of there. You and I will have a safe word to indicate you feel threatened, and if anything goes sideways, I step in."

"A code word?" That's unbelievably cool. "What—like 'purple hippo' or 'stampeding rhinos'?"

This time I'm sure his cough is a smothered laugh. "Let's keep it simple—something that's easy to work into the conversation if necessary. Since you'll probably be eating on these dates, let's say 'paprika.' Then you can say something like 'There's a lot of paprika in this.'"

"Paprika. Okay.' *It's no purple hippo.* "I say 'paprika,' and you neutralize him."

He coughs. "Exactly."

"And will I be, like, wearing a wire?"

"Not if we can help it. Wires can be compromised by technology in the surrounding area. It's also dangerous if you get spilled on, and it can spark suspicion. People tend to act very strange when they're bugged."

Not me, I think. *Two semesters of drama in high school.* But I keep this to myself.

Damon continues, "When you're not on a date, you'll be under protective surveillance by two agents at a time around the clock."

"You think that's necessary?"

"Probably not." He takes a swig of what smells like coffee. "But once you respond to these guys we don't want to take any chances."

"Better safe than a skin suit," I agree.

Damon chokes on his drink and wipes his mouth with the back of his hand. "You're resilient—to have a sense of humor about it."

"Either that or be scared out of my mind."

"We've notified your employer that you're helping local law enforcement with some clerking projects, but it's important that you tell no one about this."

"Not even my parents?"

"Not even them. We can't afford this getting out, or we lose our small advantage."

In Relief Society they start out with a good-news minute. Girls are always like, "I just got a scholarship!" Or "I just got engaged!" I never have anything worth sharing. Now I imagine standing up next Sunday and saying, "I'm a spy for the FBI. Top that!"

That would be awesome . . .

"I won't say anything." I sigh. "No one would believe me anyway."

"Assets tend to find it harder to lie to their loved ones than they first anticipate. You need to tell me now if that's going to be a problem."

"I'll be fine." I already have to edit the goings-on in my life to keep my parents from discovering how hopeless I am. This'll just be one more thing not to mention.

Another guy in a suit—everyone wears suits around here, even the women—comes in with a small metal case.

"This is for you," Damon says, accepting the case from the guy and setting it on the table. I jump up, eager to see what gadgets they have for me. I am *so* the female James Bond! Only not English. Maybe I could adopt a fake English accent. Be a little exotic—

He lifts the lid and—

It's a phone.

A very ordinary smart phone is nestled into a Styrofoam notch. True, it's all white and silver and gleaming, more high tech than any phone I've ever had. But it's still just a phone.

"Your contacts and photos have already been transferred from your old device. You know, the techs were particularly interested in this one." He taps the screen, and the photo that pops up as my screensaver—*Uggg*—is of me and Bridget. We're wearing pajamas, my hair is in pigtails, and we each have about half a tube of frosting smeared on our dopily smiling faces.

I *told* her we shouldn't have taken a picture.

"Bad breakup," I say, trying not to blush. "It's a girl thing."

He purses his lips and nods, his eyes crinkled at the edges. "I'm programmed in as speed dial 2. Speed dial 3 is Agent Terigan, my second over your protective watch. Speed dial 1 is a panic button. You push it, and it automatically calls emergency response that will follow the GPS tracker on the device."

"Speed dial 1 is usually voice mail," I say. "I'll have to be careful not to mix that up."

"Other than that, it's the newest model with all the latest technology."

He hands it to me, and I smooth the screen, saying, "Great."

He cocks his head. "You seem disappointed."

I shrug. "I was just hoping it did something else like turn into a switchblade or a parachute. Or, like, an emergency bomb I could detonate by voice command."

Damon's mouth twitches. "We're pretty picky about who we hand out emergency bombs to."

"Sure." I sigh and put the phone in the front pocket of my bag.

"You'll need that to e-mail the guys."

"Oh, right." I tug open the zipper and retrieve the phone. "I can e-mail on here? That's nifty."

"We cloned the phone so we'll be able to see and hear all your communications."

"Well, that's unsettling." I scroll through the touch screen and suddenly shriek, "Plants vs. Zombies?! Best phone ever!"

I send a mass message to the guys who've already contacted me, trying to sound nonchalant but urgent, and give my number. Almost instantly I get a text from Charles Windle. He's "excited I finally wrote back" and would like to meet at six at P.F. Chang's, which is on the approved locations list. With that quick a response time, I'm thinking this online dating thing might actually be smart.

If the guys weren't potential killers, that is.

It's four p.m. now, so Damon hands me off to Agent Terigan to take me home so I can get ready. "I have to finish prepping things here, but I'll be waiting for you at the restaurant," Damon says. "Good work so far."

I'm playing Plants vs. Zombies on my new phone and barely hear him.

Agent Terigan is a tall (and I mean football-linebacker tall) black man with a shaved head and huge fists. They're like two pumpkins coming out of his sleeves. When I first see him, I swallow my gum. Then I splutter for five minutes while he smacks my back with one of those pumpkins and tells me, "Spit it out. Just let it come."

He's actually quite sweet as he escorts me through the building and down to a dark SUV. He even holds my door. I can't remember when that last happened.

"You're very brave to do this," he comments as we speed toward Orem. "Not many people would risk their lives like this."

That's one way to burst a new-high-score bubble.

"You're awfully kind," I reply. "Aren't you supposed to be cold and calculated when you work for the FBI?"

He gives a throaty chuckle. "My mom always called me softhearted, but it's good for the job. The more I care, the harder I work."

"That must get tiring, caring so much."

"It tears you up." He nods. "But I can't imagine doing anything else."

"So," I muse, "what do I call you? Agent Terigan? Mr. Terigan. Double O Huge?"

He laughs again. "How about Samuel?"

"Samuel, okay. I'm Jack."

He glances over to shake my hand. "Pleased to meet you, Jack."

"Likewise, Samuel. I'd have gone with Double O Huge, but that's just me."

With rush hour, we don't make it to my place until five thirty. "You've got fifteen minutes," Samuel says as I hop out of the car. "Come down when you're ready, and I'll drop you off."

"You're not coming in the restaurant?"

"No, ma'am. I cover the exit while you're inside. Less conspicuous."

"Yeah." I smile. "I'm guessing you kind of stand out in a crowd."

I make a mad dash upstairs and start yanking options out of the closet. What do you wear on an undercover date for the FBI when your dining companion is a possible psycho?

My first attempt—all black with a floor-length leather jacket and sunglasses—seems a bit much. I might as well announce to the whole restaurant that I'm an amateur spy.

I'm a spy. So cool!

Attempt number two—trying *not* to look like a spy—is the other extreme: a baby-doll dress, knee-high white stockings, and a pink ribbon in my hair. I look like I'm trying too hard to be normal. Or like I stopped shopping after I turned six years old.

With five minutes left, I pull on a pair of dark jeans with a navy blazer. I slip on a pair of heels, throw my hair in a low ponytail, and head out the door, prepared to touch up my makeup in the car.

It feels strange to have Samuel drop me around the corner from the restaurant. It's like my dad taking me to school. Even the short walk has me wishing I'd rethought the heels. *No turning back now,* I think as I haul open the heavy mahogany door.

Nerves have liquefied my legs, and my hands are trembling as I glance around. Even on a Monday night, the place is decently busy, and I wonder how Charles and I will find each other—

"Jacklyn?"

I turn and see the guy I vaguely recall from the dossier: platinum blond hair, toothpaste-ad smile, preppy-boy style. "Are you Jacklyn Wyatt?" he asks, holding out his hand.

"Just Jack," I say, shaking his. "You must be Charles."

"Yes." He grins. "Your picture didn't do you justice."

"Oh." I make some awkward noise and brush back my bangs. It's a line, but it's effective. "You're . . . very nice yourself."

"I have a table for us over here." He sweeps a hand in the direction and then holds the other arm out to me.

Is he kidding?

His winning smile stays in place, his crooked elbow extended toward me.

This guy is offering me his arm. He's like Mr. Darcy!

"Thank you," I stammer and take his arm. I see others notice us as we walk toward our table—the girls with envy, the guys with surprise. *Take notes, boys,* I think. *This is what a gentleman looks like.*

When we arrive at our table, Charles holds my chair out for me. Again I'm taken aback and shimmy forward awkwardly as he pushes me up to the table. "Thank you," I repeat as he takes his own seat. "That was a new experience."

Charles gives a modest smile. "Sorry if it's a bit much. My mom was big on teaching us how women should be treated."

"She sounds amazing."

"Oh, she is." He beams. "She taught me about everything that really matters in life—faith, respect, and love."

Oh, my gosh. He's like Mr. Darcy and *a stripling warrior!*

"Well, thank her for me," I say. "It's very refreshing." I glance to my right and am startled to see Agent Wade—Damon—two tables down, perusing a menu. For a minute I'd forgotten why I'm here.

Right. This isn't a real date. Focus, Jack.

The hostess appears to take our drink orders and leave us with menus.

"I hope you're not sick of this place," Charles says once we're sipping our water. "I know it's popular for dates."

"No, this is great." I won't mention that my last date took me to Costco to eat samples. That's probably an overshare. "The lettuce wraps are my favorite. I could just eat those and no entrée."

"They are addicting," he agrees. "We're counseled against addiction, but it's hard to resist temptation."

Damon snorts and I glance his way on impulse and then snap my gaze back to the menu. *Don't notice him. He doesn't exist.*

"Hi there." A pretty girl with thick caramel hair has approached the table, pulling a pad of paper out of her apron. "I'm Tilly. I'll be your—" She looks up, and her striking green eyes widen. "Charles!"

"Tilly." Charles is rapidly turning pale. His expression leaves little doubt as to how these two are acquainted. "I didn't know you still worked here."

Still? He's brought me where his ex works? Stupendous.

"I—" She looks shocked. "I transferred to Salt Lake, but then I came back to finish school."

"Well . . . good for you. And great to see you."

"And you. You look amazing." She's a little breathless staring at him. Eventually her gaze travels to me, and I so wish I could hide behind the soy sauce.

"Who's this?" she asks, her tone glacial.

"This is Jack Wyatt."

"Your name's Jack? What, all the girl names were taken?"

I feel like she's slapped me, but I manage to nod. "Yeah, but I'm on the backorder list, so here's hoping."

Damon coughs, and I glance at him again and then back to Tilly's rigid expression.

"Are you on a *date?*" she asks Charles, her voice throbbing with betrayal.

Charles sighs. "Yes, I am. Tilly, we were never exclusive, and we haven't seen each other in months. Please don't behave this way."

Now she looks as if he's slapped her. "Fine," she says, visibly trembling. "Would you two like an appetizer?"

I'd rather call it a night than sit through the most awkward evening in history, but one look at Damon and I know I have to stick it out. For the missing girl.

Charles is watching me to confirm if I'm willing to stay, and I nod very slightly. He nods in return and tells Tilly, "We'll have an order of the lettuce wraps." Then he gives me a tiny wink.

Oh, dude. Don't wink.

Tilly scribbles on her pad so furiously the paper tears. "One order of lettuce wraps coming up." She turns and stalks back to the kitchen.

Yup. She's gonna spit in my food.

8

The. Most. Awkward. *Ever.*

The lettuce wraps are delicious despite what Tilly may have added to them—also notwithstanding her withering glares each time she drifts near to serve another table. She must've passed the word in the kitchen because we're getting glares from pretty much every waiter, hostess, and busboy in the place. Not that I blame them.

Charles can't apologize enough, insisting he had no idea Tilly would be here and that they'd only gone on a few dates nearly six months ago. Still, if I was him, I'd probably avoid P. F. Chang's altogether.

I wait until the main course arrives before pressing for information. "So," I say, spearing a piece of lemon chicken, "Charles, you seem pretty put together. Why does a guy like you need to date online?"

He chuckles. "I know. It's generally thought to be sort of a last resort, isn't it?"

"It does have a kind of negative connotation."

"It's just hard for me to meet women. Between finishing dental school and my internship with an oral surgeon, there's just no time."

"Mm-hmm." I nod knowingly as I chew—like my career in folding jeans is equally demanding.

"How about you? What led you to online dating?"

Um, my meddling sister set it up, and now I'm undercover.

"You know. It's just hard to know if a guy shares my standards. Around here pretty much everyone's Mormon, but you never know who actually takes it seriously."

"Exactly." He smiles. "So many people in Utah seem to go to church because it's expected, not because they necessarily want to."

I nod, poking at my rice. "I don't want someone who has a testimony by default." After a moment I look up and laugh. "Sorry. Too much information."

"Not at all."

I take another bite of my chicken, grimace, and dig around in my purse. As I'm pulling out the salt packets, Charles eyebrows raise. "Oh, um . . . needs salt," I explain.

"So you brought your own?" He sounds incredulous.

"Well, you know, they never have it here. A lot of places don't. Here they assume if you want saltiness, you can add soy sauce, but not everyone likes soy sauce. I've asked them before if they have regular salt in the kitchen, and they always look at me like I'm a lunatic."

There's a beat of silence.

Yeah. This was clearly the sane choice.

I hurriedly sprinkle salt on my rice and stuff the empty packets back in my purse. "So have you been doing this online thing for a while?"

He shrugs. "About two months. I've only been on a few dates, though."

"Oh, really? Were they as colorful as people say?"

He laughs. "Just regular girls, mostly."

"No one who stood out?"

"Not really. The biggest problem I have is finding someone as ambitious as me. Most seem content to have no real direction."

"Not an ambitious girl in the group?"

"No. Well," he pauses, "there was one girl, actually. She was from a grounded family and on her way to medical school. Very impressive." He's talking about her like she was a job applicant.

"Well, if she fit your standard for ambition, why didn't it go anywhere?"

"I don't know. She was maybe a little *too* ambitious, I guess. I mean, I like a girl with direction, but a doctor? That would make it really hard to raise a family."

Oh, I realize. *He's Impossible-Standards Guy.*

"I mean, don't get me wrong. I'm all for a woman having a career— any career she wants. I just need to be with someone who's driven but without too complicated a future." He smiles. "Like you."

Oh, my.

"Yep," I agree.

"You're studying literature, right?"

"Mm-hmm." *All the better to analyze our kids' bedtime stories.* "So no risk for a future there." I laugh, and he laughs with me, oblivious to my sarcasm. "I definitely couldn't handle medical school. I faint at my own paper cuts. So you never saw that doctor girl again?"

His eyes narrow slightly. "No, just the one date. I didn't think it prudent to take it further."

"Decent of you."

Damon covers a laugh, and my eyes momentarily swivel toward him.

Charles turns to look in Damon's direction and points at him with his fork. "Do you know that guy over there?"

"Hmm? What guy?"

"*That* guy. You keep looking at him."

"No, I don't."

"Yes, you do. Several times, in fact."

Crap.

I nod very slowly, my mind working frantically. "Well, actually he's"—I cover my mouth on Damon's side—"I went out with him once, and it . . . didn't go well."

"Really?" Charles lowers his voice. "Wow, the cards are really stacked against us tonight, aren't they?"

"Yeah. Old flames are coming out of the woodwork!"

"What went wrong? If it's not too presumptuous to ask."

"He, uh . . ." I fidget. "He was just kind of insulting. Called me dull."

Charles looks affronted. "Dull? Well, that's just not true."

"Thank you!" I say, more loudly than I mean to.

"If anything you're just . . ." He smiles again. "Safe."

I throw down my fork. "Safe, yes. Would you excuse me?"

I jump up, and he *stands as I leave the table.* I've never seen this happen in real life, and I feel a momentary stab of longing, but then I think, *Nope. You ruined it. Mr. Darcy would be ashamed of you.*

I saunter towards the bathroom but stop to fume as soon as I reach the marble alcove outside the doors.

"Something wrong?"

I nearly jump out of my skin. Damon is at my elbow.

"Give me a heart attack!" I exclaim. "Sheesh! Why don't you make noise when you walk?"

"You didn't say the safe word."

"I don't feel threatened. I'm just annoyed. He started out so promising."

He snorts. "That guy? Seriously?"

"He offered me his arm," I argue, "and stood up when I left the table. And I bet he opens doors."

Damon blinks. "Which automatically makes him great?"

"Opening doors is a big deal. Gentlemanly behavior is a lost art form."

"I don't think I've ever opened a door."

"Well, you should try it sometime. Girls appreciate it."

"Some of you do," he counters, "and some find it an insult. We just can't win since feminism."

"Let's not argue about this now. How much longer do I need to question the disappointment?"

"Well, I'm not picking up any red flags except the underlying chauvinism. He may just play the part well. But if anything he seems disinterested in Natalie."

"Yeah, it's not him," I agree. "If someone took her, they would have to be obsessed with her. This guy only seems interested in himself. He's an impossible-standards guy."

Damon's eyebrows scroll upward. "What exactly is that?"

"You know, the guy who's thirty in a get-married-at-twenty-one culture because he has a perfect woman list that no woman can live up to? 'Driven but not too driven.' What does that even mean? How can women compete when men have this huge list that no actual human being can live up to?"

A busboy walks by lugging a tray of dirty dishes, and I lean nonchalantly against the wall and say, "How you doing? The wraps are great tonight."

Damon is smiling as the busboy passes, but it's not a pleasant smile. "You don't think women have a list?"

"Of course we do, but it's things like funny, tall, good personality. Not 'must cure cancer before making breakfast for the children.'"

"In my experience, women tend to have some pretty outrageous expectations as well."

"Again, this is not the time to argue. Aren't you supposed to be keeping things on track here?"

"So you think Natalie didn't meet his expectation?"

"Exactly."

"A criminal psychologist might say that would be a reason to take her. Sometimes people get fixated on a person who fails to meet their fantasy. They must be destroyed so the fantasy remains intact."

"Maybe with someone less in love with himself."

"And this is your professional opinion based on years of clinical experience?"

"It's based on my years in the trenches. Guys like this are all smiles and compliments, but he'll never call again, and he'll probably still be alone at forty trying to find Dr. Mom Barbie."

Damon surveys me a moment and then buttons his suit jacket. "Well, we have a sample of how he interacts. We'll let the doc have a listen."

"The doc?"

"Our criminal psychologist. We're recording everything so it can be analyzed by a professional."

"But you said I wasn't supposed to wear a wire!"

"You're not. I am."

I scan his person as though I'll be able to see the thing poking out of his collar or something.

"If you want to ogle me, you should wait until your date is over."

I flush red instantly and say, "Don't flatter yourself." Something I never thought I'd say because when you say it, everyone knows the accusation is true. "What about 'people act strangely when they're wearing a wire'?"

"Yeah, *people* do. I'm trained. I can wear one without compromising the mission."

Normally I would've gotten goose bumps at the use of the word *mission*, but I'm throbbing with anger. "And what you said to Clemens— 'If we're going to trust her, we better trust her with the whole thing'— that was just talk?"

"We *are* trusting you. You've no idea what hoops I had to jump through to get a civilian put on something like this. Kidnappings are very serious, as I'm sure you can imagine. And with this time frame, I have one shot at this. So no, we're not taking undo risks by wiring you, and professionals will analyze what intel we gather. Did you really think the analysis would be up to you too?"

I fold my arms. "No."

"You're the Trojan horse not the army." He straightens his cuffs. "Are we clear?"

I give a venomous smile. "Absolutely. Now, when I go back to the table, am I a dull civilian or a horse?"

He doesn't even flinch. "Just run out the clock so he doesn't get suspicious. Dig a bit more if you can. Be sure to order dessert."

"Believe me, I intend to." I slouch back to the table. Charles is examining his teeth in a butter knife and looks up to flash me a smile.

"Everything all right?"

"Yes, there was a line for the ladies room." I sit and pick up my fork, but somehow my appetite has diminished, which is something that has never happened in the history of my relationship with Chinese food.

"So, Charles, tell me," I halfheartedly pick at my rice, "what are your hobbies?"

"Well," he folds his hands on the table, content to talk about himself, "I love horses. My parents have a ranch, and I go out there on weekends sometimes. It's soothing to work with the animals. They're really in tune with the things that matter . . ."

With very little guidance from me, Charles steers the conversation through the rest of the main course and into dessert. By the time the dessert plates arrive, I've learned more about him than about people I've known for years.

And said not another word about myself.

Not that I care anymore. At this point all I want is my sugar. The restaurant's best dessert—the Great Wall of Chocolate—is a towering mammoth of fudge goodness that almost makes the entire disastrous evening worth it.

". . . which is when I worked at the animal shelter and saved up money for the mission," Charles is saying, hardly touching his food. If only we'd had dessert at the beginning of the night, I would have known not to waste energy being excited by him. Never trust a man who doesn't like chocolate. "Dogs really are such majestic creatures."

"Yeah, they're great," I agree, forking another enormous bite of frosting into my mouth.

Tilly appears with the bill, her mouth set in a line. "No hurry, of course," she says, setting it on the edge of the table with more force than necessary.

"I've got this," Charles says, reaching for the check and giving me another wink. Tilly visibly flinches.

Dude, put your winker away, I think. *No tact.*

Charles slides a few bills inside and hands it back to Tilly without making eye contact with her. She hugs it to herself and goes away, looking like she's about to burst into tears.

Jerk.

He looks up. "What?"

Oh. Hadn't realized I'd spoken aloud. Suddenly I can't hold it in. Speaking low, I say, "How can you treat her like that? She's clearly still hung up on you, and you're pretending like she doesn't even exist."

He looks surprised and then pitying. "It's for her own good. If I give her any indication there's still a chance, I'll just lead her on."

"So the alternative is to pretend she's suddenly invisible? How is that better?"

"I'm not giving her false hope."

"No, but at least you'd be giving back a little of her dignity. You broke the girl's heart. The least you can do is not humiliate her by acting like she has no value."

His eyes narrow slightly. "I would've thought you'd appreciate my approach. I'm on a date with you, after all."

"What I would've appreciated is being taken to a different restaurant when you realized your ex was serving our food. I think Tilly probably would've appreciated that too."

After a moment Charles stands and shoves his chair back. "You know, I don't have to sit here for this. There are a lot of people who would be grateful to be brought to a nice place like this."

"In other words, there's a long line of women just dying to date you."

He stares at me, his face twitching mutely with anger. Then he jerkily pulls on his jacket. "You know, I'm starting to understand why you have to date online." He strides away from the table.

I sit for several moments in jilted silence. Then I take another bite of chocolate cake and murmur, "I've had worse dates."

"Well done." Damon is standing at the table.

"Well done?" I repeat, my words nearly indiscernible with such a full mouth. "I drove him off. There's no way he'll ever speak to me again."

"We got a sample of how he interacts on his best behavior, and now we have a sample of how he acts when he's angry. That should be helpful to the doctor."

"Well, I had it all planned, really." Tilly is, thankfully, nowhere to be seen, so I wave at another waiter and ask for a to-go box. "I'm not leaving this cake behind," I explain to Damon. When the Styrofoam box arrives, I pack up not only my half-eaten piece but Charles's untouched portion as well. *Thank you very much, Charles.*

"I'll drive you home," Damon says as I gather up my purse. "I need to instruct the first night watch."

"So what, you guys sit in the lot outside my place on a stakeout and look for suspicious behavior?"

"Yes."

"Oh." Again, two hours ago that would've sounded unbelievably cool to me, but the wind's been taken out of my sails a bit. At least when I get home I can watch a movie, finish my cake, and try to forget the rest of the day.

Damon is two steps behind me as we exit the restaurant. At the curb he puts a hand on my shoulder to signal me to wait for traffic. I hear a gasp of derision behind me and turn toward the side of the building.

Tilly is standing there. Surrounded by a posse of furious waitresses.

Just when I thought this day couldn't get worse.

"You're unbelievable," she hisses, advancing on me. Her face is puffy from crying, and twin trails of mascara mar her cheeks. "You sit there, right under my nose, and flirt with Charles." Her voice catches on his name. "Then you drive him away with no respect and leave with another man!"

"It's not what you think," I say, raising my palms the way they showed us at camp if approached by a wild bear.

"Oh, please. You're a man-eater. And why you had to pick poor Charles—"

"Poor Charles?" I say, incredulous. "Charles is the one who dumped you and stopped speaking to you and then just treated you like garbage in there. I defended you."

"Yeah?" she snorts. "When was that? Before or after dessert?"

I hedge. "Actually it was kind of during dessert. I didn't plan it that way. But the Great Wall of Chocolate is crazy good—"

"I just don't understand why you couldn't go to a different restaurant. Why you had to torture me—"

"That's exactly what I said!" I insist. "I told him we should've gone somewhere else."

"If you care so much, then why didn't you just leave?"

I hesitate, feet fidgeting. *Because I'm undercover for the FBI, and I had to find out if Charles is a murderer.*

"I should have," I say finally. "I should've stood up and left the minute I understood the situation, and I'm sorry. I can understand being angry with me, but you should also be angry with Charles. He's the one who threw you away, then flaunted a new girl in front of you. All those things you said to me were good, but you should be saying them to him. It's the only way you'll ever get any closure."

Her arms are folded across her chest and her expression is black, but she's listening.

"I'm sorry I didn't take a stand for you earlier," I say, softer. "I know what it's like to be treated like you're nothing by men who claim they're gentlemen. It hurts worse from that kind, doesn't it? I've been where you are. But you're not nothing. You're worth so much." My voice is trembling on those last words, and something in Tilly's expression clicks into place. She takes a halting step toward me, and I slowly extend my arms, ready to embrace her, my heart swelling with sisterly solidarity—

She slaps me.

I reel, staggering a few steps. The other waitresses are cheering, and Tilly's face is fierce with vindication.

"That's enough." Damon steps forward and takes me by the arm to steady me. "You can't understand this, but Jack did what she could in there. And for you to treat her like this makes you just as bad as that guy." Everyone falls silent as he steers me into the parking lot.

I'm massaging my jaw. I understand now why people always do that in movies. It hurts!

"Well," Damon says, "interesting night."

I glare at him. "I just got slapped in the face. By a girl."

"Actually her fist was partially closed. Technically you were punched."

"Oh, that makes it better. And she was wearing a ring. I think she cut me! Five minutes undercover, and I'm bleeding."

He chuckles. "Look, you tried to do the right thing. That gets us kicked in the pants sometimes."

We've reached the car, and I wrench open the passenger door. "Kicked in the pants?"

"Yeah. I was editing to protect your sensitivity."

Rolling my eyes, I plop into the car.

We don't speak much on the drive. P. F. Changs is less than five minutes from my house, although I doubt I'll ever go to that location again. I prefer not to be beaten when I dine out.

"By the way, there was activity on your profile while you were in there," Damon tells me. "Thomas Smythe wrote you back and wants to do lunch tomorrow."

Smythe, Smythe. I have absolutely no recollection. I'm going to have to review the dossier tonight. And start on the first draft of my medieval literature paper. Uggg. "Where's lunch?"

He takes a moment to answer, turning the corner to my complex. "Actually, he attends your university—"

"There's a possible killer on my campus?"

"Well, statistically that was bound to happen at some point."

"Comforting. Where would Hannibal Lector like to dine?"

He cracks a half smile. "In the upstairs cafeteria."

"What time?"

"One p.m.—between your Women in Literature and your Advanced Theory classes."

My eyebrows shoot up. "You know my schedule?"

"I told you, I watched you for a while." He pulls into a parking spot and glances my way. "I know everything about you."

Something flutters in my stomach, and I look away to retrieve my purse from the floor. "And you'll be there, I suppose."

"Of course."

"Maybe leave the suit at home," I suggest. "You might look odd on a college campus."

"I'll keep that in mind."

I reach for the door handle and pause. "Am I good to go now?"

"Yes. Agent Terigan checked your apartment, and it's clear."

"He was inside my place?"

"For security reasons, we need access. It's the only way to ensure your safety."

"So much for privacy." I open the door.

Damon stops me. "If you need anything, we'll be right down here. The panic button on your phone alerts my team. So if you press it, I come running."

"Goodie for me." I step out of the car and then turn back. "If you were wearing a wire tonight, does that mean that everything is on the tape? Even . . . the stuff after?"

His mouth twitches. "Yes."

"Stupendous." I slam the door.

9

SWOLLEN, PURPLE, AND SPLIT LIKE overripe fruit, my damaged cheek greets me in the vanity mirror when I wake up in the morning.

On my nightstand my new phone is queued up to the panic button.

For nearly a minute I look back and forth between the phone and the evidence of my walloping. Leaden with the confusion of sleep, I wonder if all of that actually happened yesterday. Sure, I *think* I met the FBI and went undercover on an awful date. But that couldn't have been *real*, right?

With two fingers I spread the blinds and peer out the window. In the parking lot below, a black SUV sits, seemingly inconspicuous, part of my personal surveillance.

My eyes widen. It actually happened. I'm an undercover spy!

Man, I think, gingerly touching my cheek as I climb out of bed. *Spy work hurts!*

I try to go about my regular morning routine, but as I get ready, I keep thinking, *I'm undercover!* Makeup conceals most of the bruising, but even so, my face looks different. I look tougher. With darker eyeliner and one of those head scarves women wear while driving in old movies, I could totally be a hot international spy.

Donning my sunglasses and humming the James Bond theme, I tuck and do a stealth roll from the bathroom to the kitchen—thumping into a table leg and cracking my spine. *That may need a little practice.*

I head over to the nearby school parking lot to ride the student shuttle to the main campus. As I climb onto the shuttle, I'm pretty sure I glimpse the Bureau's car half a block back. I'm tempted to just ask the agents for a ride to school instead of hoofing it. But that wouldn't be professional. And I'm a pro—as soon as I learn how to stealth roll correctly.

My first class is biology—a general requirement I've been avoiding all my years in college. It's held in one of the large lecture rooms, the better to pack in the students and give no individual attention to those of us who view science as a foreign language. I'm early for once. Usually I'm one of those who slinks in after the lecture has begun, has to do the walk of shame past the professor, and climbs over a dozen people to reach the one vacant chair. I unpack a notebook, textbook, pens, and half a bar of chocolate. It acts as my buffer to keep me from bursting into tears when I get confused.

"Hey, Jack." Peggy, a freshman with a long black ponytail sits beside me. We've chatted briefly and shared notes once or twice. "How was your weekend?" she asks.

"Fine."

"Yeah?" She glances at me. "Anything new?"

I start to answer when I'm seized with sudden suspicion. Why is Peggy so interested in my weekend? Is she some sort of enemy agent? With her exotic looks, she could easily be KGB. If the KGB is still a thing.

Or maybe she's just being polite.

"Not really," I lie. I don't think I've ever told such a bold-faced lie before. Sure, I've told the occasional that-skirt-looks-great-on-you lie to spare a friend's feelings but never something that was so blatantly untrue. Is lying still lying when it's for the safety of the country?

I maybe could ask my bishop.

By the time I've suffered through biology (I ate the entire remainder of the chocolate bar and still felt confused enough to weep) and women in literature, I've nearly forgotten about my lunch date with Thomas Smythe. I skimmed the dossier last night and learned he's an engineering student and works at Abercrombie. Same school and same mall. What are the odds?

Hmm, I think as I hurry toward the student center. Maybe it's a little too coincidental. He just happens to go to my university and work in the same mall as me? Maybe he set himself up in those places. Maybe he's been putting this in place for months.

Yes. Because he would anticipate my agreeing to help the FBI find a girl who hadn't even gone missing yet.

I'm losing it. I wonder if extreme paranoia is common in new spies. There's probably some sort of name for it—Spy Suspicion Disorder or something. I need to keep it in check.

I don't spot Thomas when I get to the upstairs cafeteria, though I mostly remember a tannish guy with dark hair. I get in line to order my food anyway.

The most coveted meal in the cafeteria is the chicken strips and fries. It's deep-fried goodness for less than you'd pay at a fast-food chain. This time of day, I'm lucky there are any left, and I only have to wait with my tray a few minutes before I'm served. I get two sides of fry sauce to go with it and grab a lemonade. I still don't see Thomas as I get in line to pay.

Paying for my own date. It's not that unusual. In fact, when I go out I make sure to have at least twenty dollars on me. Because you never know who's going to be cheap or have liberal views of equality. Or who you'll need to get a cab to run away from when he goes to the bathroom. Oh, believe me, it's happened before.

I've just finished paying when I see a dark head sitting at a center table, facing away from me. I approach cautiously so as not to creep out some guy just eating lunch. As I near him, he turns his head.

"Thomas?" I ask.

He breaks into a grin. "You must be Jack." He indicates the empty seat. "Please."

Well, we're a long way from holding out my chair now.

"Thanks." I sit. Over his shoulder, I spot Damon a few tables down with an open textbook in front of him. He's wearing a blue T-shirt, jeans, and sneakers, and looks strangely out of place in the clothing, like an actor who does period films. You're used to seeing him in a tunic and tights, and then he's suddenly in a modern movie, and the whole time you watch, you keep thinking, "Someone get this man a tunic!" It makes me smile a little as I situate my tray.

Thomas has his own tray stacked high with mashed potatoes, gravy, and chicken-fried steak. "Thanks for agreeing to meet me so soon," he says with a Cali-boy sort of laid-backness. "I know it's kind of lame to get together at school, but I was too anxious to meet you."

If it's a line, he delivers it like a well-rehearsed actor.

"Likewise." I smile. Two can play the fake game. "So you're Thomas."

"Call me Tommy." He picks up his fork. "You're hotter than your profile pic."

Is that supposed to be a compliment? "Thank you. You're not so bad yourself."

His little laugh is probably meant to be humble but comes across like, *I know*.

This is why I sometimes wish there was a two-minute escape hatch from dates. Tommy is an attractive guy with a sly smile and big biceps, and I'm sure any number of girls would be interested. Unfortunately, I can already tell this is going absolutely nowhere. It took less than two minutes to know he should move on to the next girl and save us both the time.

Then again, how many times have I hoped a guy would give me a chance, and I can tell he checks out five minutes after meeting me? I owe everyone the courtesy of seeing if my first impression is wrong.

Besides, over Tommy's shoulder, Damon turns a page of his textbook, and I'm brought back to reality. This date isn't for me anyway.

"So, Tommy, you're studying engineering?"

"Yeah." He takes a massive bite of steak and potatoes. "I love working with cars: the speed, the agility." He reaches forward and strokes the back of my hand. "The feel of the smooth metal. It's like working with a living thing."

Oh, *this* guy again.

It's twenty minutes into lunch, and I've barely touched my food. My hands have been otherwise occupied—warding Tommy's away from me. The guy must have twelve hands. He's like Doc Oc from *Spiderman* if Doc Oc's ambition was not to destroy the world but rather to publically grope a girl he barely knows. I can't figure how he's still managed to put away his pile of food while surreptitiously slipping his hand up my thigh, down the side of my neck, and once a swipe at my rib cage. Far too close for comfort.

I'm familiar with the type, the one who claims to be pious on Sundays but is Grope-y McGrabby every other day of the week. This is the kind of guy that makes it impossible to gauge if any guy, LDS or not, actually does believe in chastity and all the stuff he claims in his profile. Under normal circumstances I'd have bolted the second I realized he's really only after one thing, but I'm a stinking spy now, and when you're undercover you have to keep sitting there defending your honor until the stinking FBI gets the information they need.

I have to be subtle about my rejection so he doesn't get mad and walk away. But there are only so many ways I can coyly deflect his advances. I keep smiling in a manner I hope is mysterious and laughing girlishly to keep him at the table. It must be working because he's still sitting here. So now he thinks I'm a giant flirt who's just playing hard to get, which is only going to make him try harder.

Worst of all I can see Damon still bent over his counterfeit textbook, pretending to read but shaking with laughter each time it's a near miss.

And I've yet to find out anything about Tommy's relationship with Natalie. "So . . ." I shift back and flip my hair over my shoulder the way I've seen girls do in movies, trying to look coquettish but also moving farther out of his reach. "I've only been in this online dating game for a little bit, but there sure are some odd ducks out there." My voice is husky. Why am I talking like some leggy girl from a film noir? This must be how I attempt to flirt. All I need is a wide-brimmed hat and one of those long cigarette things. Not that I smoke.

"Oh, there are some real dogs," Tommy agrees. "Not like you."

He reaches for me, and I bat his hand away and then wag my finger at him with a smile. He laughs, but inwardly I'm cringing. I just did the finger wag in real life. Something is seriously wrong here.

"Tell me about it," I say. "What sort of encounters have you had?"

"Well, there was this one girl." He chuckles. "She was up for just about anything. Ten minutes into the date and we're making out on the side of the Taco Bell."

Classy. Why do guys think we'll find their skanky history fascinating? Do they think it'll make us realize what a catch we're with? Sometimes I feel like men talk to me and have honestly forgotten I'm not some dude from the gym.

"That is wild," I say and manage a laugh. *Oh, gosh, I'm so not built for flirting.* "Anything else? Any bad experiences?"

Tommy thinks a moment, fiddling with his paper napkin, and then snorts. "There was this one girl, hot enough but super high and mighty, real holier than thou. The minute we finished dinner, she said I was making her uncomfortable and left." His mouth twists. "What kind of crap is that? I pay for dinner, and then she thinks she can just run out on me?"

You're definitely not going to like what's coming. "Maybe she, uh, wasn't 'up for anything' like that other girl."

"Babe, I'm not asking for everything." He grins. "You don't have to buy the car to take it for a little test drive."

I give a noncommittal laugh. Partly because I don't know what to say and partly because I might puke a little if I open my mouth. After a sip of lemonade, it passes. "I knew a girl like that," I say. "A roommate of mine once. She would go on all these dates with these guys and let them take her to nice places and then just run out the minute she got dinner."

Tommy nods, jaw taut. "I swear it's like sometimes I just feel like a free meal to these chicks. It's like, I'm a person. You know?"

That's probably what they're thinking too. "Yeah. My old roommate was named Gr-Gl-Grfn-Gwen. Maybe it was the same girl."

"Naw." He takes a swig of his soda. "The chick who walked out on me was Natalie something."

Reflexively my gaze darts to Damon. He's frozen mid-page-turn, listening.

"Did you do anything to . . . get back at that girl?"

He wipes his mouth. "Like what?"

"I dunno." I reach for a lie, making it up as I go. "I had this guy friend who went out with my old roommate G . . . ina."

"I thought you said Gwen."

"Yeah, she . . . used a fake name on dates sometimes."

He snorts. "Typical."

"Yeah. So this guy friend of mine, after she ditched him, he keyed her car."

Tommy chuckles. "Harsh. But sounds like she deserved it."

My pulse quickens, and I have to swallow with effort. "Think so?"

"Yeah. Chick shows a guy that kind of disrespect, she deserves what she gets."

My palms are sweating. I blot them as casually as I can on my jeans. "And did, uh . . . Natalie get what she deserved?"

"Naw. Tramp wasn't worth my time."

"So you didn't like"—I force a shaky smile—"punish her?"

"Naw." He leans forward, catching my hands in his. "But I'd be happy to punish you, babe."

Yup, there's the vomit. I give a strangled laugh. "Sounds fun. But"—I glance at my wrist with no watch and grimace—"unfortunately, I have to get to class."

"No."

"Yeah. Class at two."

His hand is on my neck again. "You've got time."

"I have to print off a paper first." I snag his hands and lace his fingers through mine. "Besides, we don't want to rush it."

Tommy chuckles and kisses my fingers. Did he just *lick* me? "Delayed gratification. I like it. You busy later this week?"

"I'm not sure. Why don't you text me?"

"I'll do that." He stands, shoulders his backpack, and says, "Pleasure to meet you, Jack."

"And you."

Tommy leans down, moving in toward my mouth, and I turn my head. He chuckles, kisses my cheek, and struts away.

Once he's out of sight, I give a full body shudder. After a moment Damon ambles over, books under his arm. "You all right?" he asks.

"Sure. Once I get a chemical body peel."

"Yeah, he was a bit of a creep."

"He is king of creeps. The other creeps take seminars from him." I push my tray away and notice Tommy has left his for me to deal with too. Nice. "Do you think he had anything to do with . . . ?"

"Hard to say. He certainly seemed angry with her, but it could mostly be bravado."

"I almost wish he were involved, just to get him off the street." A horrible thought hits me. "Am I going to have to see him again?"

"Possibly. We'll know more once the recordings are analyzed."

"Ah, yes. The great doctor. So glad I could gather intel like a good horsey."

He cocks his head. "You were really insulted by that, weren't you?"

"You've insulted me so many times in the last twenty-four hours that I don't really know how to pick my favorite."

"Sorry. I don't sugarcoat things. It can upset touchy people."

I blink at him. "I'm not sure, but that might've been another insult." At the payment counter I retrieve a takeout box. At least I'm getting some pretty great leftovers from this gig.

After depositing both trays on the cleaning racks, I continue out of the student center, back toward the language arts building with Damon drifting along in my wake. "Are you following me now?"

"Just making sure you get to class."

"I thought you guys were supposed to keep a low profile."

He spreads his arms. "Have you seen what I'm wearing? I am grunge-tastic."

I give him a once-over and shrug. "Still look like a cop."

"Say it a little louder, please."

"Nobody cares." The grounds are in full bloom, the grass lush, and the trees full of sweet wind. It's a perfect, blustery spring day—the kind of day that poets write about. Sometimes I dream of that kind of life, quietly sitting on a terrace somewhere penning sonnets about spring breezes. Other times I think about moving to New York to become a journalist. Too many ambitions and no direction.

"Nice day," Damon observes, walking beside me now.

"Mm-hmm." I glance sidelong at him. "Do you get out a lot, or are you more of desk guy?"

His mouth twitches. "Do you mean do they keep me chained to a cubicle and refuse me access to sunlight?"

"Just making conversation," I say, peeved.

"I explained before—I coordinate task forces and act as a liaison between government and state agencies here in Utah."

"And what does that mean in human-speak?"

"I get teams and field offices organized so we can protect people."

"How'd you get into that?"

"After school and the police academy, I worked in private security for a while. Did pretty well. Then applied to the FBI."

My eyes narrow. "How old are you?"

"Thirty-two. Don't I look it?"

"You're only thirty-two and you've already done college, the police academy, private security, and now the FBI?"

"Pretty much."

I hug my textbooks tighter, suddenly feeling stupid for holding literary anthologies. I'm studying Milton while this guy's saving the world.

"I've been called too driven," he says as though he can read my mind. "Never took a second to breathe."

"Where did that drive come from?"

He hesitates and flashes a guarded half smile. "Who's to say?" He nods toward the language arts building on our left. "This your stop?"

"Yep." I hurry up the few cement steps then turn to look down at him. "What do I do now?"

"Go to class, I'm assuming."

"I mean about the . . ." I trail off and widen my eyes meaningfully.

He always looks like he's about to laugh at me. "We're trying to set up meeting times. We should hear back soon."

"In the meantime?"

Damon shrugs. "Got papers to write, don't you? We'll be in touch."

Hurrying into the building, I turn a corner to cut down toward my classroom. Just as I'm about to step through the door, I glimpse a familiar face out of the corner of my eye. By the time I turn toward it, he's gone. But I'm almost sure it was him.

Did Tommy follow me?

10

THEY NEVER SHOULD'VE OUTLAWED BEING tortured on the rack. If it was still around, I'd insist Chaucer be placed on it.

Why, oh, why did I ever decide to take medieval literature? Okay, I love the era, but Chaucer is impossible to understand. I've been poring over the same three paragraphs for more than an hour, trying to sift out a quote for my paper, and I still have no clue what he's talking about. This cannot be English!

My phone trills a musical tone, and I see Delia's number on the caller ID before I pick up. "Hey there," I answer, folding my legs under me on the couch. "How are things at the zoo?"

"The animals are restless. Patrick!" she shouts at a child running somewhere in the background. "Leave her alone, already! Go find something else to do, please." Now she's back to me. "What are you up to?"

"Sweating out a paper."

"How's it coming? Shelby! Your sister's trying to feed a cookie to your fish."

"It's not," I answer, ignoring the side commentary. I'm used to this form of communication—half to me, half to the crew, like any good captain. I can't imagine how she keeps track of all them *and* what we're talking about at the same time. "If Chaucer were alive, I'd kick him."

"If he were alive, his language would be seriously outdated. Matthew, food goes in your mouth, not your hair, sweetie."

"Calling to see if I'd expired from excessive studying?"

"General check. You seemed a little down at Sunday dinner."

"Just finals," I hedge. Family dinner always gives me a long, hard look at how I'm going nowhere.

"Really?" she presses.

I pluck a Red Vine from the turbo bin beside me on the cushion. "Yeah, really."

"Jack," she's taken on a serious tone, "you're doing the thing."

"What thing?"

The thing."

"I'm not doing a thing!"

"Your voice is doing the thing. What's wrong?"

I can't go into it for her safety as well as the missing girl's. "Really, Lia. I'm just overworked. Stressed in all directions. Once the semester is over, I'll be able to breathe a bit, and I'll be right as rain."

"Really?"

"Positively." I take another bite of Red Vine and smile even though she can't see me.

"Okay," she says. Clearly she's not sold, but she's backing off a pace. "After midterms we'll have movie night."

"It's a deal."

"So what paper are you—Anna. Anna!" she scolds. "Spit out those rocks. Do *not* eat those rocks. I have to go," she tells me.

Even as she hangs up, my phone bleeps again. Bridget's calling. No one wants me to finish this paper. Least of all Chaucer.

"I am super popular today," I answer.

"Must be your magnetic personality." I can hear voices in the background. "Guess where I am."

"The fourteenth century murdering Chaucer for me?"

"Close. The mall."

I gasp loudly. "Traitor! You know you're not allowed to go there without me."

"I had to pick up shoes for my mom. Guess who's here? Terry Templeton."

"Terry Templeton? Who went to school with us?"

"Yeah and get this—he asked me if we still hang out."

"Urch," I say.

"And if you're still single."

"Ew! Please tell me you said I was dead."

"Relax. I sidestepped. Although I could've just told him you were seeing a dark, mysterious stranger. Is the reception guy still stalking you?"

I fidget. "Not stalking, no."

"So you haven't seen him again?"

"No-o," I reply, making the word sound more like a question than I meant it to.

There's a beat. "You're doing the thing."

"What thing?"

"The avoiding thing."

"Oh, my gosh—I'm doing the most thing-less thing ever."

"Then why is your voice like that?"

I shove a Red Vine in my mouth. "Eating junk food. You caught me."

"That's not your junk-food voice."

"I have a junk-food voice?"

"You have voices for different kinds of junk food. It's part of your guilt thing."

"Oh, really? Then tell me, Yoda, what am I eating right now?"

After a beat she says, "Licorice."

Stunned, I stammer, "That's incredible. How did you do that?"

"I bought you that tub of Red Vines, remember?"

"Less impressed." Completely monotone I say, "Oh, look. The house is on fire. I have to go lest I burn to a crisp."

"This isn't over."

"Loves."

I hang up, and instantly there's a rap of knuckles on my front door. I look over from my seat on the couch. It's laundry day, so I'm wearing mismatched pajamas and a Mickey Mouse sweatshirt. My hair is piled in a messy bun atop my head, and my makeup is smudged from an afternoon power nap.

"Never going to finish," I mutter, shuffling to the door. I open it with the chain still engaged and see Damon on the doorstep.

"Why did you open the door?" he asks.

My brow furrows. "Because you . . . knocked?"

"You're in danger, and you just open without even asking who's there?"

"I left the chain on."

"Do you know how easy it is to kick through one of these?"

"C'mon," I snort. "Can't be that easy—"

The door slams inward as the chain snaps, and I jump out of the way with a shriek. "Whoa!" I cry, shocked that he actually did it. "Overreact much?"

"Just proving my point."

"Then draw a diagram or something!" I examine the damage. The base of the chain that was screwed into the wall is now dangling with a chunk of plaster still attached to it. "You broke my apartment!"

"Relax. I'll have it fixed."

"Relax? Says the guy who just kicked in a door to prove a point." I pull on the useless chain and sigh. "You have aggression issues."

"I'll work on that. Meanwhile, we have to go."

"Go?"

"Drake Spalecki wrote back and wants to meet for dinner."

My eyes widen. "Tonight?"

"In about half an hour, and it's a bit of a drive . . ." He trails off, his gaze traveling from my messy hair to the mismatched socks.

I shift self-consciously. "It's laundry day."

"Well, throw something on. He has a reservation."

"I'm not remotely ready!" I protest. "Everything I own is soaking wet."

"Then wring it out, and let's go."

Damon waits wordlessly, his expression deadpan. "You're serious?" I ask. "You're going to make me go like this?"

He glances at his watch. "The car is leaving in five. So whatever you're wearing then, you'll wear to dinner. Your call."

My mouth opens to argue, but he just brandishes his watch at me. I turn and stomp toward my room, huffing in frustration.

"Pout all you want," he calls after me, "as long as you pout in the car."

Literally four minutes later he's hustling me down the stairs while I drag a brush through my hair. "See, you found something fine to wear," Damon says, pointing toward the SUV.

"Fine?" I'm wearing a shapeless white dress about four times my size. "This is an angel costume I wore in a church Christmas pageant." I show him two small holes at the back of the dress. "I had to rip the wings off."

"Well, you're dressed. That's the important thing."

"I'm just saying, if you want these guys to be interested enough to ask me out again, you have to give me more than thirty seconds to get ready."

"It was easily more than thirty seconds," he says, holding the back door open for me. I glare and climb in.

"Hello, Jack," Samuel says from the driver's seat.

"Hey, Samuel," I answer, braiding my hair for lack of another option. "How's Double O Huge this evening?"

He gives a throaty chuckle. "Just fine, just fine. And you?"

"Earning my money."

Damon slides into the passenger seat and types an address into the GPS.

"I know the place," Samuel says as he steers the car out of the lot. "Great tacos."

"Who're we meeting again?" I ask, messily reapplying foundation from my purse.

"Drake Spalecki. What do you know about him?"

Feeling like I'm being quizzed, I grope in my brain for what was in the dossier. "Um . . . He's twenty."

"Twenty-one," Damon corrects.

"One," I add quickly. "You didn't let me finish. He's a . . ." I got nothing. "Human being."

Samuel laughs, but Damon turns to give me a stern look. "Have you even looked at the file? You need to know these things."

"If it were a regular first date, I wouldn't know his credit history and social security number."

"It's not a regular date, and the more you know going in, the better chance you have of getting information out of him."

"Okay, I'll study next time," I say. "Just give me a clue on this guy."

"Attending BYU."

I meet his gaze in the rearview mirror. "That's like saying he has feet."

He sounds impatient. "Currently doing general studies because he just got—"

"Back from his mission," I finish, triumphant. "He's a brand-new RM!"

"Yeah, *that's* like saying he has feet."

"True, but I remember he went on his mission to"—I bite my lip—"somewhere in Latin America. Nicara . . . no. Cuba!" I smack the back of Damon's seat. "He went to Cuba! Haha!"

"Honduras," he corrects.

"Oh, can it, Magellan," I grumble and sink against the seat.

11

As I step into the restaurant, there's a stampeding bull with steam billowing from its flared nostrils rearing over me.

Yikes. I stop short and stare. The ceiling and walls have been painted with a vivid mural of a Spanish bullfight. Beside the curved doorway leading toward the dining room, a gored matador lies in the sand, bleeding out. His tongue lolls in death. That's the image you want burned into your mind right before you eat dinner.

"Hello!" chirps the hostess behind the brightly painted counter. "Welcome to—" she rattles off the name of the restaurant, something very long and complicated in Spanish that I could never hope to repeat back. I wonder if that's the requirement for working here. You have to be able to say the name correctly.

"Hi." I smile, fidgety in my ridiculous getup. I'm one of those never-go-out-in-public-without-makeup-on people. Even when my appendix burst, I put on cute pajamas and mascara before leaving the house. Standing here in this angel costume is more painful for me than the appendix thing.

She beams at me from beneath an enormous sombrero. That thing must weigh a ton. Maybe that's another job requirement. You must be able to wear twenty extra pounds on your head for an eight-hour shift. "How many in your party?" she asks.

"Actually, I'm meeting someone, but I'm not sure if he's here yet."

"It wouldn't happen to be Drake Spalecki, would it?"

I blink, surprised, and think, *Oh, my gosh, she's in on it. They've laid a trap in the restaurant of death.*

"Yes," I respond warily, and her smile broadens.

"Drake is a regular. He said he had a date coming." She leans toward the curved doorway and calls, "Drake, your lady is here."

After a moment a guy strides through the doorway, and again I wonder why I haven't given online dating a chance. He's average height and has somewhat nondescript features and brownish hair. But when he smiles, twin dimples flash in his cheeks and make him instantly cute.

"Drake?" I ask, holding out my hand.

"Indeed. Jacklyn Wyatt, I presume?"

"Guilty." His eyes sweep over my outfit, and I find myself blushing. "Sorry about my dress," I say hurriedly. "It's a long—"

"No need to apologize; you look very nice." He shakes my hand, keeping it for a moment. "Very wholesome. It's refreshing."

Wholesome. Yeah, that's what girls like to hear. But I'm relieved he's a nice guy who doesn't mind me looking like a reject from the nativity display. "Well, thanks." We drop our hands, and I motion around the little lobby. "Nice place. I've never been here before."

His eyes light up. "You haven't? Oh, you're in for such a treat! They have the most authentic Latin food in all of Utah Valley. Trust me, I've done my research."

Oh yeah. He's a newly returned missionary, I remember. *Just got back from Nicara—no.*

"I actually just got back from Honduras," he says.

Honduras! I was close.

"I've been homesick for the food. That's why I eat here a lot."

"We get more business from Drake than all our other customers combined," the hostess puts in, and I see a little glimmer there. Maybe I can do a bit of matchmaking later on.

You know. After I'm sure he's not a killer.

Drake laughs and waves her off modestly. "Well, you won't find better food than here at—" He rattles off the name but with extra emphasis on each syllable, like a giant sneeze in Spanish. Then he laughs and the hostess laughs and I join in, even though I'm not quite sure what we're laughing at.

"Well, shall we go to our table?" he asks, motioning to the doorway.

"Sure."

I go to follow him, but he stops to stare at the gutted matador on the wall. "Beautiful, isn't it?" he asks wistfully.

"Yeah," I agree, squeamish even at the fake blood. "Really gets the appetite going."

On a Tuesday night, there are only a handful of other diners in the restaurant, and Drake clearly had his pick of seating. We're at a table in the center of the large room on a slightly raised platform under a sort of stone cabana. A wooden lattice overhead is strewn with artificial vines and grapes; a mariachi band circles the place, serenading each table in turn with upbeat music.

"Isn't this great?" Drake asks. "You know, the food isn't exactly the same as it is in Honduras. Obviously there are differences since the cultures are entirely different. But this is the closest I've been able to find." He plucks a hot scone from the basket in the center of the table and inhales its scent, eyes closed a moment. "I tell you, eating here for the first time was like coming home."

"I can imagine," I agree, drizzling honey on my own scone. *Wow, that's good. Yeah. I'd come back here just for the scones.*

The mariachi band is making its way toward us. Behind them, at the closest table to our platform, Damon is sipping his water. I nearly call to him, "Dude, try the scones!" before I remember I'm not supposed to know him.

"So," I say around another hot mouthful, "tell me, what you're—"

The mariachi band has arrived at our table and breaks into a loud rendition of some Spanish song. Their instruments are literally right in my face, and I reel back at the volume.

Drake is clapping along with their song, and I try again, louder this time, "What are—"

A trumpet beside my left ear blares a trill, and I jerk, grabbing my head. The maraca player is dancing a bit, leaning toward me. I smile back, trying to cover my annoyance. I scoot toward Drake and nearly shout, "What're you—"

"*Mi amore!*" the singers belt, taking up the lyrics now. They continue on, and Drake is beaming, my half question clearly forgotten. Normally I love this kind of thing, but I've never so wanted to stuff a scone down a trumpet before.

"Don't they ever move on to the other tables?" I holler to Drake.

"A little, but they always come back to this center area," he calls back. "That's why I chose this table. Best spot in the whole place."

"Awesome." I sink back and take a huge bite of my scone, defeated.

"Ma'am?" The hostess is at my right elbow, and I jerk, startled. With the music blaring, a machete-wielding assassin could've crept up and I would never have known. "There's a phone call for you."

"A phone call?" I repeat, confused. I open my purse and check my phone. No missed calls or texts, and there are full service bars in here. Weird. "Okay. Where do I go?"

She motions back toward the lobby, and I excuse myself—though I'm sure Drake didn't hear me—and follow her.

"Right down there." She points down a tiny hallway at a green phone with the receiver sitting on top.

I thank her and make my way down the hall, putting the receiver to my ear. "Hello?" I ask. But the line is dead.

"Hey." Damon is suddenly beside me, and I jerk again, heart racing.

"Will everyone stop scaring me?" I say. "That dead matador made me edgy."

"I need to put a wire on you."

My eyes widen. "You serious?"

"It's too loud with the music. I'm not picking up anything."

A wire, yay! I think but try to appear nonchalant. "That's cool, whatever." He leads the way to the exit door, and I stifle the urge to hum James Bond again. Samuel is waiting in the alley, device in hand.

"Hey, Double O," I'm barely containing my excitement, "is that for me?"

"It is, indeed." He hands me the fat end—a small black box.

"This is the battery pack," Damon explains. "Put it down the back of your dress and hook it to . . . whatever." His shoulders shift as though he's uncomfortable. It's awkward, especially with two men watching, but I manage to slip the battery pack into my dress and hook the clip to the top of my tank top. Samuel is already winding the flesh-colored wire up the back of my neck, securing it with clear tape, looping it over my ear, and nestling a tiny bud into my ear.

"That's the receiver and microphone. This enterprise being what it is, we didn't exactly get up-to-date equipment. We can't put a mic any closer to your mouth without it being seen, so speak up."

"Not a problem," I holler, and they both cringe.

Damon glares. "Not that loud."

I'm unabashed. "Then you should clarify."

"You'll also be able to hear us."

"Testing," Samuel says, and his deep voice registers in my ear.

"That's so cool!" I smile. "I'm official."

Samuel smiles back. "Just be careful of the pack. Try to keep it dry, and don't slam your back against anything."

"Do I want to know how much this thing costs?" I ask.

They both respond, "No."

"And act natural," Damon says, tugging the rubber band off the bottom of my hair and unraveling my braid. "If you get weird, you'll tip him off."

"What're you doing?" I ask as he continues to run his fingers through my long hair, arranging it around my shoulders.

"Hiding the wire on your neck," he responds. Something about the way he's handling my hair makes me feel like he must have sisters or something. My sisters and I assured our brothers that learning how to braid would impress girls. I wonder briefly what siblings he has, what he was like as a kid. His hand brushes my face as he finishes his work, and for some reason I glance away.

"There," Samuel says, striding back toward the SUV. "You're a pro."

"Act natural," Damon admonishes again and motions for me to return to the restaurant.

I roll my eyes at him and stride inside, but making my way back to the table, I notice the difference. I'm walking a little funny. I can't quite remember how to swing my arms with the stride of my legs. Is it the same arm with the same leg or opposite? I'm swinging my arms too vigorously now, and finally I lock them stiff at my sides.

Drake is watching me as I return to my seat. Over the music he asks, "You okay?"

"Fiiiinnnne," I respond, over-enunciating. That's exactly what I'm not supposed to do, so I try again, "Fine." The band has moved off a few paces, still *right there* but not rattling my teeth with their volume. Again I try to start a conversation. "So, Drake, you say you just got back."

"Yes." His eyes are alive. "Honduras was incredible. The best experience of my life."

"Missions are amazing things," I agree. "Absolutely life changing, I'm sure."

"So much. Not just the missionary work, but I fell in love with the country itself. Honduras has to be the most gorgeous place in the world."

"Really?" Well, he's certainly not hard to get talking. "Why don't you tell me about it?"

Worse thing I could possibly have said.

The next thing I know I'm wearing a sombrero, drinking some sugary concoction with an umbrella in it, and swaying as the band serenades me with a mournful ballad. Once you get over the hearing loss, the band is pretty great. Their mustaches defy the laws of gravity, and the maraca player has serious moves. Otherwise, this date is a bust.

This guy has done nothing but talk about Honduras for the past *hour and a half.* Every time I try to steer the conversation toward Natalie (or anything else, for that matter), he manages to find a way to get it back on track. Not even in smooth ways but like, "Speaking of McDonald's trans-fat content, did you know that in Honduras . . ." I could do a full presentation on Honduras tomorrow if I had to, complete with a working diorama of its "humble workers in the beautiful cane fields." I appreciate how much this guy loved his mission; I really do. There can be no nobler set of people than missionaries who completely give themselves to serve the Lord like that. I just wish we could talk about something, *anything* else for two minutes.

He's signaling the waiter. "Can we have some more guacamole, please?" he asks—but he pronounces it with a crazy elongated accent like *hguacchhhamoleh*! Then he gives a little shrug and smile. "Sorry. It's so hard to give up proper pronunciation."

I'm chewing on my straw. "I'll bet."

"The Spanish language is just so beautiful, so physical. Like you're not saying it right if you don't taste the words. Like guace-che-che—" He's spraying spittle in my face. "Do you hear the difference?"

"Mm-hmm," I say, surreptitiously wiping my cheeks. "And feel it."

"What?"

"Nothing. Good drink."

I take a noisy slurp, and Damon says in my earpiece, "You're losing this guy. You've got to take control of the situation." Hearing him in my ear is so strange. And he's done nothing but tell me how I'm doing this all wrong. Maybe the wire isn't as cool as I thought it would be.

"So." I scoop another chip of *hguacchhhamoleh* into my mouth. "Tell me. Have you dated much since the mission?"

"Not really." He sighs. "It's just been so hard to acclimate back to American culture, you know?"

"That's probably why you tried online dating."

"Yeah. It seemed like an easy way to break the ice." He pauses. "Did you know in Honduras in the winter—"

"Yeah, that's great," I interrupt, "but tell me more about your online dating experience. Have you been doing it long?"

"No, not long. In fact, you're only the third girl I've asked out."

Bingo.

"Really? Well, I'm flattered." I smile and can feel tomato in my teeth. I try to subtly suck it out as I ask, "Who were the other two?"

He looks a little embarrassed. "Surely you don't want to hear about that?"

"No, I do. I *really* do. I, uh, find it interesting."

"Well," he takes a sip of horchata. Or, as he calls it, *hhhorchaatuh*, with extra spittle. "The first girl was named Lucy, and she was studying at BYU to be a therapist." His eyes light up. "Did you know that in Honduras—"

"That's fascinating, Drake," I say loudly. "But tell me more. Who else have you dated?"

He thinks a moment. "The other girl was named Natalie. Studying at the U, I think. Premed. I told her that once she has her degree, she should really consider working in Honduras. They have such a need for professionals there. I'm thinking of going into the medical business myself and starting a clinic down there."

"That would be stupendous. So you and this Natalie got along pretty well?"

Drake shrugs. "Sure. She didn't, uh, seem all that interested in me, to be honest. She acted rather bored with our conversation."

I wonder why. "So you didn't see her again?"

"No. She was a nice enough girl, and really I would've loved to team up with her and run a joint clinic someday. But if a girl's not interested in me, I move on. They tell us when we're coming home from the mission, 'Don't rush too much into marriage, but don't wait too long either. There are a lot of amazing ladies out there.'"

I'm noisily eating salsa, the peak of my ladylike conduct. I wipe my mouth on a napkin and nod. "So true."

"You've got to dig deeper," Damon instructs in my ear. He's like an annoying Jiminy Cricket who just won't shut up. Like a bossy little insect wearing a dark suit and an earpiece. The thought gives me a sudden giggle.

"What's so funny?" Drake asks.

"Oh, nothing." I fight to rein in my expression. "I was just thinking how amazing it would be to run a clinic. I mean, think of all the good you could do."

He's nodding. "Exactly. That's exactly what I thought."

"I mean, there's so much to be done for those poor, beautiful, beleaguered people."

Drake is looking at me like I'm Mother Theresa. "Jack," he says with sudden passion. "Would you like to run a clinic with me?"

"Me?" I gasp, spurting salsa from my nose. *Wow, that burns!* I try to blow it out in my napkin. The ladylike moments just keep coming. "No, no, no—I, uh . . . I have no training."

"We could get the training together." He seizes my hand, eyes shining. "We could start premed together, study together, help each other with exams. Then we could find a medical school and attend together. We could be setting up our clinic in Honduras in ten years."

Ten years? Of constant studying? That sounds awful. Kudos to all the doctors out there.

"Drake." I gently pat his hand. "You're very sweet, and it's a super tempting offer. But I'm not made for that kind of life. I already have my passion. Besides, I'd be the worst doctor on the planet. The sight of ketchup makes me woozy."

"Oh." His face is slowly falling.

"But that doesn't mean there aren't plenty of girls out there who would love to have the Patch Adams thing with you. It's such a noble dream! Like that Natalie girl, for instance. Maybe she didn't seem that interested last time, but doctors are pretty serious people. Well, except Patch Adams. Maybe she's just quiet like that."

He takes his hand back, deliberating. "Maybe."

"So maybe you should call her back and see what she thinks about your idea."

He's nodding slowly, some of the light returning to his eyes. "Yeah. Yeah, maybe I should."

"So you would do that? You would . . . go out with her again?"

"Absolutely. As you say, maybe she's just a reserved person. The kind of work we'd be doing demands a serious, dedicated mind. And she was awfully nice."

Now that I've come down this track, I feel bad for giving him hope about a girl who's not even there. I lean forward. "But even if Natalie's not the one, I'm sure you'll find some girl who is. Don't give up on that. She's out there just waiting for her Dr. McDreamy."

His brow furrows. "Who?"

"Never mind. She's just out there. Trust me."

Drake regards me for a moment. "I must say, it's rather unusual to have a girl I'm on a date with encouraging me to date other women."

"Well," I shrug, "that dream of yours sounds amazing. I'd like you to have it with a girl who can hold her cookies when someone starts bleeding."

He laughs. "That's kind of you." He pauses. "So what's your passion?"

"My what?"

"Your passion. You said you already had one. What is it?"

"Oh." I'm taken aback. I hadn't even realized I said that. "Literature, I guess. That's what I'm studying." I don't mention the thing that went through my mind when he asked—*spying*.

"Well, good for you," he says. Then he gets that dreamy expression again. "Did you know that in Honduras they have—"

I slump down beneath my sombrero and signal for another drink.

When I tramp unevenly toward the car after the date (too much sugar makes me just a little tipsy), Samuel is a few paces off, talking quietly on his cell phone. Damon is sitting in the passenger's seat looking disapproving.

"Oh, shut up," I say.

He blinks. "I didn't say anything."

"Yes, but you were about to say something rude, and I'm very tired, so I wanted to preempt it."

He ignores my comment. "You didn't push that guy hard enough. Not nearly hard enough. You did a half-rate job."

"See, there it is. I must be psychic."

"Jack, don't you get it? Now we have to spend more time—more precious time that we absolutely do not have—waiting and setting up another meeting so you can question him again."

"If you're so keen to question him, why not just drag him in and interrogate him?"

"We could've done that at the beginning with all these guys and left you completely out of it. The idea was to identify the kidnapper and see if he could lead us to Natalie. We let him know we're onto him, and she's as good as dead—if she's not already."

"I got Drake to admit he wants to go out with her again. Why would he say that if he already had her in his lair?"

"Maybe so you would stop talking about it. You're not the most subtle bullet in the box."

"So first I didn't push him hard enough, and now I'm too forward? Pick your insults, Damon."

"That's not proof. He talks a good line, but we can't know that he intends—" His phone buzzes. He takes it from his pocket and answers with a curt, "Yes?"

I use the lull to slip off my heels and lean against the door. My stomach hurts. Way too much guacamole. And salsa. And tacos. And rice . . .

"Thanks." Damon hangs up and is silent several seconds. "Drake just called Natalie."

I perk up instantly. "He did?"

"Yes. When she didn't answer, he left a message saying he'd like to get together again. He even suggested a specific night, if she was available."

I'm smiling. "Surely he wouldn't do that if—"

"If he was the one who took her. It indicates he thinks she's still out there living her life."

"So . . ." I know I'm treading on dangerous ground but can't help it. "So I actually did get some proof."

His eyebrow crooks, but he doesn't look over at me. "Yes, you did."

I press, "So what I did in there was actually *good*."

Now he's smiling a little, albeit with annoyance. "Yes. It was good."

"I'm a good spy." I'm dancing a bit now, like the maraca player. "You can say it, Damon. It's okay. No one else will hear you."

His face is overly rigid, like a little kid fighting not to grin. But he just says, "Don't push it."

12

SUGAR COMAS ARE REAL THINGS. And they're as bad as hangovers. I don't care what anyone says.

Not that I've been drunk or hungover, but I cannot imagine it being worse than this.

In the morning I have a blinding headache that follows me through my classes and drives me home onto the couch by early afternoon. Throbbing from the base of my neck all the way through both eyeballs, I spread the notes for my women in literature paper on the couch and try to focus. Never before have I noticed how *small* my own handwriting is. Does that say "exultant" or "excrement?" It makes a real difference to the direction this paper will go.

Without meaning to, I've slipped down and am resting on my side, face pressed to my notes, blurry eyes falling shut. *Just going to close my eyes for five minutes. Just five minutes . . .*

The mariachi trumpets blare in my ear, and I jerk awake, sitting up on the couch. My neck is kinked to the right, and I've been drooling all over my notes. The trumpets are actually my phone ringing. I grope for it, try to swipe the touch screen to answer about ten times before it works. "Hello?"

"Did I wake you?" It's Damon. The guy that never goes away.

"No," I say, my voice clearly slurred with sleep. "I was ssstudying."

"Ssstudying? Aren't there a few extra syllables in there?"

"Sshut up. What do you want?"

"Have you checked your e-mails?"

"Not today, no."

His voice is disapproving as he asks, "How can you make contact with these guys if you don't stay on top of it?"

I drag my sleeve across my mouth to remove excess drool. "Sorry. Was still recovering from my success last night. You remember it, I'm sure."

There's a beat. "I vaguely recall."

"So stubborn. What's on my e-mail?"

"Ned Craven. He wants to meet."

"Tonight? You seriously have to give me time to put the hotness together."

Another beat. Then, "The hotness?"

"You know, at least an attempt at some hotness. Luke-warmness, maybe."

"It's tomorrow night."

"Oh. Well, that's good. I'm a royal wreck right now."

"Good, sure." There's something about his voice.

"Not good?" I ask.

"It's just twenty-four more hours that we have to wait."

I'm nodding. "You hate the waiting."

"I hate thinking of what it means to the girl."

Natalie. I keep forgetting. I'd gotten caught up in the cool wires and the oddball dates and forgot *why*. "Yeah, I'm sorry," I say, genuinely humbled. "I should've been pushing harder to set up the meetings. Maybe I can get this Ned guy to meet tonight."

"No, he said he wants to take you to a specific event."

"What event?"

"He didn't say."

"I just hope it doesn't involve carving knives." There's a noise on the line that confuses me. "Are you *laughing?*" I ask.

Silence. "Maybe."

"Wow." I get up and wander to the fridge, pulling out my chicken-and-fries leftovers. "Stoic Special Agent Damon Wade laughs. That's one for the books."

"You caught me off guard. Won't happen again."

I munch on a cold fry. "Yeah. Keep that buttoned, Agent. This is serious business."

"Yes, it is."

"I'll check in with the guys I haven't met yet and see what's up. And I'll study my dossier so I can annihilate Ned tomorrow."

"Sounds good."

I put my leftovers in the microwave.

"You should rip off the lid," Damon says.

"What?"

"On your leftovers. You should rip the lid off the Styrofoam so it can vent as it heats up."

I turn toward the kitchen window. "You watching?"

"No. But I'm starting to get you." He hangs up.

After the call I'm anxious. There's a ten-day clock on this mission, and we're already through two days. That's eight days left and six guys still to meet. Not to mention the ones I'll have to go out with a second time. I'm not great at math, but even I know it's looking grim.

As I inhale the leftovers, I check my e-mail on my phone, scrolling through the list of suspects I already messaged. Ned can't meet until tomorrow, but there are five others who might be available. Three of those have already contacted me and shown interest. I quickly compose a short message—*I know it's late notice, but are you up for some ice cream?*—and shoot it off to all three. Might as well stack my chances.

Twenty minutes later I'm bent back over my notes when my phone dings, signaling an e-mail.

Stu Clarkson has written back: *Ice cream sounds cool, I guess. I mean cool like fine. You know. Want to meet at Cold Stone? I guess I could be there. How about in an hour? Or maybe forty-five. I can probably show up.*

Even on the second read the e-mail is weird. He sounds nervous or confused maybe. Who agrees to a date, proposes a location and time, and then says they can "probably show up"?

The point is he answered! Already I'm jerking a brush through my hair with one hand and texting Damon with the other.

In ten minutes there's a knock on my door. I answer in jeans and a gray, loose-knit sweater, still putting in earrings. My hair is down around my shoulders in case I need to wear a wire.

Damon's on the doorstep, looking surprised. "You have a date with Stu?"

"Yep, and I brought the hotness in record time." I snap my fingers. Sauntering past him, I add, "Feel free to be impressed."

The line at Cold Stone extends from the order counter all the way to the door. It's so packed I can only open the door a crack and shimmy through it sideways, nearly losing some valuable body parts in the process. I resist the urge to reach back and be sure I didn't snag my wire on the way in. When he saw how crowded it was from outside, Damon conceded my wearing the pack again. It would be more suspicious for him to stick close in such a cramped space.

The walls are lined with photographs of the sinful ice cream creations they offer, and the whole place smells like sugar and bliss. Just walking in is enough to fill my mouth with saliva.

I arranged this meeting in such a rush there was no chance to review the dossier, so I have no clue what Stu looks like. The tables are occupied by couples and small groups, and everyone in the line seems to be with someone. On the opposite side of the room, my gaze lands on a guy standing alone. His posture is impressive, his build stocky, and his dark eyes keep darting toward the exit like he's mapping his getaway.

Jostling past laughing couples with towering bowls of ice cream (restraining myself from taking a lick of every cone I pass), I reach the loner and offer a smiling, "Hey, are you Stu?"

His gaze swivels to me, his eyes instantly narrowed under a shock of long, reddish hair. "Who wants to know?"

"I'm Jack Wyatt. You agreed to meet me?"

He shrugs, but it's a sharp movement—like he's wound so tightly every action is executed in double time. "I guess. More or less. But you're the one who suggested it."

"Yes, I did," I say slowly. "And . . . thanks for coming."

His eyes are on the exit again. "Sure, that's . . . fine."

After a long moment I motion toward the counter. "Well, should we order?"

Stu wets his lips, sizing up the counter as though it might be some kind of trap. "I guess so. We could." He doesn't move.

I take a halting step but pause when he makes no effort to follow. "We should probably, uh, get in line then."

"Yeah." He nods and takes a shuddering breath like he's psyching himself up the way I do before getting a shot. "Yeah, I guess we should." Still, he doesn't move.

I think I'm starting to understand what's going on here. "Well," I say, trying to sound casual and nonthreatening, like I'm talking to a man on a ledge. "I'm going to go over here and get in line. If you feel like you want to join me, that's where I'll be."

The line has increased and curled around back toward us. Moving slowly so as not to startle Stu, I amble over, keeping my gaze forward. What animal is it that only attacks if you make eye contact? I can't remember, but I think the same might be true here. Except instead of attacking he'll bolt for the door or take up permanent refuge under a table.

After a full minute he shuffles into place beside me, but still I don't look over at him. Maybe thirty seconds more pass before he says, "I guess we could order."

Yep. He's Terrified-to-Commit guy.

It takes nearly forty-five minutes to get through the line to order, and in that time I learn almost nothing about Stu. I'm afraid to push the conversation and scare him off, so I ease into each subject like treading a minefield. By the time we're carrying our bowls of ice cream to a vacant table, I've learned that he is currently undecided on his major, lives with his parents but is thinking of maybe possibly moving in with some roommates, and hates fish.

Although he's not entirely positive about that.

Even Damon is silent, loitering at a nearby table but saying nothing in my earpiece. Last night he couldn't shut up about me pushing Drake Spalecki, but apparently he too can see that Stu is a whole other thing.

The portion sizes are so enormous I've probably gained five pounds before I finally work my way around to the subject of Natalie. "So, Stu." I take a bite of cake batter ice cream smothered in caramel with cookie dough chunks. Just looking at it gives me cavities. "Have you been online dating very long?"

Stu is staring into his bowl—a combination of five different kinds of ice cream and twelve toppings. He anguished so long over which flavor to get that the girl behind the counter finally dished up all of them. "A while," he says finally. "I've e-mailed a few girls but only met with you."

That would be flattering if it wasn't clear he'd been regretting it ever since. I do remember Clemens saying that according to the e-mails two of the guys who contacted Natalie had yet to arrange dates with her. "But," Clemens intoned, "that doesn't mean they didn't observe her without her knowledge. They're still suspects."

Personally, I've got my doubts about Stu.

"So there weren't any other girls who caught your eye?" I ask.

His fevered gaze darts up to me then back to studying his sludge of flavors. "There were some nice girls. Just no one I was ready to see yet."

Shocker. Just signing up for the dating service probably gave him the sweats. "Any that you might ask out in the future?"

His knee starts bouncing erratically, and he drags his pale fingers through his hair. "I don't know. Maybe. Maybe not. It's a lot of pressure." His Adam's apple bobs as he swallows and tugs at the collar of his shirt. "Is it hot in here?"

"A little bit." I chuckle. "Here, have a napkin."

I hold one out to him, and he reaches for it, then retracts his hand. This continues several seconds before he launches to his feet.

"You know what?" he says loudly, his forehead flooded with sweat. "This is just too much. You know? It's like, we just met and suddenly you're giving me things? You're a nice girl, but this is like a speeding train. I don't care how much my mother pushes me, I'm too young to have nine kids and a minivan." He sprints for the door, shouting, "I hate minivans!"

As the door closes behind him, the entire place has fallen silent, and all eyes are on me.

Feebly I hold it up and say, "It's just a napkin."

13

Pigs must be flying this morning. Damon and I actually agree on something.

Last night he reluctantly concluded, as I had, that Stu is an unlikely candidate for kidnapper. It seems to me kidnapping is a highly committed act. The guy who balked at accepting my napkin could hardly have taken Natalie for fear of what she'd read into it.

More and more I'm convinced Tommy could be the guy.

The ice cream incident was so short it unfortunately left me with time enough to be obligated to study. As I agonized over every single word of my first draft on femme fatales in literature, Tommy texted me almost constantly. Cheesy lines straight out of the Player's Handbook: *You tired, baby? Been running through my mind all day.* Gross.

Even at one a.m. when I finally closed the computer on my finished draft and dragged myself to bed, he messaged: *Want to come over?*

Hoping I came across playful and not just annoyed I wrote back: *Booty call, much?*

To which he responded: *You read my mind, babe. ;)*

And when I declined, insisting I was too tired but would talk to him tomorrow, he said good night.

Then thirty seconds later, he wrote: *Hey, Amy. Want to come over?*

And fourteen seconds after that: *Sorry. Wrong person.*

First thing this morning, there were more texts. Sure, he seems like your average player, but the behavior's getting stalker-ish enough that I think he warrants a second look.

Tired from the late night, I'm sluggish and run into biology two minutes late. The professor barely glances my way as I slouch through the door, but I still duck down behind my collar as I creep toward my seat. I have to climb over four people—including Peggy, who gives me a little smile—before stumbling into my chair.

The lecture has already started, and I scramble in my bag for my notebook and a pen. Everything long and skinny and remotely pen-like I grab and extract but no. Lip liner. Highlighter. Stick of packaged Slim Jim. Not a single stinking pen in the whole bag?

Frustrated, I dump the entire contents on the table and ignore the people who turn to look at the racket. No pen. And no chocolate bar. I'm off my game today.

The guy next to me holds out a pen. "Here you go."

"Thanks." I reach to take it and give an almighty gasp.

It's Damon.

He's wearing another calculated casual look and reclining in his chair like the average student with bad posture, head cocked and expression amused.

It takes me a moment to realize the professor has stopped talking. The room is silent. It takes another moment to realize that everyone is looking at me. I guess I did gasp pretty loudly.

"Sorry!" My voice is still louder than I mean it to be. "Thought I saw a rat. But it was . . . my foot."

The professor's brow is furrowed. "Your . . . foot?"

"Yes. Yes, sir." When he keeps staring, I say, "I have . . . hairy feet."

Peggy shrinks back from me.

The professor shakes his head and returns to the whiteboard. "Well, then. Let's continue. The cell structure is labeled as follows—"

I snatch the pen from Damon and furiously start scribbling notes, trying to ignore him. After a moment he leans toward me and whispers directly in my ear, "The phrase you're looking for is thank you."

Without taking my eyes off the whiteboard, I hiss, "What are you doing here? Has the perimeter for the protective watch suddenly shrunk to two feet?"

"As a matter of fact, yes. We had reason to worry about your safety."

A tiny panic flutters in my stomach. "Why? What happened?"

"You received some mail this morning."

"I didn't pick up any mail."

"We intercepted it. We're monitoring all incoming." He slides a paper onto my notes, and I instantly go cold.

A single phrase is on the paper, strewn together with letters cut from a magazine: *I could be your great adventure.*

"You want to tell me something?" Damon asks. His voice makes me finally glance at him. He looks angry.

I shrink down a bit in my seat. "Okay. Maybe I wrote all the guys again last night. Maybe I used some . . . carefully worded phrasing . . ."

"You commented that you didn't have enough adventure in your life." His voice is like flint.

"Well, I know time is running out, and I thought maybe I could spark something in them like Natalie did."

"Were you trying to blow your cover? Or just get yourself killed faster?"

I turn to glare. "You can't put me in the field and keep me in a box at the same time. Pick one!"

A guy on the row behind us gives a sharp, "Shh!" and I nearly throw my Slim Jim at him.

"Besides," I shove the paper back at him, trying to keep my hands from shaking, "clearly it worked. If I got the guy's attention and you're watching me, you'll catch him."

"Do you realize what you're saying? We only wanted to gather information. What you've done is practically stamped 'Kidnap me!' on your forehead and broadcast it to every suspect we have."

I shrug. "If it gets results."

"If it gets results?" He slides his chair closer to mine, buzzing in my ear. "Since when did you become Rambo? You were hesitant to even work with us, and now you want to use yourself as bait?"

"Excuse me." The professor's talking to me again, and once more all eyes dart toward us. "Would you two like to share with the class?"

"Nope," I holler back. "Thought there might be another rat. But it was just—"

The professor crosses his arms. "Your other foot?"

"Yes. But I'm, uh, looking into laser hair removal. So . . ." I keep nodding, my cheeks burning. Eventually the professor shakes his head and resumes teaching.

Damon slides his chair back to its place and remains silent for the rest of the lecture. I don't look his way again but feverishly scrawl notes. Not that it matters. I'm so failing this class.

"So, what now?" I ask as he trails behind me out of the lecture hall. "You tag along and ruin my entire academic career?"

"Your protective detail's been doubled. From now on there'll be two agents close by at all times and another two running constant surveillance."

"Two? Where was the other agent during class?"

"Blending in. Clearly he's more 'ninja' than I am."

"And when does the detail turn over?"

He glances at me, head cocked. "Trying to get rid of me already?"

"Yes. The sooner the better."

"Well, sorry to disappoint, but I'm on daytime detail. You don't get rid of me until after the date tonight."

"Right. Ned Craven. The accountant."

"You did your studying?"

"Yes." I sidestep a group of dancers flitting out of one of the ballet studios. "I was trying to help. Wouldn't have tried so hard if I'd known you were going to make me flunk biology."

My phone beeps, a text from Bridget: *Lunch?*

Thursdays we have our class break at the same time and often meet for a bite. I type back, *For sure. Cafeteria?* To which she replies a smiley face. It'll be good to see her, to ground myself to reality for a bit. Just one more hour.

"So," Damon says. "What women will we be studying in literature today?"

This could be a long hour.

14

I'm going to slap him.

Sure, Damon behaved himself during my second class. He sat several seats behind me and had the decency to stay quiet, but now that class is over he's on my heels again. I know it's my fault the detail got multiplied, and I appreciate the security measures, but he's in full Jiminy mode again—always picking. When we reach the entrance to the cafeteria, I turn to face him. "What're you doing?"

"Going to eat lunch," he says. "I hear the hamburgers are good."

"You're not sitting with me."

"Why not?"

"Because I'm meeting Bridget, and I don't want to explain how I'm suddenly cozy with the guy I thought was stalking me a few days ago."

He looks interested. "You talked to her about me?"

"Yes. Back when I thought you were following me around. Oh, wait. Guess I was right." I lope away from him, and he lets me out on an invisible tether. But I can almost feel it tugging, assuring he's nearby.

Bridget's already seated at a table under an umbrella, tapping on her phone. "Hey," I say and bend to hug her. "It's so good to see you."

She smiles. "Rough day?"

"Rough week. I need fatty foods and girl talk."

"Then you've come to the right place. Should we get our food one at a time? I don't want to lose our table."

"No. I'll just leave my stuff here."

Her brow knits. "You sure? You're not worried someone will take it?"

"Hey, if they want my biology book"—I dump my textbooks on the table—"they can have it."

We each wait for chicken strips, though Bridget pairs hers with a modest salad, and I go for fries and double sauce again. Eating my frustration.

"Are finals bugging you?" she asks, selecting a fruit cup from one of the large fridges.

"No, just . . . annoying people."

She adds an apple to her tray. I add cake to mine.

"Yeah, like who?"

"Oh, I don't even want to talk about it. How're you doing with finals?"

She shrugs. "Easy classes this semester. Not real worried."

The guy at the register gets tongue-tied when Bridget hands over her salad for weighing. I swear it's like being best friends with a Greek goddess. Except she can't curse pesky mortals for me.

"Would you do the world a favor and just pick a guy?" I grumble as we return to our table. "At least if you had a rock on your finger, they'd realize there was no hope and might notice the rest of us."

She looks me over carefully. "You're edgy."

I blow out my breath. "Yeah. I'm being a brat. Sorry."

"What's up? Really?"

Nothing would feel better than spilling the whole thing to her, but there's that whole confidentiality bit I signed back at the field office. At the time I was more concerned with the waiver absolving the FBI of any responsibility should I be injured or killed during the mission. Now I wish there had been some loophole so I could confide in just *one* person.

Well, maybe there is. "It's this, uh . . . this case," I say slowly.

Bridget starts into her salad. "Case?"

"Yeah. For my lit class. We're . . . studying the origin of the detective novel, and for our final, we have to solve a mystery." My pulse is throbbing in my temple from lying, but Bridget looks unsuspecting.

"And you're having a hard time with it?" she asks.

"Yeah. It's a modern mystery with very realistic characters, and I just can't get a handle on who could have done it."

"Well, lay it out for me. I'll help."

"Okay." I glance around and spot Damon across the cafeteria, eating a sandwich. According to him there's another agent somewhere

in the room and two more watching, maybe from outside. The entire far wall of the dining area is glass looking out onto the upper walkways of campus. Students bustle by, but I don't notice anyone who looks like an agent. Chances are they can't hear me right now. And I'm not actually telling her it's real, right?

Rationalizing is another of my major sins.

"We haven't been introduced to all the characters yet," I say, still taut with nerves. "But so far there's a guy who's like Mr. Perfect. You know, the kind of guy who has impossible expectations of women?"

"I've dated three." Bridget nods. "What's the crime?"

"Kidnapping. The victim is a girl, midtwenties. She was on her way to becoming a doctor."

She brightens. "Just like me!"

"You're becoming a doctor now?"

"I don't know, maybe. I was thinking about it. Continue."

"For suspects so far there's Mr. Perfect. There's also a super groping, pervert guy."

Bridget's nodding again. "Dated two of those."

"There's also a good guy who just got back from a mission and a guy who can't even commit to what socks to put on in the morning."

She chews thoughtfully for several moments before answering. "Well, you're much more of an expert on literary stuff than I am, but isn't it usually the person you least suspect? And there's always that person they try to make it seem like it is."

"A red herring. A character that looks guilty to throw you off."

"I'd say that the pervert is too obvious to be guilty. Mr. Perfect is the one people wouldn't suspect, but the fact that I *wouldn't* suspect him makes me suspect him a little. So he's probably the red herring. My bet would be on the good guy. That's the best twist."

"Yeah," I muse. "But there's some evidence that it wasn't the good guy."

"Is the evidence solid?"

"Relatively."

"Then it's just further proof that it could be him, because we think it couldn't possibly be."

I pop a fry into my mouth. "That's a good point. I don't know. There are like five other suspects to be introduced."

"Well, when you read that far, call me, and we'll brainstorm some more." Bridget smiles. "I'm sure you'll figure it out. But don't be too hard on yourself. It's just a grade."

There's a sudden lump in my throat. "Yeah, sure. Just a grade."

The second I part ways with Bridget, Damon's at my elbow again. "Nice chat?" he asks.

My heart constricts, certain this is a loaded question and he knows what I did. But his expression looks neutral enough so I respond, "Yes. It was great, thanks."

"Ned Craven e-mailed a response about your date tonight."

"You didn't read the e-mail?"

Damon shrugs. "Thought I'd let you do that yourself."

"The illusion of privacy. How thoughtful." My brow furrows as I look at my phone. "He didn't name a restaurant. He gave me an address."

"An address?" Damon takes my phone and types the address into his own to do a search. "This is a church building."

"Like a Mormon church building?"

"Yeah. It's up in Cedar Hills."

"What's he planning to have us do? Play basketball? Vacuum the chapel?"

Damon's face suddenly clears with realization, and he starts laughing. "Oh, I think I have a pretty good idea."

15

It's a stake dance.

It's a *stake dance.*

The dances LDS kids attend when they're ages 14–18, but mostly they only go until they're 16 and allowed to date. For the 14- and 15-year-olds, it's mostly just a good excuse to flirt with members of the opposite sex without breaking the dating rule.

My grown-up, adult date has brought me to a teenybopper dance.

I stare for several minutes at the front of the church, watching the preteens file in. They're all dressed so carefully, so excited about the prospects of the evening. I was the same way when I was their age. But I'm not their age anymore. I'm *twenty-five.*

"He can't be serious," I say for probably the fourth time.

Damon hasn't stopped laughing since we pulled up. "You know, I suspected," he says. "But I didn't think it could actually be true."

"You can't expect me to go through with this," I implore.

"Oh, on the contrary. I expect you to dance and drink bad punch and be generous when it's time for the girl's choice. There are a lot of lonely, acne-ridden boys in there whose self-esteem could really benefit from a dance with a woman like you."

I fiddle with the earpiece, stalling. Remembering the deafening music at these things as well as I do, Damon once again suggested I go in wired. "Isn't this evidence enough? No man who brings a woman to a *stake dance* on a date could possibly be a psycho killer."

"I think this does the opposite for your argument, actually. Face it. You're not getting out of this."

I open the door and glare as I climb out. I'm just another girl getting dropped off at the stake dance. It's like I'm fifteen years old all over again.

I try to cover my face and slouch so as not to be so tall as I walk inside, but there's a congregation of kids in the foyer who all turn to look at me with confusion as I enter.

The FBI is *so* not paying me enough for this.

There's a tall, lanky guy behind the table. He's dressed in a white shirt buttoned all the way up and dark pants several sizes too big for his small frame. His hair is combed to the side, and his long face reminds me of those dogs with the mournful eyes and all that slouchy skin. He's marking names on a clipboard as the kids come in. Beside him an older couple scrutinizes those entering to be sure the boys are wearing ties and the girls' skirts come to the knee.

When the tall guy sees me, his face breaks into a shy smile, and he comes around the table. "You must be Jack," he says and leans forward to give me a hug. Surprised, I hug him back. It's like embracing a bony tree. He really needs a good, square meal, as Mom would say.

He leans back and instantly looks ashamed. "I'm sorry. That was awfully forward of me when we've just met."

"No, no," I say. "I'm a big hugger."

"Well, maybe after we've become more acquainted. Thanks for meeting me here."

"Yeah . . ." I look around, searching for something to say. "This is certainly familiar."

"I had already agreed to chaperone this dance when you said you were available tonight, so I thought"—he spreads his arms—"two birds, one stone!"

I give a strangled laugh. "That's a . . . way to do it!"

"I figured, what's better than a little wholesome fun, getting to serve the youth. But don't worry." He nudges me with his clipboard. "We'll have plenty of time to get our groove on."

"Oh good," I say. But I don't say more because I can't hear over Damon laughing in my earpiece.

We sit behind the table, ticking off names as the kids swarm in. The old couple deliberates over this one poor girl's skirt for so long ("It sort of hovers in front of the knee but doesn't fully come *to* the knee.") that

I'm sure she'll burst into tears and go running home. But finally she passes inspection and gratefully hurries into the gym with her friends.

After about an hour they stop coming through. Even the kids who decided to arrive fashionably late are inside.

"Well, now it's time for phase two." Ned turns to me, deadly serious. "Are you ready to go into law enforcement?"

My heart skips a beat. *Oh my gosh, he knows.* "What do you mean?" I ask, turning the ear with the receiver farther from him.

"I mean, it's time to do the most important part of our job." He hands me a flexible tape measure with a flourish. "Keeping the morality."

I take the tape measure. "So with this I'm supposed to . . ."

"Use it to be sure the kids aren't dancing too close. If they're standing a solid foot apart, they're good. But if they're any closer," he sucks in his breath sharply, "we have a problem."

"Right." I nod. "Well, okay then. I'll go get measuring."

I start to get up from the table, but he stops me. "Wait, let me escort you." He comes around to my side and holds out his arm. I take it with a little laugh and walk with him into the darkened gym.

The room is lit with flameless tiki torches, part of a luau-themed décor. Paper grass hangs across the front of the stage and fringes the doorways, and a cardboard cabana painted to look like bamboo houses the refreshment table. Each kid obviously had a plastic lei forced on them when they came through the door. Several are still wearing them, but some of the boys have adjusted them to be headbands, bicep bands, or belts for the very skinny. The cheaply decorated room and the swell of Backstreet Boys from the speakers hit me with a sudden bittersweet wave of nostalgia.

It was the best of times, it was the worst of times. When Dickens wrote about the French Revolution, he'd never been to a stake dance.

"Oh, I almost forgot!" Ned exclaims. "Excuse me for a moment." He darts off, and I lean against the wall, watching the crowd. It's a good turnout. Surprising in a day when texting has become the new hanging out, and hanging out has become the new dating. There are probably seventy-five kids here. As I thought, most of them are no older than sixteen. The groups are pretty much the same as they were when I was here a decade ago.

The too-cool guys cluster near the middle, pants hanging low once they passed inspection at the entrance. Sometimes they spontaneously create a circle in which they badly break-dance and high-five each other a lot. Those who are here to flirt and nothing else gather near the back in twos and threes of cute girls to which the guys can circulate to select who'll be next for the slow song.

There are throngs of all-girl groups near the perimeter that came en masse to feel more secure and have a good time with their friends. Most of these girls look so sure of themselves when they're bopping and laughing with their friends, but they're the same girls who, as soon as the music slows, drift to the walls in hopes they'll be asked to dance. And many times that just won't happen.

I was one of those girls. Showed up with my ward friends and honestly had a great time during the fast stuff. But the minute a slow one came on, I was hugging the wall so I wouldn't look pathetic and just praying that someone would come for me—anyone really. Sometimes they did. But mostly I just drank a lot of punch and tried to pretend I wasn't bothered.

Ned is back. "I got these for us!" From behind his back he produces two matching grass skirts. "Festive, right?" He laughs and holds mine out to me.

What the heck? I don't know these kids. It's not the first time in my life I'll look like an idiot. Sometimes when you look stupid, you have the most fun. "Very festive," I agree and slip the skirt down over my head and onto my hips. "Thank you, Ned."

"You're welcome." The song changes, and he lights up. "I love this song." He instantly starts doing a bad rendition of the hula, and I can't help laughing.

It's clear the DJ thinks no music has been produced for the past fifteen years, which gives Ned the chance to demonstrate a lot of his sweet moves. He's pretty good at the running man, the shopping cart, and the sprinkler, but he fails at the worm and has to nurse his back for a minute.

It's so loud in here I can't do much besides let him flail in circles around me and try to keep up. I'm hoping a slow song will provide the opportunity to talk, but the second the music slows his expression turns somber.

"Time to protect morality." He unclips his industrial tape measure from his belt. He's snaking off through the crowd before I can say anything.

Resigned and wishing I'd worn tennis shoes, I pull my own tape measure out and circle the room, trying to look like I'm doing my job. Most of the kids are behaving themselves, but when I do pass a couple getting a little close, I just say, "Keep it PG, guys." I got the measuring tape used on me once while dancing with a junior version of Grabby McFeely, and it was utterly humiliating. I'd like to spare them one more traumatizing experience.

The second slow song is "Lady in Red." *Classic.* I can't locate Ned, which is ridiculous as he's taller than all these kids by two heads.

"He's by the refreshment cabana," Damon's voice says in my ear, and I visibly jump. I'd forgotten he was listening in.

"Yup, I'm still here," he says as though reading my thoughts. "Miss me?"

"Well, I haven't been insulted in nearly thirty minutes. That's unsettling."

"All right. Your sprinkler is a little rigid."

"It's supposed to be rigid. It's a *sprinkler*," I hiss. Two kids dancing at arm's length look over at me, concerned that I'm talking to myself. I just smile and move toward the cabana.

". . . which is why it's so important to maintain standards even in peer pressure situations," Ned is telling a pair of teenagers. He must've caught them making out. More of her lipstick is on his mouth than her own, and they're standing about four feet apart, looking ashamed. "The choices you make now about what you will and won't do are the choices you'll carry with you the rest of your life. If you don't decide now where the line is, you won't be able to decide in the critical moment." Ned places a fatherly hand on each of their shoulders. "Understand, guys?"

They both nod mutely and slouch off in different directions.

Ned sighs, shaking his head. "Technically I should've thrown them out. But I like to give them a second chance. Sometimes one good, stern talking to is all it takes."

"It was nice of you to reason with them," I say, and I mean it. "Most people wouldn't take the time."

"I take chaperoning very seriously. I might sound silly, but these formative years are so important. I like them to know someone who really cares is looking out for them."

And here it is again. A cliché is, underneath, just the very best of something.

"It's good of you," I say. Suddenly I realize that "Lady in Red" is ending and a faster song is picking up in its place. "I was hoping we could talk," I say, already having to shout over the swell of music.

"Maybe on the next slow song," he yells back. "I need to have a word with the DJ. I think some of these songs might be questionable." He strides off, and now I understand why the poor DJ is playing only songs from when I was first battling acne. I pocket my measuring tape and amble along the perimeter.

"You'll have to do better than that," Damon speaks in my ear again, and I jump.

"We've been here thirty minutes, and it's LOUD," I intentionally holler into the microphone. "Cut me a break."

"Then you've got to get him somewhere that's quiet. Fake an ankle sprain or something. Get him into another room."

"This guy wouldn't be in a room alone with me. He's probably still operating on the honor system."

"Just get moving."

I pull a face, and Damon adds, "Don't make that face at me. I can see you, you know."

I glance around the shadowy gymnasium but don't spot him. "Creepy," I murmur.

Slinking on, I encounter a group of about ten girls sitting along a wall in folding chairs, looking sullen. "What's wrong, guys?" I ask. "This is a fast song. You should get up and dance."

"Why?" asks one girl with a mouthful of braces. "So we can just get ignored again on the slow ones? None of us has danced with a guy yet. Not once!"

"They all want the perfect, pretty girls," another chimes in, wearing glasses much too large for her face. "The same girls keep dancing to every song while the rest of us get ignored."

I wish I could tell you that changes.

"Look, guys." I crouch down by the braces girl. "Truth is boys are probably going to disappoint you a lot. Even if you do get asked to dance or you go out with the guy you like, he's not going to be perfect. Nothing with boys will ever be exactly how you want. The key is to be okay with yourself and have fun on your own, independent of boys."

The glasses girl is staring at me. "What are you—Oprah? We just want to dance."

"Fair enough." I stand again.

The song changes to the twangy "Cotton-Eyed Joe," and I laugh. "Wow. This was my favorite when I was your age."

"This song?" Glasses says with disdain.

"Yeah. We had the best line dance to it." Already I'm bopping a little.

A girl with red braids has shifted forward in her seat. "Could you teach it to us?"

"Teach you?"

"Yeah."

"It would be something to do, at least," Braces agrees.

"No." I laugh nervously, gripped with sudden stage fright. "I really couldn't."

"Come on," Braids implores.

"Yeah," says Glasses. "What about all that 'have fun on your own' stuff?"

My eyes narrow. "You're on."

Next thing I know I've kicked off my heels and am at the head of the room. The girls pick it up in one verse. The steps aren't really hard. Right, left, right, together. Left, right, left, together. Lasso slide forward. Jump, jump, jump back. Kick right double, left double, right, left, right, pivot! And repeat.

They're all laughing, and after another chorus when I glance back, half the room has joined in. It's been a decade since I did this, and I'd forgotten how exhausting it is. But I keep it up, lungs burning, and after another verse almost everyone is dancing with us.

I laugh out loud, spurred by their involvement, and dance harder. For the first time this evening, I glimpse Damon standing off to the left. He's smiling. I've never seen a real smile on his face before—like with his teeth and everything. It's so startling that I nearly falter in my steps.

By the last chorus the room is full of laughter and feet stomping, and I'm pouring sweat. *Man, this is a long song!* On the very last "Cotton-Eyed Joe," I turn and throw my arms up in the air, and the room bursts into applause.

And I fall over.

There's a general gasp, then laughter, and Braids and Braces are instantly at my side. They pull me to my stand on my rubbery legs.

"That was awesome!" Braids says. "You okay?"

"Oh yeah, yeah," I stammer. "Just a tad old."

"It was . . . pretty cool," Glasses concedes.

I nod, my head still spinning a bit. "Glad to help."

The girls go off together, and after a moment Ned appears. "Well done! I saw you getting your thang on."

I'm mopping my dripping brow. "Yeah, just, uh, serving the youth."

He pulls an apologetic face. "I'm so sorry to do this to you, but one of the kids collapsed a few minutes ago."

"Oh my gosh—was it my fault?"

"No, no. It was during the previous song. I think he's just a little overheated. His parents are going to meet us at the ER."

"Oh no!" I'm gripped with sudden panic. "I mean, that's uh, awful for the kid. I'll uh—I'll go with you."

"No, I wouldn't inconvenience you like that," Ned insists. "Besides, I really need to focus on making sure the kid gets what he needs."

"Of course. Well, maybe we can do this again."

"Sure. There's a dance every month."

"No, I mean . . ." I motion back and forth between the two of us.

"Oh—oh!" Ned smiles, looking surprised. "Yes, I'd like that. I'll call you." He starts to turn away, then wheels back and plants a forceful kiss on my cheek before hurrying away.

Shocked, I stare after him. Knowing what that kiss must've cost him, I suddenly feel terrible for leading him on. Beneath the awkwardness, he's just a nice guy.

"Well," I'm talking to Damon now, "want to wait until later or tell me now how I blew that?"

"You did fine."

I limp over to my heels—my legs are still wobbly, and I think I have blisters. "Now we have to waste time setting things up with him again."

"He seems pretty eager to go out with you again. Who wouldn't be after that dance routine?"

"Yes, I'm sure you have some serious insults for that one."

"Actually I thought it was cute."

Cute?

I run a hand through my sweaty hair, self-conscious. "Where are you, anyway? It's creepy talking to a disembodied voice."

"I'm right behind you."

I turn, and there he is, leaning against the wall, shirt sleeves rolled up to the elbows. My stomach does a flip that I pointedly ignore as I approach him, holding my shoes.

"Scoping out a dance partner?" I ask, my cheeks unusually warm.

He shrugs one shoulder. "Maybe. There's plenty for you to choose from as well."

I shrug in return. "Jail bait. You know the funny thing is I'd find this date adorable if I actually knew the guy a little."

The music transitions into Brian Adams's rock ballad "Everything I Do, I Do for You."

Damon straightens and holds his hand out to me.

"You serious?" I ask.

"Shouldn't waste a good ballad."

I'm suddenly acutely aware of just how sweaty and disheveled I am but take his hand. He slowly eases into me, placing his other hand on my waist. My stomach swoops again as we start to sway.

"Better not get too close," Damon says. "Or you'll bust out your tape measure."

I manage a little laugh, aware of the texture of his fingers on mine, of how he tugs on my hip to lead me, of how he smells—not like cologne but like some musky soap. He's only a head taller than me, and his chin keeps brushing my forehead as we move.

To fill the silence, I say, "I love this movie. The song's from *Robin Hood: Prince of Thieves*. Ever seen it?"

"Yes."

I squint up at him. "Do I detect distain for Robin Hood?"

"I don't know. It's an okay movie, I guess. But in the end the guy has himself catapulted over a wall to rescue Marian. *Catapulted.* Do you know what his actual chances of surviving that were?"

"Are you speaking from experience on this?"

"I just find it hard to believe."

"He does it for her."

"What—he couldn't go around?"

I'm getting mad. "He does it because he loves her and it's courageous. Stupid, yeah. But brave. It means more because it was dangerous."

Damon just gazes at me a long moment. "You're a real romantic, aren't you?"

"You're just realizing this?"

"I don't know. You're naïve, sure—"

I start to pull back. "And the insults begin—"

He holds on to me. "But you also seem a little bitter. Kind of a cynic about relationships."

I snort. "Cynics are romantics who've been badly burned." *That was a tad more revealing than I meant it to be.* Luckily he doesn't respond.

We dance in silence for a minute, listening to Bryan Adams rock out.

"Damon, can I ask you something?"

He looks suspicious but nods.

"What happened to you? Why did you leave the Church?"

He blows out his breath. "I've got no real beef with the Church. I didn't leave so much as just . . . stopped going."

"Isn't that the same thing?"

"No. Leaving implies it was some dramatic exit, and it wasn't. I just found no more need for it in my life."

"So you . . . didn't have a testimony?"

"Having a testimony doesn't guarantee you can stay with it."

"Then you just found it too hard?"

He gives a mirthless smile. "Why do you care?"

I glance away. "I don't know. I want to help you."

"Well, I don't need help." He keeps my hand and spins me out, then in again, and drops me into a dip.

"Pretty smooth moves." I laugh.

"Oh, I honed my skills at dances like this. I was the dipping king."

"I'm sure you were a real ladies' man."

He looks down at me. "Why do you say that?"

"Because you're . . ." I shrug, "you?"

He cocks his head. "Are you saying you find me attractive?"

My cheeks blaze red, but I fake a smile. "I can't tell. It is pretty dark in here."

"Well avoided." He smiles. "I like your skirt, by the way."

"Yes. It's the height of Hawaiian fashion. But you better stop complimenting me. It'll throw me all off."

"I've been a tad hard on you, I guess."

"You *guess*?"

"It's the job. I have bigger things to worry about than being nice."

"Samuel told me the more he cares, the better an agent he is."

"Samuel's stronger than I am. Caring clouds my judgment."

I smile and keep my tone light. "So you have to be a jerk instead?"

"If I want to stay objective. Especially around someone like you."

I'm startled. "Like me?"

"You're unexpected. I never quite know what you're going to do."

"Is that bad?"

"No." He pauses, his expression unreadable. "But it is getting a little cloudy."

I'm not sure what to make of that, so I don't respond. Damon, too, seems to draw back, and we finish the dance in silence.

At the end he just drops my hand and says, "Come on. I'll take you home." When he turns toward the exit, he adds, "We're on the move." For a second I think he's talking to me, but then I realize he's telling the other agents.

It's like being the president. If the president were frequenting a stake dance in Utah.

I retrieve my jacket from the front table and slip it on as I follow him out the glass doors. The spring evening is chilly. My breath mists the air, and I hug myself as we move toward the far end of the lot. Since most kids were dropped off, only a handful of cars are parked right up front. The SUV all the way at the edge of the lot looks silly. It's like saying, "Hey, surveillance car here!"

Samuel is coming around to get my door when headlights suddenly blaze on, blinding me. I'm so disoriented by the unexpected brightness that I don't even register the squeal of tires until hands are hauling me off my feet and tumbling me onto the blacktop.

Stunned, I lie on my back, wind knocked out of me, blinking up at the night sky. Then several faces are hovering over mine.

"Are you okay?!"

"What . . . happened?" I manage. "Who knocked me over?"

"I did," Damon says. "Forgive me. I'll be gentler next time I knock you out of the path of a speeding car."

"Car?" They each take one of my hands, and I cry out, gripping my left wrist. They slowly sit me up, propping me against the SUV. The whole parking lot lurches drunkenly. "Teenage drivers," I say through teeth clenched in pain. "Sheesh!"

"I'm not sure that was it," Samuel muses, looking at Damon. I follow his gaze, and everything swirls again.

"Then what?" Nausea fills my mouth, and I swallow gingerly. "Ew, not feeling great."

"Are you dizzy? Sick to your stomach?"

I'm not sure who is talking. "A bit."

"Does anything hurt besides your wrist?"

I feel something at the back of my neck, and when I swipe at it with my good hand, my fingers come away red. I hold out my crimson palm. "Am I'm leaking?"

Then I pass out.

16

SOMEONE TRIED TO KILL ME.

Nightmare fragments of squealing tires and blazing headlights cling to me as I swim up from unconsciousness. Again and again I see the car bearing down and feel myself flying through the air—like when I would go boating as a kid. It's that moment when, soaring out past the wake, I was thrown from the tube—the feeling of dread before hitting the concrete slab of cold water.

Amid that lurid memory the knowledge is there, distant but growing louder by the instant.

Someone tried to kill me.

Tires squeal again, right in my ear. I jerk, coming awake with a strangled shriek.

"Hey there, easy." There are hands on my shoulders, and a round, sweet-faced nurse holding on to me. Her hospital scrubs are decorated with kittens chasing string. This absurd detail, the first thing I notice upon waking, only furthers my disorientation, and for a moment I flail, fighting her grip.

"It's okay, sweetie," she insists, easing me back toward the pillows. "You're just fine now. A little bump on the head and a broken wrist, that's all."

I settle back uneasily, taking in the small room walled by sliding green curtains on every side. Near the plastic bed railing, a metal tray is cluttered with bottles of prescription medication, and a machine monitors the frenzied bleeps of my heart. Above the stiff sheets I'm wearing a thin hospital gown and a pair of blue socks. My left wrist, throbbing dully, is encased in a white cast that hooks up around my thumb. An

IV snakes down my arm and into the back of my right hand. The second I see it I look away, biting my lip. I really hate needles. And tubes coming out of me.

"Your friends are filling out paperwork," the kitten-wearing nurse explains, wrapping a blood pressure cuff around my arm. "They should be in any minute now."

"Why am I naked?" I manage, and my tongue feels fatter than usual.

The nurse chuckles and adjusts the drip on my IV. "We changed you to check for further injury. Your wrist fracture was small, so you should only have to wear the cast for a few weeks. You've got a few scratches and, like I said, a bit of a head bump. But the concussion was minor, and the wound on the back of your scalp was shallow. Head wounds always look scarier than they are."

The room is moving a bit, and I feel floaty—like I'm up above my body somewhere. "Am I . . ." I have the sudden urge to giggle. "Am I on something?"

"The doctor gave you morphine for the pain in your wrist. Mr. Wade provided us with a copy of your medical background so we knew you weren't allergic to anything."

"Mr. Wade." This time I'm unsuccessful at holding back a giggle. "He does *not* wear kittens."

Her eyebrows lift slightly. "No, he does not. Would you like me to get him?"

"No, nooo," I can hear myself slurring and try to enunciate, "That's not good. I need to not be naked before he comes in."

"Well, you're not in much of a state for getting dressed right now, sweetie. The doctor wants to keep you under observation for a few hours to be sure that concussion doesn't cause trouble. Why don't we pull the covers up?"

"Okay, then."

She helps me hitch the covers up to my chin, which makes me feel better some. Besides, I think she turned the morphine up because I'm starting to not care so much. About anything really. Not even the fact that—

"Someone tried to kill me!" I blurt, my eyes wide.

The nurse glances over at me but doesn't look terribly concerned. "Did they?"

"Yes. They tried to splat me with a car!" My face feels itchy, and I rub my nose. "My money is on the tan guy, Mr. Impossible—or Mr. Standards." I frown. "I can't remember which. His hair was shiny."

"And this shiny-haired man tried to splat you?"

"Yes." I'm nodding emphatically. "Because he pulled my chair out, and then I left with all the cake. So Mr. Darcy is ashamed of him."

"I'm sure he is, sweetie. I'll just be right back."

In the silence the heart machine beeps away. It sounds like a submarine on movies. The light coming through the IV bag is shiny, like Charles's hair. I reach up with my left hand and turn it this way and that, wondering if I can make a rainbow like with a crystal.

There are footsteps, and the curtain is pushed open. "Jack?" Damon asks. "You all right?"

"Shh." I try to put a finger to my lips and miss a bit. I point up toward the rainbow. "I'm talking to Mr. IV Bag."

Damon moves into view beside my bed. "Really? And what does Mr. IV Bag say?"

I roll my eyes. "He doesn't say anything, Damon. He's an IV bag."

He's nodding. "My mistake."

"I turned up her morphine drip when she woke up," the nurse is saying.

"Mr. Wade," I say and giggle. "Mr. Wade, Mr. Wade. You should wear kittens on your suit."

Damon looks amused. "Should I?"

"Yes, because then they could chase string. Kittens need to chase string." I lean toward him even though it makes me queasy. "Did you know that someone tried to kill me?"

"Did they?"

"Yes. Not a kitten. I think it was Mr. Shiny." I lower my voice to a whisper. "He took cake from Mr. Darcy."

"I see."

"So he tried to make me a pancake. Splat on the tires." I point at Damon, though he refuses to stand still. "You needa go find him, Wade."

"I do?"

"Yes. You find the Shiny, not the Darcy." I pause and giggle. "Although, if you find the Darcy, bring him back here." I turn onto my side and snuggle my face into the pillow. "Pcrmbcrley is lovely this time of year."

The fuzziness has settled over my whole body now, and I float into it, drifting . . .

Next I feel the harshness of the bed and hear the beeping monitor before I open my eyes. It is far too bright in here. There's a sour taste in my mouth, and when I try to sit up, nausea forces me back.

My wrist *aches* and my head is pounding, and when I reach back, there's a wide bandage at the base of my skull. The nurse said something about a head wound. They must've given me stitches.

Oh, if they shaved a piece of my head to stitch me up, I'll sue.

My hands tremble as I pull my arms out from under the sheets. Despite the cast, my left wrist feels fragile as straw. Everything hurts.

Beyond the curtain, two men are conversing in lowered voices. I catch Samuel's unmistakable baritone and another voice that sounds like Damon's.

". . . for not containing the situation."

". . . couldn't know she would send out that message," Samuel is saying.

"But I pushed her to it. We're not getting results fast enough, and she reacted. Now I can't have more manpower, and we're responsible for her as well as trying to solve a kidnapping." Damon sighs. "We don't have time to babysit her."

Babysit. Despite the lingering disorientation, I know exactly who they're talking about.

"Then we drop the charade and drag them all in for questioning. Put them in a box for a few hours and sweat them out."

"And Natalie is totally lost to us. That was the point of this whole fiasco—a chance to recover her. Now we've just compounded the problem."

Samuel pauses. "Then what do you want to do?"

After several moments Damon responds, "I don't know," then pushes open the curtain. When he sees me, his tone softens. "Hey there."

"Hey." I pull the covers up, trying to act like I'm just waking.

"How do you feel?"

"Like I got knocked on the head."

"Yeah." He slides his hands into his pockets, smiling a little. "Well, doc says you're a tough cookie. He cleared you to go home. You need to come back in a week to have your wrist checked, but the concussion was mild and you should be fine."

"Stitches?"

"Only three. Just a precaution."

"Did they shave my head at all?"

"No. It was a small enough area, they just sewed around it."

The thought of a needle in my scalp makes my skin crawl, but I nod, forcing myself to sit up despite the dizziness. "Good. Otherwise the Bureau would be paying for my new wig collection."

Damon chuckles. "Lucky for us."

I rake my tangled hair back from my face and drag a hand across my mouth. I've been drooling in my sleep. *Excellent.* "The car," I say, still groggy. "It was on purpose, wasn't it?"

He sighs. "We think so, yes. It seemed pretty deliberate."

"Did you see the driver?"

"No. Neither did Samuel. He looked for plates, but there were none on the front and the back was smudged with mud, which was probably intentional. We have the make of the car—a dark blue or black Geo Metro. But for college students that's pretty common. We're checking DMV records to see if any of our guys drives one or is related to someone with one. It's also possible it was a stolen vehicle, so unfortunately it's not much to go on. But one thing it has proved is you've definitely rattled someone's chain."

"Yeah." I ease my legs over the side of the bed, wincing at the soreness from where I hit the concrete. "Rattling chains is more painful than I expected."

"At the very least it means we're on the right track." He pauses, watching me. "I'm sorry you've landed here."

"I jumped, as I recall."

"I told you there were possible dangers, but I honestly thought there would be no risk to you. I certainly didn't think this would happen."

"Well, I'm in it now. Might as well be useful."

Damon gives a minuscule smile. "You're braver than I gave you credit for."

The compliment, though apparently genuine, directly contradicts what I just heard him say in the hall. I just nod, my chest feeling heavy. "Any idea where my clothes are?"

"Over here." He motions to a chair and says, "I'll call a nurse to help you get dressed. They'll bring a wheelchair once you're ready to go."

"Please. I don't need a wheelchair," I scoff, edging onto my feet. "I'm perfectly capable of—"

My legs fold, flopping me onto the linoleum. "Yeah," I say. "A wheelchair would be good."

"Thought so."

17

Battered, bruised, and bandaged, I hobble up the stairs to my apartment with Samuel in tow. He claimed he wanted to clear my apartment, but I suspect he was there to make sure I didn't fall down again. I perch, shaky-legged from the short walk, on the couch until he finishes scouring closets and corners. He leaves with a promise to be "just down the hall."

As of today the Bureau has temporarily rented a vacant apartment a few doors down to be closer in case I need help. The coolness of this is dimmed by Damon's recent disapproval. Not to mention the way my head throbs every time I blink.

Morning classes have already come and gone, and I was in no condition to attend even if there was still time. Maybe I can get the FBI to write me a sick note. That definitely should be legit enough for my professors.

Alone, I drag myself to bed and fall into it, still wearing my dress from the stake dance. I don't even have the energy to remove my heels before passing out again.

It's late afternoon by the time I wake, my face smashed in a puddle of my own drool. The soreness has only increased while I slept, and I have to unkink myself like the tin man after a long lull between oiling. The clock reads 3:11 p.m., and there are four new texts on my phone.

From Delia: *Suffocated under a mound of papers yet? Check in. Love you.*

From Ralph Timen: *Hello, Jack. Would love to meet for dinner as you suggested. Does seven work?*

From Damon: *Let me know when you're awake. D.*

From Tommy: *Hey, hottie. Missing me?*

This is overload for my aching brain. Damon being annoying. Ralph Thompson wanting dinner—possibly to get another shot at making me roadkill. Tommy getting one step closer to that restraining order. Only Delia's message makes me smile. For a moment I have the desire to text her and whine about the pain I'm in, but I'd never be able to explain.

It must be hard, I muse. Being an agent who can never discuss their work and what they go through with anyone. It seems like a lonely life.

This moment of insight explains a lot about Damon. When you spend every day unable to tell people about your work and dealing with the ugliest aspects of mankind, it would get easier to shut down rather than let it all in—let others in. Under it all, maybe he's just a lonely guy.

Too much. Need food and medicine.

I kick off my heels and exchange the dress for a pair of fleece pajamas. The warm fabric is soothing on my aching skin. Shuffling into the kitchen, I fish out the lemon-chicken leftovers and snack on a good chunk of chocolate cake while I wait for the meal to heat up. To an episode of some sitcom I scarf down the chicken and chug half a carton of root beer before my hands stop shaking.

First I respond to Ralph: *Seven is perfect! Where would you like to meet?*

Then I text Damon: *Awake. Meeting Ralph at seven.*

I consider writing to Tommy: *Dear Grabby, please answer yes or no if you're a serial killer so I can get you out of my life.* But I restrain myself.

Almost instantly Damon returns: *Wow. Well done. Where?*

Wow? I think, irked. Did he have to write *wow?* Like, *Wow, Jack. Guess you're not a total waste of space. Wow!*

A moment later he adds: *How are you feeling? You okay?*

Which only irks me further. *Sure, now you're nice to me.* I blow a raspberry at the phone and keep eating cake.

Three hours until I need to leave to meet Ralph. Just the thought of pulling myself together to go out and perform an interrogation masked as a conversation makes me want to cry. But now this guy is after me too, and he won't stop with me. No time to whine.

Still waiting on Ralph's response, I drag myself to the bathroom and soak in a hot bath for thirty minutes, careful to keep my cast out of the water. Only one other time in my life had I ever worn a cast. As a kid I broke my foot playing kickball with my brothers and had a leg cast for eight weeks. Already the claustrophobia is setting in.

Out of the tub again, I put my fleece pajamas back on—can't face real clothes until I absolutely have to—when there's a sharp knock on the door.

Instantly the squeal of tires and flash of headlights rush at me, disorienting me a moment. Fear prickles cold sweat along my hairline. Only last night someone tried to run me down. What if that person comes knocking when they realize it didn't work? I stifle the urge to get the kitchen knife again and edge toward the front door.

Remembering Damon's scolding the other night, I call, "Who is it?"

"Damon Wade."

I roll my eyes and unlock the door, muttering, "Damon Wade. How many Damons do you think I know?"

He's on the doorstep, eyebrows knit together in apparent concern. "You okay?" he asks, slightly out of breath.

"Fine," I answer. "Why?"

"You didn't respond to my texts. I thought maybe you passed out or something."

"No. I just happen to have a life sometimes." I sound confident, but since I'm saying this in fleecy blue pajamas while keeping company with my TV, the argument doesn't hold much weight. "I thought maybe you were the killer."

"There are two agents down the hall watching your front door at all times. Believe me, if the guy comes calling, he won't even get to knock before we've got him."

"That's good. Although I wouldn't mind a few more dates first. I'm running out of leftovers."

He chuckles. "We can arrange that. I could add a few more suspects to the list if you'd like."

He's being nice again, and it nettles me. I hate when people are nice just when I'm determined to detest them.

When I don't respond he presses, "Did Ralph give a location?"

"Not yet." I step toward the kitchen and glance back. He's still hovering on the threshold. "You coming in?"

"If it's all right?" He steps inside and closes the door behind him. "It's impressive you got this set up with him so quickly. There are only a few more meetings that are really vital at this point."

"Two more guys, right?"

"And . . . maybe a repeat or two."

I pause pouring more root beer. "Like who?"

He hesitates. "We want you to get a second date with Tommy."

"Oh no," I groan. "I don't have enough hands to deal with that guy."

"He wasn't that bad."

"Not that bad? He said he wants to get to know me *biblically*. He actually said that."

"Well, it's risky work."

"Can't I just get run over again?" I flop into a kitchen chair and wince.

"Spies can't be choosy."

"I counted on having to defend my life, not my honor."

Damon chuckles. "Can you get the date?"

"Of course I can get it. I've been dodging him all week. But I'll have to explain how I recovered from the Bulgarian flu so fast."

"Is that a thing?"

"If it is, then the fake Wikipedia page I made to back me up is going to confuse a lot of people."

He laughs again. "You're funny. And resourceful."

"Am I?" I take a drink. "And here I thought I was in need of a babysitter."

It's silent a moment. Then Damon blows out his breath. "You heard that."

"Yup. Hospital curtains aren't very soundproof."

"You have to understand"—he places his hands on the back of a kitchen chair—"I was stressed and frustrated."

"Yes, I know. I've just compounded the problem."

"Not you, me. By bringing you into this."

I'm nodding. "Sorry to have screwed things up for you."

"You haven't. You've done exactly what I wanted. But Natalie is my responsibility, and I'm failing her. Now you're my responsibility, and you're in danger too." He pauses, and his face is more open than I've ever seen it. "At the end of the day, I'm the one to blame if something happens to you. So this car thing is on me. And anything else that could go wrong. It's a lot to carry."

I hold his gaze, and I do understand. I took it personally, but for him it isn't about me. It's about his failure to keep me safe and what that means about him.

"Good thing nothing will happen then," I say at last. "From now on, I'm on high alert around cars. And you. You did throw me down, after all."

He cracks half a smile. "Got to keep an eye on me, huh?"

"Oh, I'm watching. Corner of my eye at all times."

Damon remains on my couch, watching whatever noisy sitcom is playing, while I rebuild my face with makeup and coax my hair into some semblance of order. When at last I emerge from the bathroom, dressed in jeans and an enormous black sweater to hide my cast, I can almost pass for normal.

Damon glances my way. "You look nice. Definitely better than the angel costume." He stands. "Do we have a location?"

"Yep." I hold up my phone with Ralph's response. "Café Rio."

Café Rio is always packed; the line from the counter snakes through the waiting zone and often across the sitting area to the door. The décor is brightly painted wood and faux stone with rustic touches like hanging chili peppers. Serving classic Mexican dishes from burritos smothered in sour cream to milk-soaked tres leches cake, everything at the café is wickedly delicious. But *I* wait in line for the special salad dressing. I also appreciate there are no dying matadors on the walls.

When I arrive I don't see Ralph anywhere. Surreptitiously I check his dossier picture on my phone. With a head of jet-black hair, six foot two and smiling, he would be hard to miss even in this crowd. He must not be here yet. *No harm in getting us a spot in line.*

I slide into place behind a group of chatty teens and pop one of the painkillers the doctor prescribed. If the pain in my wrist doesn't die down soon, I'll be of no use to anyone.

"Hurting?"

It's Damon's voice in my ear, and I jump slightly. He handed over the wire during the drive without a word—a small sign of the trust I've gained. Too close to listening ears to respond out loud, I quickly text: *I swear, sometime I'll get used to you being in my head.*

"Enjoy me whispering in your ear, do you?"

The question makes my stomach swoop a little, though I'm not sure why. Or maybe I'm choosing not to know. *Maybe. But your sweet nothings need work.*

He laughs, and I wonder where he is. Certainly somewhere he can talk without drawing attention. *Where are you?* I write.

"At an outdoor table. I'll move closer once he arrives."

You're not eating?

"I might get something. What's good here?"

I consider before writing: *Try a pork salad and horchata.*

"Really? Just a salad?"

It's not just a salad, I respond. *It's like a small planet.* Then I add: *How can you live in Utah and not have had Café Rio???*

"Clearly my education's been neglected. You may have to teach me some things."

Again, my stomach does a ridiculous flip. *Knock it off,* I think.

I reach the front of the line, place my order, and pay at the end of the counter. Once I have my drink, I swoop down on a bright yellow table as another group vacates it. I sip my soda and watch the door, but there's no sign of my date.

My phone beeps, and I expect it's Ralph telling me he's running late or something. But it's Damon. *Bad date etiquette.* I see he's moved inside to a table to my right.

I write back: *He might also be a kidnapper. Worse date etiquette.*

He chuckles to himself, reading my response. It's strange, like being on a date with someone who's sitting across the room.

Except you're not on a date with Damon, and you wouldn't actually want a date with Damon. Focus.

A few minutes pass, and I drain my drink. Eventually I tear off the very edge of my tortilla and nibble on it. I smell the hot chicken and rice, and the dressing looks so creamy . . .

My phone bleeps. From Damon: *Do it.*

Surprised, I answer: *Do what?*

Dig in.

Freaky. It's like he read my mind. Or spotted the drool on my chin.

A moment later he adds: *You know you want to.*

It's rude to start without your dinner companion, I argue.

It's also rude to be sixteen minutes late.

I glance at my watch, and he's right. I'm consistently five minutes late for everything, but five minutes is understandable. It's like inflation on a busy life. Sixteen minutes with no word at all is something else.

I tear off another chunk of my tortilla.

Five more minutes, and Damon gets in line. He pretends to be absorbed with his phone but keeps glancing my direction. "We're not supposed to know each other, remember?" I murmur into the microphone and see him smile, though he's not looking at me.

By the time Damon is carrying his tray back to his table, I've eaten away the entire edge of the tortilla, and Ralph still isn't here. Thirty-one minutes late. Driven by hunger, I pull out my phone and text him: *Hey, Ralph. Just want to see if you're all right?*

While I wait I pluck a few crunchy chip strips and snack on them. Out of the corner of my eye I see Damon start into his salad, and I'm filled with envy. Stupid date etiquette. My phone beeps, and I grab it, hoping it's Ralph's response. But it's Damon again: *You were right.*

About the salad?

Yes. Amazing.

I know, right?!

My foot is tapping impatiently now. Ralph hasn't answered, and I texted him a whole . . . minute and fifteen seconds ago. The digital age is supposed to give us responses instantly, especially when we're starving and waiting to eat a scrumptious salad.

Five more minutes, and my frustration is mounting. I didn't even want to come tonight. I've been groped, slapped, nearly run over, and now this guy is denying me my dinner. That's seriously the last straw.

Forty-five minutes late for a date. I think there's an unofficial rule about this. If your date is forty-five minutes late, you're cleared to eat without them.

The second I put the first delicious bite in my mouth, my phone beeps. For a wild moment I think it's Ralph saying, *I saw that!*

But it's Damon: *Atta girl.*

18

STOOD UP BY A POSSIBLE killer. That's a new low for me.

Still, things are really looking up after the salad. I'm definitely a person who needs to eat in order to be happy. On an empty stomach, the world is a dark place.

Well, this is clearly a bust, I text Damon once my dinner's gone. Three more texts to Ralph have gained no response, and he still hasn't shown. Maybe he changed his mind and just didn't have the guts to tell me. Or maybe he saw me scarfing my salad and got scared away. Wouldn't surprise me.

Appears so, Damon responds.

What do you want me to do? Try calling or e-mailing maybe?

No. This whole thing feels a little off. Let me take you home.

I'm not quite sure why we're still texting instead of giving up the charade and talking. Maybe in case Ralph happens to walk in. Or just because we're used to it. Gathering the trash onto my tray, I clean up the table and get my purse. As I walk toward Damon, he suddenly holds a few fingers out toward me and shakes his head slightly, like he's telling me to back off.

Confused, I retrace my steps to my table like I forgot something and riffle through my purse to buy time. There's an incoming text from Damon: *Sorry. Samuel's checking something. Hang out a minute.*

To stall, I refill my drink, replenish the salt packet collection in my purse, and touch up my lip gloss. Finally another text from Damon: *We're trying something. Go out of the restaurant, turn left, and walk down to the Laundromat at the end of the strip mall. Okay?*

Ooookaaay . . . I head for the door. Wondering what in the world is going on, I follow his instructions and wander along the sidewalk until I see a rusting sign for Larry's Laundromat. Store hours on the window say it's still open, so I push through the door and step inside.

Directly opposite the door, a girl sits behind a counter. She has long blonde dreadlocks, oversize hipster glasses, and doodle-covered sneakers, which she is resting against the cash register. To the right a single row of washers followed by a single row of dryers sit on cracked yellow linoleum. Orange plastic chairs line either wall, and a stooped man is pushing a single laundry cart with squeaky wheels. This is a very sad place.

The girl and old man both look up, and suddenly I realize how strange I must look with no laundry. "Hello," I say, leaning against the wall as casually as possible.

The girl pops her gum and returns to a magazine in her lap. The hunched man pushes his shrill cart toward the washers to change loads.

Trying to appear like I'm browsing—like people often check out Laundromats before they choose one—I wander along and finally sink onto a plastic chair. My fingers are already texting Damon when the door opens—even the entry bell sounds depressing—and he comes in.

"What the trash?" I ask, standing to meet him.

"Sorry. It's an experiment."

"Do you mind cluing in the lab rat?"

He keeps his gaze directly on me but says, "Don't be obvious about it; don't turn your head, but look out toward the parking lot."

Confused, I move just my eyes and look outside. There's a smattering of cars and a few people strolling along the sidewalk. Glancing back at him I ask, "What am I looking for exactly?"

"The car on the far left."

I look again, and this time I notice some kind of dark vehicle. "Is that—"

"Possibly the car that tried to run you down. It's the same make and model. An agent noticed it while we were in the restaurant. We think maybe Ralph isn't Ralph."

"Ralph isn't Ralph?"

"All the background we found on Ralph Timen was surface stuff obtained by search engines online—legitimate websites but nothing concrete. With the other guys, we found people who knew them, current work histories. Ralph's stuff is all boxed, like it could've been manufactured."

"But why? Why would someone do that?"

"As a smokescreen. Say Drake Spalecki, or any of them, became fixated on Natalie, but after the date, she wouldn't see him again. So he creates a fake profile, contacts her, and convinces her to meet him. She goes thinking he's somebody else."

"And now me," I say, feeling chills creep along my arms.

"It's just a theory, but it tracks with Ralph's profile and standing you up."

"So what—you're going to"—I drop my voice—"bust the car?"

"Samuel's trying to get a warrant right now to search it."

"Why not just walk up and see who it is?"

"That's fine if we want to do nothing but alert the guy. If it's one of our suspects, the warrant will allow us to get evidence in the car. And if he transported Natalie in his car, there might be something."

"Sweet! Let's do that."

He smiles a little. "The trick is finding a judge this time of night, especially one who'll give us a warrant with so little to go on. We'll just need to stay here awhile."

I glance around the Laundromat with its peeling walls, rundown washers, and depressing clientele. "You sure know how to show a girl a good time," I say blandly.

"Excuse me?" the girl behind the counter is speaking to us. "Are you here to wash something?" She points to a sign: *Restrooms for customers only. No loitering.*

"Absolutely," Damon says. "We're here to wash something."

The girl looks at him for several seconds, waiting. "Well?" she asks. "What are you washing?"

Damon looks around. "Uh, this." He strips off his T-shirt, and my eyebrows shoot up. "Got something on it. Need to wash it right away."

The girl chomps her gum. "You got soap?"

Damon glances around again as though some might materialize.

"We sell soap." She points at an array of detergents on the shelf behind her. "What kind would you like?"

"The cheap one." Damon walks up to the counter.

The girl sets a generic box in front of him and says, "That'll be $9.99."

"Ten bucks?" Damon gasps. He holds up the box. "This'll barely wash a pair of socks!"

The girl shrugs in a way that clearly says, "Not my problem," and after a moment Damon pulls out his wallet, cursing under his breath. I stifle a giggle.

Once he's paid for the soap, the girl asks, "You got quarters?"

He grits his teeth. "I forgot them. Can I get some change?"

"Sure." She pops open the cash drawer. "Exchange fee is two dollars."

"Two—" Damon bites off his response and hands her a five-dollar bill. She pours the coins into his hand, and with a sharp, "Thank you," he slouches to the closest machine.

"This machine costs $3.50 a load?" he says incredulously. "I'm fifty cents short. Do you have any change?"

I dump out my wallet and search the crevices of my purse but find only twenty-nine cents. "We have to get more change, I guess."

His expression turns dark, but he nods curtly and strolls back to the counter. "Hello again."

Dreads holds up a finger, tapping her sneakers on the counter as she reads an article in her magazine. At last she finishes, sets it aside, looks up, and says, "Hey."

"Hi." Damon smiles, leaning against the counter in a calculated way.

He's flirting with her, I realize. *He's trying to use his charm.* Normally this kind of thing would irk me, but in this situation I find it highly amusing.

"I underestimated the price," he says, dropping his voice to an intimate decibel and giving her a mysterious little smile. "Could I get some more change?"

She smiles back. "Sure."

"Great." He lightly touches the back of her hand. "Thanks so much."

Her smile widens. "Exchange fee is two dollars."

Damon stares. "I'm only fifty cents short!"

"Bummer." She nods. "Two dollars."

He rips his wallet out of his pocket, muttering a little more loudly this time, and slaps a twenty-dollar bill on the counter.

"Oh, I can't change that, sir," the girl says. "It's too big for my till."

"I only have twenties left. What do you expect me to do?"

"Well, if you were to purchase say, some candy and spend about five dollars, then it would be a more reasonable amount for me to give change for."

"Five dollars in candy?" he repeats.

She motions to the selection of candy bars in front of the register. "The Mike and Ikes are quite nice."

"Fine." He grabs a random handful of bars and tosses them on the counter.

"One more, I think," Dreads instructs, and he practically hurls a Twix in her face. She gives him change, including a dollar's worth of quarters.

This time he fully snaps, "Thank you," before turning away from the counter.

He stalks back to his machine, tosses in the shirt, selects a setting, pours in about half the meager box of detergent, and shoves quarters into the slot. The machine churns to life, and only then, when his shirt is soaked, does the girl clear her throat.

When we look over she's pointing at another sign: *No shoes, no shirt, no service.*

"You have got to be kidding!" Damon explodes.

Dreads motions to the display to the right of the counter. "We do have Larry's Laundromat T-shirts for sale."

Five minutes later I'm sitting on a dryer next to Damon, who's slumped, his expression murderous, in a tiny pink T-shirt with little dresses and bikinis on a clothesline across the front. They were out of men's shirts. Of course, Dreads didn't reveal that until he'd already paid the thirty dollars.

I'm sniggering silently, my hands pressed over my mouth.

"Stop laughing," he snaps without looking over.

"I'm not," I choke out.

"I can feel it—you're shaking the whole dryer."

"At least they had women's sizes and not just the kiddie left."

"What's the difference?" He pulls on the hem, which still remains stubbornly above his navel. "What kind of woman could actually wear this?"

"The kind who only eats celery. There are lots of them."

"This place is a serious racket." He glances toward the counter. "That girl should be in high-stakes sales. She'd make a killing."

"Seems like she does fine for herself here." As he continues to pout, I turn toward him, tucking my feet under me. "Come on, now. It's not so bad. At least we have a lot of candy to keep us going."

"True." He places the pile of bars between us, and I select a Kit Kat.

"And be glad I'm not one of those crazy social networking girls. They'd have plastered your picture all over Twitter by now."

"Yes, thank you for your mercy." He rolls his eyes. After a moment he picks up a Snickers and tears into it. "Is this what it's like being a girl?"

"Eating chocolate and feeling sorry for yourself?" I nod. "Pretty much."

He glances around, chewing. "It's been years since I was in a Laundromat."

"Really? I'm in one every week. Living the dream!"

"You know, sometimes I think I missed out. I tore through college so fast. Got done in three years and then went on to the academy. I never did the regular school thing."

"Bad apartments, walking eight blocks with a full laundry basket, living off peanut butter and crackers. It's an experience."

"You've done it the fun way."

"I don't know about that. Most people my age graduated about three years ago."

"What's taken you so long?"

I shrug and fold the empty wrapper into sections. "I didn't want to rush it. I love learning, corny as that is. And I took off a couple of semesters here and there to work or just hang around. I don't know. I've sort of liked just doing it."

"You're the free spirit type?"

"Not really. I definitely have to have some kind of destination. I just haven't minded taking a while to get there."

"And what is the destination?"

"Grad school, maybe. I could just become a perpetual student. At least that would be picking something. Oh my gosh!" I seize a small white packet. "You got Fun Dip!"

"Is that a good thing?"

I stare at him, aghast. "You've never had Fun Dip?"

"No."

"Oh! I mourn for your childhood." I tear off the top of the packet and break the white dipping stick in half, presenting him with the bigger part. "Here."

He stares at it like I'm offering him a vial of small pox. "What am I supposed to do with that?"

"You dunk it in the sugar stuff and lick it off." When he hesitates, I add, "It's delicious!"

After a moment he dips the stick into the blue powder and slowly licks it clean, looking utterly uncomfortable.

"Well?" I ask.

He's nodding slowly. "It's all right."

I roll my eyes. "You can never just compliment anything, can you?"

When I go to dip my stick, he pulls the powder away. "Whoa, whoa. We share the same sugar?"

"Yeah. Why not?"

He stares at me like I've asked to share his vaccination needle. "Our saliva will get all mixed up."

I snort. "So what? I'm sure you've swapped saliva with plenty of women in your time."

He doesn't deny it but hedges, "This is different."

"Yeah, it's probably more sanitary, and you won't have to debate about calling me tomorrow." I point at the packet. "Come on."

After a long minute, he relinquishes the powder.

"Now, was that so difficult?" I ask. "Sheesh. You're a special agent, and you're scared of a little saliva?"

"I'm serious about personal hygiene."

"We get so weird about that as adults. Kids share suckers and ice cream cones and never think twice about it."

Damon nods, deadpan. "And that's how herpes started."

I laugh and dribble blue drool. "You're a bit of a pessimist, aren't you?"

"I just like to keep to myself."

"You mean you keep yourself safe. From germs, emotions . . ." I trail off, scooping more sugar, but I stop when I notice Damon's expression—half surprise, half annoyance. "Sorry. Just making an observation."

He makes a noncommittal noise and hesitantly dips into the powder again. He looks like he really thinks he might contract the plague while he eats.

"You're very buttoned-up, aren't you?" I ask.

"Says the girl who eats the same thing every day for lunch."

"Well, I'm boring, right? We established that pretty early on."

He's cleaning blue powder off his fingers. "You've really got to get over that."

"One doesn't forget spot-on insults from strangers very fast."

"All I meant was you live a quiet life. It's admirable, really."

"Sure, because you value order. But quiet and buttoned-up can be different. I may be a quiet person, but I have a loud personality."

Damon cocks his head. "Sometimes I have no idea what you're talking about."

"I mean—do you ever do anything besides work in your suits and go to the post office in your suits and run on the treadmill in your suits . . . ?"

"It's work attire."

"Yeah, but are you ever not working?"

"Of course. I have hobbies. I go on dates."

"Oh," I laugh, "I can just imagine the kind of women you date."

He leans forward and folds his hands. "Do tell."

"The kind of girl who wears blouses every day. You know, not like a shirt but a blouse, with buttons and a collar and everything. A very serious scholar, perhaps, with her hair in a bun. Maybe she plays the flute and has an interest in ancient Mayan artifacts, and for fun she likes to go to the museum and then to a tofu bar."

"There's nothing wrong with that kind of girl."

"No, absolutely not. In some ways I'd like to be more like that girl. But she's just so wrong for you."

"Because?"

"Because people who are too much alike cancel each other out. You can't have two people saying, 'Hey, let's go to the museum today' because then where's the challenge? How do you ever grow with that person?"

"Maybe being alike means you can grow faster in the same direction."

I'm shaking my head. "There's a reason opposites attract. Opposites push each other. They balance."

"So who do I need?"

"I don't know." I'm chomping on my candy stick now. "Someone more relaxed and whimsical—silly even. Someone to make you chill and to bring a little lightness into your heavy work."

"Someone like you?" He's looking at me in that unreadable way, and I feel my cheeks color.

"No." I laugh, hastily reaching for a Twix. "No, I'm way too much fun for you. You need someone slightly more buttoned."

"Then opposites don't attract?"

I look up, and he's still watching me evenly. *Is he trying to say—?* "You tell me," I challenge, feeling my stomach clench. I brush my hair back and give him full view of my face. "How does the average slacker look to you?"

"I don't know about the average slacker," he says, "but you are beautiful."

I draw back, surprised, and try to open the candy bar with fumbling fingers.

"Now who's being guarded?" he asks, his voice a little softer.

"You caught me off guard," I admit, still struggling with the foil.

"Because I called you beautiful? Do you not hear that very often?"

"Not a lot, no." What is this wrapper—childproof?

He takes the bar from me, his fingers lingering on mine, and I feel an electric current at his touch. Stupid attraction. He opens it easily and hands me one stick, keeping the other.

"Hoarding, are you?"

"Sharing," he corrects. Damon takes a bite, his eyes never leaving mine.

I finally demand, "What?"

He chuckles. "You're really not comfortable with people finding you attractive, are you?"

"I haven't had much practice."

"I doubt that. Guys are attracted to you; you just can't see it."

"How would you know they're attracted to me?"

"I watch you interact with people. Believe me, there have been guys looking. Although I've noticed for such a fun person you sure can't flirt."

"I beg your pardon," I say, affronted. "I *can* flirt. You've just never seen me turn it on."

"I haven't?"

"No."

"Okay." He clears the candy from between us and faces me. "Go."

I blink. "What?"

"You said you can flirt. Go ahead. Show me your mad skills."

"No!" I laugh, cheeks burning again. "I'm not doing that!"

"Why not?"

"Because it's weird when you put me on the spot. It has to happen naturally."

He's nodding. "Or maybe you're just incapable."

"Oh, fine!" I take several deep breaths and shake out my shoulders like an actor prepping for a big scene; then I look at him. He's watching me with a smug look. Little punk.

I smile my most mysterious smile and toss my hair back the way I see girls do. "Damon," I say, my voice husky. I touch his arm, running my fingers up to his shoulder. For good measure I toss my hair again and a chunk sticks to my lip gloss. I try to subtly spit it off and end up sputtering everywhere. When finally I pull it free, I have to scrape gloss off the strands with my fingernails. Eventually I smile at him again, refocused. "Damon," I repeat and try to play idly with his hair. "You're so . . ."

His eyebrows are up, expectant.

I cock my head, trailing my fingers in his sideburns. "You're so very . . ."

He squints as though he can see how blank my brain is.

I drop my hand and scoot back, scowling. "Fine. I can't flirt."

"Keep going." He chuckles. "I'm waiting to hear what 'You're so very' leads up to."

"I don't know! That's the problem. I don't know what you're supposed to say. Or do. I fail at hair flipping."

"Hair flipping is kind of overrated anyway. More often than not you get hit in the eye."

"No wonder I'm still single," I grumble, reaching for more candy. "I'm the only woman who was born with a faulty flirter."

"Not the only one. There are a lot of unfortunate souls like you."

"You make me sound like a mutant."

He shrugs. "It's just odd to me. Flirting seems so natural."

"To you maybe. You don't even have to try. It's like—" I roll the sleeves of my sweater up to my elbows and badly imitate him: "I'm Damon. I'm brooding and boyish, and I have a beautiful jawline."

His eyebrows shoot up. "Beautiful jawline?"

"You know—that's what you think of yourself."

"Actually I've never given much thought to my jawline, let alone called it beautiful." He smiles that ridiculous crooked smile. *"You* must be the one who likes my jaw."

"I've never even noticed your jaw."

"You must have since you commented on it."

"Fine. You have a lovely jaw. Happy?"

"Just surprised that you've been ogling me."

"Puh-lease," I scoff. "I have not ogled you."

"My beautiful jawline would say otherwise."

"I don't want to talk about this anymore." I stuff a Nut Roll in my mouth. "I can't flirt. I'll die alone. End of story."

"You could be taught."

"What?" A peanut falls out of my mouth. "To flirt?"

"Sure."

"What're we—gentlemen in a forties movie?"

"It's not that hard," he presses. "It's about being intent."

"Intent?"

"Your focus on the other person. If a guy keeps serious eye contact with you," he pauses, just watching me for several long moments, "he's interested in you."

My gut tightens. "I see."

"If he's watching you, focused as he speaks to you, and if he looks for some reason to touch you . . ." He reaches out and skims my knee with his fingertips. "That's flirting."

I try to swallow, making some kind of gurgling noise in my throat.

His eyes haven't moved from mine. "You try it."

"Me?" I laugh.

"You. Pretend we've just met." He doesn't move back at all but holds out his hand in the small space between us. "Hi, there. I'm Damon."

I glance down at his hand then remember the eye contact thing and look up again. I take his hand in both of mine, saying, "Hi, Damon. Jack."

He keeps my hand and my gaze. "Interesting name, Jack."

"Well, you know what they say." I laugh lightly, dropping our hands to the dryer but still holding on.

He seems to have moved closer. "What do they say?"

I can barely breathe, but I force myself to keep my gaze steady. "You know? A rose by any other name."

He leans in, his face in my hair, and inhales. "Would smell as sweet," he murmurs.

"Exactly," I whisper. Without realizing it, I've caught his shoulder, keeping him close to me. He leans back slightly, his nose brushing mine, and I can scarcely breathe. "But don't take my word for it."

His eyes are on my lips now, and he's leaning in—

A dryer goes off; a deafening buzzer that makes us jump apart. The man at the end of the aisle shuffles toward the dryer two down, shooting us a glance of amusement.

"Well," I say, shaking as I turn to drape my feet over the front of the dryer. "How'd I do?"

Damon looks unruffled. "An excellent student. You're better than you give yourself credit for."

"Maybe there's hope for me yet."

Damon's phone beeps, and he answers with, "Yes?" After listening a bit, he blows out his breath, says, "All right," and disconnects.

"Samuel?" I ask, my pulse still descending.

He nods, jaw taut. "Couldn't get the warrant. He decided to approach, but when he did the car sped off. He got some pictures of it first but still couldn't see the driver—only a black hoodie."

"So . . . back to square one?"

"I'm wearing a pink shirt. We wish we were at square one."

I chuckle and motion to the washer. "I think your load is done."

He hesitates, and I think maybe he's still watching me, but I don't look up. Finally he slides off the dryer and goes to retrieve his sopping shirt. Coming back, he taps my legs out of the way and tosses the shirt into the machine I'm sitting on. As he adjusts the setting, his arms are on either side of my legs, casual but close enough to make my pulse race.

"I don't believe it," he mutters. "The dryers are more expensive. Between this catastrophe of a shirt and tax, I'm fifty cents short again."

"You're kidding." I giggle.

"I wish I was." Resigned, he marches to the counter. "Hi again," he says, and Dreads sets aside her magazine. "I'm going to need a bit more change."

"Of course." She smiles and pops her gum. "Exchange fee is two dollars."

19

WHAT I NEED IS A gun.

Not for whoever tried to run me down and is now stalking me, but for this upcoming breakfast date with the pervert. Although I think IHOP frowns on firearms in the restaurant.

The stupid broken wrist won't stop aching, and my scrapes are now starting to itch too. I slather them with prescription cream the doctor recommended before dressing in a red turtleneck with long sleeves and a solid pair of jeans—defensive clothing. At the last minute I exchange my heels for a pair of flat, slouchy boots. The better to run in should the need arise.

Damon knocks on my door at precisely ten minutes to the hour and scrutinizes me with a calculated, "Very nice. You ready?"

As he drops me around the corner from the restaurant, I say, "Remind me of the emergency word. I'm probably going to need it today."

"Paprika." He smiles.

"Okay. Paprika, paprika, paprika," I chant. "Promise you'll come running?"

He meets my gaze. "Of course."

Something about his expression makes me swallow before climbing out of the car.

Once again, Tommy is already seated. And once again he's already *ordered.* He's digging into a giant omelet and stays seated as I arrive at the table.

"Hey there, hottie." He grins. "Sit."

I drop into my chair, feeling like the fly sitting down to a meal with the spider. Saturday morning at IHOP is always a madhouse, and today is no exception. Families gather at long tables; friends and couples dine in booths, and waiters bustle continuously throughout. Lots of noise. Lots of witnesses.

"Didn't know what you wanted," he says, motioning to the food. "But there's a menu there. Get whatever you want."

Generous. A harassed-looking waitress scurries over. Luckily she and Tommy don't seem to know each other. I order eggs, bacon, and French fries with no fear she'll spit in it.

The second she's gone he reaches for my hand. "Miss me, babe?"

"Absolutely," I respond, retrieving my hand under the pretense of taking a drink of water.

"I was psyched to hear from you. Just when I was starting to think you didn't like me."

Okay, flirting. What did I learn last night? "Can't make it too easy for you, can I?" I say, keeping his eye contact.

Tommy chuckles. "True. The chase is half the fun."

"Think so? Then you've clearly been catching the wrong girls."

We laugh, and I see, over his shoulder, Damon looking at me from a booth with unchecked shock.

Somehow I manage to keep up with the flirting and avoiding his hands throughout the meal. I finish the last of my eggs with a sense of serious accomplishment. It's like running a marathon and dodging an octopus at the same time.

But I haven't managed to glean any other information about Natalie. When I tried to bring it up, he just shook his head, muttered, "Cold chick," and then started comparing cars to women in details I won't repeat. No matter how I try, he won't return to the subject at all, and no advice is coming through the earpiece from Damon. He's gone totally silent. The time I actually need him he chooses to finally clam up.

"Remember my old roommate I told you about?" I say in a final attempt to learn something—anything. "You know the one who walked out on that guy after dinner?"

Tommy pushes aside his bare plate. "I don't want to talk about them."

"Then what *do* you want to talk about?"

He slides his chair around next to mine. "Us."

"Us?" I laugh nervously and try to shift away, but his arm is stealing around my waist.

"Yeah." His breath is hot in my hair, and I swear he just nibbled on my earlobe. "You smell great."

I turn my head and mutter furiously into the microphone, "Cayenne. Cayenne, cayenne."

"What?" Tommy asks.

"Cayenne. I think there was cayenne on my eggs."

He looks perplexed at the turn of conversation. "What are you talking about?"

"My eggs. I think there was cayenne on them. You know the spice? Cayenne. *Cayenne!*"

"Never mind that." He brushes my hair back, his fingers lingering on my neck. They really don't make turtlenecks high enough. "You want to check out my parents' place?"

"Your parents' place?"

"My folks are out of town all summer, and I'm looking after their place in Lehi. It's on a couple acres of farmland." He's talking in my ear again. "Very secluded."

I'm about to jump up and shout the name of every spice I can think of when his words sink in. Parents gone all summer. Secluded little farmhouse.

The perfect place for a lair.

"Sure," I say impulsively. "Yeah, let's check it out."

"Really?"

"What're you doing?" Damon demands in my earpiece.

"Yeah." I manage a smile. "Sounds like fun."

"Great. Well then, let's pay the check and we'll go. Do you need to freshen up or anything?"

"No," I say quickly. If I'm alone for even a second, Damon will stop me. "No, let's just get going."

"So eager." Tommy chuckles, standing and pulling me with him. "I like that."

We wait in line to pay, and I stay close to Tommy's side, holding tight to his hand on my waist so it doesn't wander. After a few minutes, I realize that Damon's in line directly behind us.

While Tommy is signing the receipt, Damon steps up close to me and murmurs into my hair, "Don't do this, Jack. *Don't do this.*"

I step away and follow Tommy out the door.

20

Okay, maybe this was a bad idea.

Maybe it was a *really* bad idea.

When we get off the Lehi exit, Tommy steers the car down through the main part of the city, past the old roller mills, and keeps going out into open country.

This is seriously the middle of *nowhere.* Damon's been keeping up a running commentary about how stupid I'm being in my earpiece, but I haven't once seen the SUV behind us. True, it's an FBI vehicle, so we're not supposed to see it, but still. I'd feel better if I knew they were close.

Finally the car skirts a length of fields and pulls into a gravel driveway beside a cute little yellow house. It's so charming I wonder how the sort of people who live here could've raised such a pervy son.

This could be where Natalie's being kept. My pulse races at the thought, and I steel myself for whatever's coming. I can't regret coming when it's possible I could find her here.

Tommy shifts the car into park and looks over, grinning. "Well, here it is."

"It's beautiful," I manage, my breath short. "How long have they lived here?"

He shrugs. "Most of their marriage. I grew up here. But I couldn't get out of here fast enough. Not enough excitement for me."

Yes, Orem really is a thriving metropolis. Well, by comparison.

He gets out, and I hurry to do the same before he can come around to my side. Already I'm striding toward the house, calculating a means of getting away from him so I can have a look around.

"What's your hurry?" Tommy asks.

"Just excited to see the inside," I say.

"You idiot," Damon hisses in my ear. "He thinks you're still flirting. You are in so far over your head."

The front steps are flanked with ferns and greenery. I wait on the stoop, looking out at horses grazing in the lush fields while Tommy unlocks the door. It really is a gorgeous spot.

And from here no one can hear me scream.

The moment he unlocks the door I slip inside, strolling through a small but comfortable sitting room, kitchen, and living room. The furniture is well-worn, but there are ornate quilts on the backs of the couches and chairs, quaint painted pots on the shelves, and a general feeling of warmth. It's so out of character with Tommy I wonder again how he possibly could've been raised here.

Moving to a narrow hall, I glimpse several doors on either side. All closed. Natalie could be behind any one of them. I need to get down there and check.

"Where are you going?" Tommy asks, coming up behind me. "Looking for the bedroom already?"

"No," I say emphatically and flash a smile. "Just . . . exploring." I hurry back into the living room, pretending to examine a needlepoint wall hanging.

"I know it's cheesy," he says. "But after rooming with a bunch of guys, it's nice to have some privacy."

I bet.

"Now." He moves up behind me and brushes the hair off my neck. "Why were you so eager to get here?"

Uh-oh.

"Just, uh, love a good farmhouse." Can't say the emergency word until I've had a chance to look around.

"Really." He slides his hands around my waist and turns me toward him. "And does it disappoint?"

"I wouldn't really—"

He's kissing me. It's so abrupt that I don't immediately pull away. I've been kissed before, but I've never been kiss-attacked like this. I had no chance to block it!

"Hey, now," I say, extracting myself. "Slow down there."

"Can't help it." Tommy grins. "You're hot, you know?" He leans in again, and I cover his mouth.

"I'm, uh, feeling . . ." *What? What can I say?* "A little bit sick."

"Oh, don't play hard to get." He chuckles. "I've caught you, remember?"

"No, not playing," I insist. "Really, I'm queasy."

"You look fine to me, babe. More than fine." His mouth is already back on mine.

"No, I'm—" I fake a gag, and Tommy instantly jumps back. *Ha!* I put my hand to my lips. "I just need to . . ."

"Down the hall, first door on the left," he says, keeping his distance and pointing.

I scurry up the hall, pausing only long enough to close the bathroom door, then bypass it and go to the second door on the left. The door creaks slightly as I push it open.

It's a tidy bedroom with a quilt on the bed and a doily across the nightstand with a ceramic rooster perched atop. Probably a guest bedroom. I duck quickly to check under the bed, and then pull open the small closet. Nothing.

"What are you doing?" Damon asks in my ear.

"Snooping," I mutter. "Hush up and let me do it." Peeking back into the hall to be sure it's still clear, I slip out and slide along the wall toward the next door.

"What is that?" Damon asks. "Are you humming?"

"No," I scoff and open the next door. It looks like Tommy's mom uses this room for crafts. A quilt frame is strung with a partially stitched project, and a set of shelves overflows with ribbon, scrapbook paper, tape, and gift bags. Another closet is full of more supplies but nothing else.

I peer back into the hall.

"You are!" Damon says, triumphant. "You're humming the *Mission Impossible* theme!"

"Maybe." I slink down the hallway to the next door, humming unabashed now. Got to have a soundtrack to this moment. Master bedroom is empty.

There are only two doors on the right side of the hall. First is a sort of pantry lined with jar-laden shelves. They clearly have a handle on their food storage. There are peaches, peas, and vats of sugar and flour. My food storage consists of a single can of beans at the back of my shelf. And I'm pretty sure it's expired.

I'm about to exit when I notice a rug on the floor with a strange shape underneath. When I crouch and peel back the rug, my pulse races. It's a trap door for a basement.

"You doing all right?" Tommy calls from the living room.

"No, no, awful!" I shout back, hoping he doesn't notice exactly where my voice is coming from. "Oozing, vomitus . . . It's bad. Just don't come back here!" To Damon I say, "There's a basement. I'm going in."

"Don't go in, don't go in!" he says furiously. "Do you hear me, Jack? *Jack!*"

I'm already removing the rug and tugging on the metal ring. With my mighty heave, the door squeals open on rusty hinges. *Please let Tommy have suddenly gone deaf.*

The stairs descend into total darkness, and for a moment I'm gripped with fear. If this really is a lair, I'm about to walk right into it. Isn't that what you're not supposed to do in this situation?

Just when I'm about to back away, I imagine Natalie huddled down in that darkness. I grit my teeth and move onto the steps. The old wood groans under my weight, and I pray it won't break. All I need is to fall into a lair and break my legs. Wouldn't that be dandy?

Several steps down, the light from the room above is swallowed by the dark. The childish compulsion to turn and run intensifies, but I plod on, groping in front of me—there! A string! I grip it and pull and a dim yellow cast of light brightens the space below.

It's smaller than I expected, more like a closet than a room. Dusty boxes are stacked practically wall to wall. *No, no, this can't be all there is.* I hurry to the bottom and circle the boxes on every side, looking for something—a nook, a cranny. I even feel along the length of exposed wall, shuddering at the cobwebs that tangle around my fingers. But no secret walls swing open. It's just a regular basement. And Tommy's going to find me any second.

"There's nothing here," I whisper.

"Then get yourself out of there," Damon orders.

I scurry back up the stairs, snap off the light, shut the door, and replace the rug with trembling fingers. Was it like that or more angled? Oh, never mind.

The hallway is still empty, so I slip into the final room.

This must've been Tommy's room. The walls are covered in posters of cars and Halle Berry. Automotive magazines litter the old dresser, and the bed is unkempt. Clothes obscure the floor, and the closet stands open, filled with old rackets and hockey sticks and various junk. He must be sleeping here while he looks after the place.

Nothing here either. I was so sure—

"Feeling better, I see."

I whirl. Tommy is leaning in the doorway. "Well, you get right to it, don't you?" He chuckles, ambling into the room.

"I, uh . . ." I scramble for an explanation, but what else can he think when I'm in his bedroom? Can't say that I was searching for a secret lair.

"I like a girl who knows what she wants." His hands are on my waist, and before I can react, he's kiss attacking again.

"No, no—I think I feel sick again," I manage, trying to push him away.

"No more playing," he whispers. Suddenly he's dragging me back toward the bed.

Not good, not good, not good—"Really, wait!" I insist, trying to dig my heels into the carpet. "I don't—I can't—"

Suddenly there's pounding on the front door. "Jacklyn!" someone shouts, and the deep, rich timbre of the voice can only belong to—

"Samuel?" I murmur.

Tommy looks confused. "Who's Samuel?"

"He's, uh—"

"Jacklyn, open up! I know you're in there!"

Looking shaken, Tommy disappears through the bedroom door. A moment later I hear him saying, "Look, man. I don't know what you—"

"I know Jacklyn's here," Samuel counters. *Wow, he can be loud!*

I scamper down the hall to the front door, and he's standing there, so enormous he fills the doorway, looking terrifying.

Sent in the huge guy. Nice move.

"Jack, we're going," he says.

"Whoa, whoa, buddy," Tommy says. "I don't know who you are, but she's not—"

"She's my girlfriend," Samuel says. "And she's leaving. Jack?"

"Yeah, yeah." I grab my purse, but Tommy stops me as I try to cross the threshold.

"Wait a sec, you're not going anywhere." His hands are digging into my arms, his face furious.

"Let go, Tommy," I say, trying to pull away.

"You can go when I say." He turns to Samuel. "As for you—"

Samuel's fist hits him so fast I don't even register it's happened until Tommy's head snaps back and he tumbles onto the carpet. My jaw has dropped open, and Tommy's spluttering and dabbing blood from his nose. Then Samuel has tossed me over his shoulder in a fireman carry and is lugging me down the driveway.

"Bye, Tommy," I say, waving as I'm carried off. "Call me!"

21

"You could've been killed," Damon says for the thousandth time.

All the way back to my apartment, I've gotten the extended lecture on how stupid I was and how much danger I was in, blah, blah, blah. I stopped listening after a while. Bottom line is he was not pleased with me.

There was a moment of total terror, but it was so worth it to see Samuel knock that guy out. He looks pretty ashamed of himself now.

"Don't worry, Samuel," I say as we pull up to the apartment. "You're still a gentle giant."

"I used unnecessary force," he argues quietly.

"After what he tried to do to Jack, I think it was entirely necessary," Damon says.

I look over at him. "You were really worried about me, huh?"

"Of course I was. If something happened to you in there, it would mean a mountain of paperwork."

I roll my eyes. "You know, just because I didn't find anything doesn't mean Natalie isn't there. If the house is on a couple of acres, there could be another place. Maybe a barn or something underground."

"Just leave it to the professionals," Damon says, consulting his phone. "And try not to get attacked on your way up the stairs."

I slam the door louder than necessary when I get out.

A nap and the rest of my Great Wall of Chocolate later, I've nearly recovered from my narrow escape. When I think about what could've happened, I still get the chills. I really am lucky they were there to get me out of it. The Lord heard my prayers.

Too many papers sit unfinished on my computer, but I can't concentrate. After a while I'm drawn to the window that overlooks the parking lot. The SUV is parked near the back of the lot, the hood propped open. I can see someone tinkering underneath but can't quite tell who it is.

Slipping on a sweatshirt, I wander down to the car. "Something wrong?" I ask.

Damon pokes his head out from under the hood and then comes around, wiping his hands on a rag. "Oil change."

I nod, suddenly quiet. Okay, maybe it's just me, but guys in white T-shirts . . . there's something about it. Especially when they're doing something physical like working on a car or digging a hole. It's just really masculine. I'm not big into guy's guys, but for some reason this is a weakness of mine. His hair is disheveled, and there's a smudge of oil on his forehead. It's such a different look than his suit.

"Can't you take it to the dealer for that?" I ask.

"Sure." He leans back against the driver's door. "But then we have to switch cars. Too much of a hassle."

"You know, I've hardly seen anyone but you on my protective detail."

"It's a small team. Normally I'm off when you're asleep."

"Yeah, but that's not much time to be off. You're spending a lot of hours on this assignment."

He shrugs, still scouring his hands. "This sort of thing is more of a lifestyle than a job."

I nod and blow out my breath. "Look, I'm sorry. It was stupid to go to Tommy's today. It could've been seriously bad, and I was wrong. The opportunity just presented itself, and I thought—"

"No, you were right." He cracks a reluctant smile. "We asked you to get close to these guys to gain information. What you did was gutsy. I just didn't like thinking of you in danger."

I'm tempted to ask why exactly that is, but I stop myself. "Well, it could've been worse." I laugh. "At least he finally paid for my meal."

Damon circles back to the engine. "You know, it's become painfully clear to me that no one knows how to date anymore. Even the guys who manage to avert disaster have no style."

"Style? It is Utah Valley. Dating options are sort of limited."

He looks up. "It's not about doing something huge or even spending a lot. It's about arranging something she'll like, doing a little research."

"Research?" I laugh. "What—do you, like, do a background check on a girl before you take her out?"

"Oh, of course. Background, credit, and general surveillance. Never date a girl without it."

"I hope you're joking."

He sets aside the oil. "I'm one of those wacky guys who likes to talk to a girl and learn a little about her before I ask her out. Otherwise, how would I know if I'm even interested?"

I shrug. "Looks. It's what most guys go on."

"Sure you've got to be attracted. But I've seen plenty of gorgeous women and had no connection with them."

"Plenty, huh? You must get around."

"There has to be more happening than just attraction."

"Well, you're unusual then."

He meets my gaze, unflinching. "Yes, I am. I'm also very good at dating."

I snort. "Is it your humility that's such a draw?"

"It's just a fact."

"So you're like the king of dates? Best date a girl ever had?"

"That's right."

I lift my face to the sun. "Okay, then."

I hear the clink of metal, and when I look back, he's coming toward me, holding out his hand. "I accept your challenge."

"What challenge?"

"To take you on the best date you've ever had."

I'm a little shocked and recover with, "Considering the dates I've been on lately, the bar's not real high."

"Good. Then I won't have to try very hard."

He's still holding out his hand, and after a moment I ask, "Are you serious?"

"Deadly serious."

Dang white T-shirt. "Fine," I say, shaking his hand. "You're on."

22

Calm down.

Calmdowncalmdowncalmdowncalmdown!

Call in reinforcements.

Standing in the center of my bedroom in tall, stripy socks, dress shorts, and a Crab Shack T-shirt, I frantically dial Bridget.

"Hey." She picks up on the second ring. "You're still alive, I take it."

"Barely. Listen, Bridget. This is an emergency."

Her tone turns somber. "Like a 'bring *The Notebook* and ice cream' emergency or 'bring *Titanic* and straight frosting' emergency?"

"Like a 'bring all the clothes you own and the accessories to go with them' emergency."

She gasps. "You have a date!"

"Yeah. And nothing to wear. Seriously, nothing. I had no idea my closet was total crap."

"Who's it with?"

"I don't . . . really want to say."

"Oh, come on! No info, no clothes."

I hesitate. "The stalker guy."

There's a beat, then she bursts out laughing. "I knew it! I knew it, I knew it—"

"Bridget, can I get the second chorus of 'I Told You So' once you're here?"

"Of course. Be there in fifteen!"

True to her word, she knocks exactly fourteen minutes later. How she knocked I've no idea. When I open the door, I can barely see her eyes over the pile of jackets, dresses, and purses in her arms.

She totters in and dumps the lot on the living room floor, then surveys me with a sad, "Oh, sweetie."

"I know." I tug on one striped sock. "I'm not sure how this happened."

She gasps and grabs ahold of my cast. "What happened to your arm?"

"Oh, it's a long story, and we don't have time."

"And your hair?" She touches the long strands gingerly. "Half of it's curled, and half of it's straight."

"Yeah. I thought I wanted to go curly, but then I felt like curly was making my face look fat. So I straightened half of it to see the difference, and now I can't decide."

"Okay." She nods, and I can see the wheels turning in her head. "Let's narrow down wardrobe a bit. What kind of date are we talking about? Active? Sitting? Half and half?"

"No idea. He just gave me a time."

"Men," she scoffs, quickly laying out options. "Don't they understand that an itinerary would help us prepare properly? No, they just give us a time and then complain when our heels get stuck in the golf course. We'll go with something neutral. You have jeans?"

"Yes." I scuttle back to my room and start yanking things out of the hamper. My favorite pair of jeans is near the bottom, rumpled but still smelling clean enough. I bring them back for inspection, and Bridget nods approval.

"Good, good. We've got a skinny jean. Better to go with pants since you don't know what kind of activity you're looking at."

"But are jeans too informal?"

"No. Better to do jeans with a dressy top. We don't want to reenact the Overdressed Incident of 2009."

"Oh, yeah." I grimace. Bridget tried to convince me my new sequin dress was too much—an opinion I shared when my date took me to an arcade.

"Okay, jeans." I'm hopping from one sock to the other. "What next?"

"Dressy top." She holds several up to me in a rapid-fire sequence, discarding each over her shoulder. "No, not right, not right. Let me mull while you finish the hair."

"Okay!" I scamper toward the bathroom and then come right back, panicked. "What am I doing with it?!"

"Go with loose waves. That way if you get sweaty, you won't wilt as bad."

"Right. Loose waves!" I scurry back into the bathroom and snatch up the hot curling iron.

"So," she says from the living room, "the stalker guy, huh?"

"Mm-hmm," I say, concentrating on my hair.

"How did that happen?"

"I have no idea." I spritz the finished wave with a touch of hairspray. "We met finally. But I wasn't interested. One minute he hates me, he's insulting me, he's telling me what an idiot I am. The next minute he's asking me out."

"Sounds pretty normal. How about a nice wedge shoe?"

"They make me trip, remember?"

"Oh yeah. So what do you think of this guy? Do you like him?"

"I'm not sure." I pause, musing. "He's cute. I'm definitely attracted. But he's kind of severe sometimes. He seems a bit lost. But still, there's something . . ."

"Keep curling!" Bridget shouts, and I snatch up the iron again.

Nine minutes before I'm supposed to meet Damon, I hurry back into the living room, hair done.

"Okay, I have it," Bridget says, holding a top up to me. It's dark, navy lace—delicate, beautiful, a perfect match for the jeans.

"I can't wear this," I protest. "This is your third-date shirt!"

"So you know how much I love you then. Put it on."

While I pull it over my head, she's debating over shoes. "Yep, these," she decides, proffering a pair of pointy black boots.

"Will I be able to walk?"

"The heel is pretty short. You've got a good four hours before your feet go numb." She tugs the hem of the top into place and nods, satisfied. "Perfect. That looks great on you."

"Really?" I'm hopping to wrestle the boots on. "Not too much?"

"Just the right amount. And, oh, I totally have a purse the same color as that shirt! Where's your regular purse?"

"On the coffee table." I manage to wrangle myself into the boots (her feet are a size smaller than mine, but her shoes are so beautiful that

I've learned to live with the pain) while she dumps everything from my purse into the one that matches.

"Four minutes." Suddenly I panic. "Jewelry. I don't have jewelry!"

"Plenty of time; calm down." She retrieves a bag of accessories and paws through it, coming up with a handful of silver bangles and diamond-studded hoops to match. "Put these on." I pop in the earrings while she shoves bangles onto my wrist and pushes me toward the bathroom mirror to survey our work. Wow. I have to admit, I look all right. Bridget could do this for a living.

"Thank you!" I throw my arms around her. "You're a lifesaver!"

"You'd do the same for me."

I blow out my breath, twisting the bracelets. "I think I do."

"Do what?"

"Like him."

She smiles. "I know. So go knock him dead."

"Okay." I peck her cheek and am already out the door before I have to come back. She's holding out my forgotten purse and a leather jacket. I snatch them and call, "Thanks again!"

Dusk is just starting to fall as I head down to the SUV. Damon leans against the car, talking on his phone like he's been there the whole time. But somehow he's managed to change his clothes. He's wearing a fitted gray sweater and jeans, and I have to stop for a second to get my breath back. Yeah, he can definitely pull that look off.

"Get back to me as soon as you hear." He looks up, sees me, and does a double take. "Mm-hmm," he continues into the phone, but he's giving me the up-and-down. "Yeah. Just text me, but don't call. Thanks." He hangs up, straightens, and says, "Well, aren't you stunning?"

Stunning. A huge smile breaks out across my face before I can pull it back. "Stunning, huh?" I say, trying to sound casual. "That's a far cry from boring."

He just smiles. Those smiles come so rarely that when a real one appears I feel like I've won the lottery. "Shall we go?"

"Sure." I head toward the SUV, but he's walking around the car, and, confused, I follow.

"You'll need that jacket," he says, stepping up to a gleaming black motorcycle.

I stop short, shaking my head. "Oh no, no, no. I can't get on that."

"What?" He pulls a helmet from the side compartment. "You scared of bikes?"

"No, I like bikes. Bikes are the thing with the basket on the front and ribbons coming off the handlebars. This is a *motorcycle.* Machine of death."

"Didn't know that was its technical name."

"Well, you should really do your research. We could take my car?" I offer.

Damon swings one leg over the bike, and there it is again—that manly thing that makes my stupid heart jump. "Who's buttoned-up now?" His eyes are challenging.

"You're right. I underestimated you. You're a wild thang. Now let's take my car."

He's holding a spare helmet out to me. "Just get on the bike, Wyatt."

I grit my teeth and climb on behind him. "You know, this helmet will do nothing for my hair."

"Your hair doesn't need the help." He starts the bike, and the engine roars to life, menacing. "Now, remember, you need to hold on to me."

"Don't have to tell me twice." I fit snug right behind him, both arms wrapped as far around as I can get them.

"But still let me breathe," he says.

"Nope," I respond, my voice muffled inside the helmet. "If you wanted to breathe, you should've brought a car."

He chuckles and takes off across the parking lot.

To my credit, I do manage to stop screaming. About fifteen minutes later when we pull up to our destination.

The second the bike is stationary I stagger off, stifling the urge to fall down and kiss the pavement.

"See?" Damon says, taking off his helmet. "Now was that so bad?"

"No, much worse." I remove my helmet, and my hair stands on end, full of static. "Every time we went around a corner my life flashed before my eyes."

"You must not have done much then." He takes my helmet and locks them both into the side box. "Believe me, it was worth the ride."

I look around, not recognizing this piece of downtown Provo. "Where are we?"

"The best Chinese food place in the state."

"Oh, really?" The squat building in front of us with the banner "Saigon Noodle House" looks ordinary, even rundown. "You sure this is it?"

"What's that they say about little faith?" He leads the way toward the front door. "This is the best kept secret in Utah. I noticed you liked the lemon chicken the other night. But you haven't had lemon chicken until you've had it here."

I glance over at him, surprised he would notice something like that. "Doing recon on me?"

He smiles. "Just a little research, as I said."

When he opens the door, my faith wavers even more. The walls are mostly bare, the carpet dull, the space littered with only a few tables. Nothing special.

A small Asian woman comes up to the counter as we enter and with a wordless smile leads us to a table. Paper menus are already waiting, but Damon ignores them and orders us each the lemon chicken.

As our elderly waitress shuffles away, he asks, "Sorry. Did I cross a line there?"

"How so?"

"By ordering for you. I did that for a girl once, and she threw her drink in my face."

I chuckle. "I don't mind. It means you know what I like. As long as it's actually as good as you say."

"No problem there."

When our food arrives, the plates are heaped with enormous portions of ham-fried rice and lemon-smothered chicken. I spear some chicken with my chopstick, but when I look up, Damon's hands are folded in his lap. "You're not eating?"

"I need to see your reaction first."

I take a bite and nearly die, it's so good. "Oh my gosh," I manage around the mouthful.

He's smiling, triumphant. "I told you."

"Oh my gosh!" I repeat, shoveling in rice. "That is seriously the best Chinese food I've ever had!"

"I know. Sometimes the most inconspicuous places have the best stuff."

"How'd you find this place, anyway?"

He's eating now and takes a moment to answer. "Uh, my sister found it, actually."

Shocked, I look up. "You have a sister?"

"Yeah." He takes a bite, and I feel like he's avoiding the topic.

"What's she like?"

"She's sweet. She's a student, and you know that's all about budgeting. You can get a whole meal here for roughly six bucks."

"Another reason I'm moving in." I realize how messily I'm eating, but he just chuckles. He successfully sidestepped the conversation about his sister, but I leave it alone. A private guy like him needs to give up things in doses.

Still can't believe I'm on a date with Agent Wade. How exactly did this happen?

We chat comfortably through dinner, but it's mostly likes and dislikes. He admits an affinity for sardines, and I tell him my biggest pet peeve is wet socks.

"Wet socks?" He laughs, choking on rice.

"Absolutely," I say. "You know, you put on a pair of clean, warm, fluffy socks, and you go into the bathroom or the kitchen or something and step in water. So disappointing."

"You're really all about creature comforts, aren't you?"

"I am. Give me good food, a warm blanket, and an old movie, and I'm set. That's really the best of life."

"You're low maintenance."

I pull a face. "I sound like an easy-to-clean lawn mower or something."

"I just mean you don't require big, flashy things. You like the stuff that's real and simple." He nods. "It's a good way to be."

"Or maybe I'm just mediocre."

"No. There's a difference between mediocre and content."

I'm smiling. "I like that. It makes me sound highly evolved instead of boring."

"You're not boring."

"But you said—"

"I know what I said." Damon looks weary. "I made a snap judgment based on what I saw of you from a distance. Up close, it's a different story."

"Up close I'm not just sitting around watching Hitchcock?"

"You're still watching Hitchcock, but it's because you think like he did—all in your own mind where there are these enigmas and this humor." He chuckles. "I can't imagine what it's like inside your brain."

"Trust me, you don't want to."

"You're a lot smarter than you give yourself credit for, Jack. You're content to downplay your own light, but the truth is"—he looks up at me—"you're dazzling."

I'm so surprised I can't speak, can't find words. I just look back at him, wondering if he really means it. He doesn't look away either, and soon the waitress approaches and quietly asks if we need anything else. Damon pays the check, leaves a generous tip, and puts his hand on the small of my back to lead me out of the restaurant.

"Well, how am I doing so far?" he asks as we walk back toward the bike.

"With what?"

"Your challenge? Giving you the best date of your life."

"Is that all this is? A challenge?"

He slides his hands into his pockets, watching the ground as we walk. "You know how serious I am about my work."

"Yeah."

"Then do you think I would take the time if that's all this was?"

Again, I'm speechless. Eventually I manage, "I guess it depends on how much you like Chinese food."

We've reached the bike, and he gets out the helmets. "Think you're up for it again?"

"That depends. Are we just going across this parking lot?"

"It was worth the first stop, wasn't it?"

"Absolutely. But you can only have one really great restaurant up your sleeve per date."

He climbs back onto the bike. "Then come see what else I've got up there."

This time I only scream for half the ride. The other half I keep my eyes clamped shut, squeeze Damon's middle until I've probably condensed most of his organs, and pray for my life.

My eyes are still shut as we pull up, so it's a total surprise when he says, "We've arrived," and I see where we are.

Skate City. He's brought me roller skating.

"Seriously?" I peel myself off the bike and hand him my helmet, grinning. "Roller skating?"

"Looks like it."

A delighted laugh bursts out of me. "I haven't been here in years. I used to love roller skating!"

"I know."

I stop and turn to look at him. "Were you serious about that background-check thing?"

"You mentioned it to Drake. You said that you practically lived here in high school."

"I just said that to Drake randomly. How did you remember it?"

Damon shrugs. "I remember important things." He motions to the front door. "Shall we?"

The pubescent teenage girl behind the counter looks dreamily at Damon as she takes his money and stamps our hands. Walking through the black curtain into the main room is like stepping back ten years. To the left, workers tender roller skates over a long counter, and farther down, kids wait in line at the neon-lit snack bar for pretzels and blue Icees. To the right, teens duck in and out of a flashing photo booth. Moving lights zigzag across the surface of the circular rink, where teen couples and groups of singles skate to some pop song.

We're easily the oldest people in the room, discounting the parents dragging their small kids along, but I don't care. This is easily the cutest thing a guy has ever done for me.

"So, you want to get a snack or start skating?"

"Skate first!" I say, ridiculously excited. "Got to work up an appetite again."

We get our skates and find an empty patch of velvet bench to sit on while we switch shoes. "Lace it up tight," Damon instructs as I double-knot my laces. "That's how you keep your ankles secure."

"Oh, believe me, I know. By the time I graduated, I could've gone pro." I hop up, a little shaky after so long. I move back and forth across the carpet a few times to get my legs under me. "Okay. A few wipeouts and I should be back in the swing." Damon hasn't moved from the bench. "You coming?"

He looks nervous, I realize. "Truth is I haven't really done this."

My jaw drops. "What? You've never been skating?"

"Well, I think I remember going once as a kid, but I did more falling than skating and haven't tried it since."

"Oh, wow, something you're actually bad at." I tug him up from the bench. "Come on, now. It's not that scary."

He shuffles over to one of the carpeted pillars. "What if I fall?"

I shrug. "Then you fall."

"Okay." He's looking at the floor. "It's just—the ground seems much farther away than it used to."

"Yeah, well, when you're a kid it's a shorter fall. That's part of why kids are so much braver than adults. Just come on. If we biff it, we'll biff it together."

I step out onto the skating floor, just outside of the flow of traffic, and wait for him to step out next to me. It takes him about three minutes, and even then he's pretty unsteady.

"You're doing great," I insist, but I'm giggling under my breath.

"I hear you laughing," he says.

"Look at the bright side—at least you're not wearing that tiny pink T-shirt."

I keep his hand as we go very slowly around the floor a few times. We're so slow we nearly cause several collisions with people coming up behind us at regular speed. But after about the fifth time around, he's not shaking so badly anymore.

"See?" I say. "You're getting the rhythm."

"Yeah, I'm really moving." Sweat has broken out across his hairline. "You know, I think I'll get us a snack. What would you like?"

"Icee, please." As he shuffles off the floor, I call after him, "You sure you're not just avoiding skating?"

"Can't hear you," he hollers back. "Music's too loud."

I laugh and pick up the speed to circle again. I'd forgotten how much I love skating! Soaring along is this incredibly freeing thing. As a kid, I imagined it was the closest I would get to flying. I stick my arms straight out and shut my eyes like I used to, feeling more content than I have in a long time.

By the time Damon's finished at the snack counter, I'm ready for a break. I glide to a stop and step off the floor, plopping onto the bench next to him. "Icee for the lady," he says, handing it to me.

"Thank you." I take a long drag on the straw. "You got me a red one. How did you know?"

He shrugs, looking a little sheepish. "I noticed when you get sodas and things on campus, you prefer cherry to other flavors."

I'm ludicrously touched by this. "You really have paid attention, haven't you?"

"It's my job to pay attention. But it has come in handy."

"You were really serious about catering to a girl."

"How else can you make it memorable?"

"I don't know. Most guys don't think so much about the individual girl, I guess."

Damon nods, holding my gaze. "That's what makes me good."

"Yes." I nod back. "A great dater. And a horrible skater."

"You had to bring that up."

It takes some coaxing to get him back out onto the skating floor, and we alternate between shuffling awkwardly around and taking breaks to work on our snacks. After a while Damon insists I skate without him again, and I don't push him. Even *my* ankles are aching, and I've had far more experience than him.

He watches me from our bench while I sweep around a few times. Then the music changes to a slow song, and the DJ announces, "This one is a girl's choice."

I glide to a stop in front of Damon and step up onto the carpet.

"Girl's choice, I hear," he says.

"Oh." I feign surprise. "Were you under the impression I was going to ask you to skate? Sorry to disappoint, but I actually had my eye on that guy over there." I point over his shoulder at a kid—redheaded, freckled, and probably about twelve—chomping on a piece of pizza.

"Can't really blame you." Damon shrugs. "Who can compete with that stud?"

"I do have a thing for the shorties. But he seems a bit preoccupied so . . ." I sigh. "I guess we could skate together."

"I only hope I can satisfy your high expectations."

Damon's slower and shakier than most of the tiny kids going around and gritting his teeth on our second rotation.

"You really don't like this, do you?" I ask.

"I'm just . . . not a huge fan of not being in control."

"Yeah, I've noticed. You don't ever put yourself in situations you're not comfortable with." He wobbles, and I hold on to him, laughing a little. "If you're so uncomfortable, why'd you come?"

He glances over. "Because I knew how much you'd like it." He's been gripping my hand for dear life this whole time, but now he interlaces his fingers with mine.

My heart skips a beat.

And then we crash into another couple and collapse in a tangle of turning wheels and bruised knees.

I'm still laughing as we limp out to the motorcycle. "If you don't wipeout at least once, you don't get the full experience."

Damon grimaces as he climbs astride the bike. "That's one experience I could've lived without." He sighs. "I'm sorry. This was supposed to be—"

"Are you kidding?" I interject. "It was perfect. Fun with a touch of whimsy."

He's smiling. "I liked watching you skate with your arms out like that."

"I was flying," I correct him. "And it's impolite to spy on someone while they're flying."

"Well, you shouldn't have looked so cute then." He hands me my helmet. "Come on, be brave. One more stop."

"Well, it's been good so far," I concede and slip on the helmet.

"Good?" He sounds affronted. "We have to crank it up to a better adjective."

This ride is longer—a solid twenty minutes before we stop. When I open my eyes, we're beside a dark stretch of trees flanked by a dirt road.

"Ahh," I say as I swing myself off. "I see we've arrived at the point in the evening when you kill me and bury my body."

"I think you've confused me with your other suitors of late." He packs the helmets away, then motions to a path around the trees. "Come on."

I follow him along the curve of grass and brush, our path lit by the solitary slice of moon overhead. A chorus of night creatures murmurs to us as we stroll, but otherwise it's quiet. Just when I'm starting to wonder if he really is planning something shady, the trees clear.

We're standing in a field of grass. A sheet has been stretched between two trees, and a projector behind it is running the opening credits of an old film.

"What's this?" I ask, wonderstruck.

"This," Damon leads me to a blanket laid out on the grass, "is a private showing of one of your favorites."

The credits transition to the opening scene of a film I know well, Hitchcock's *Rear Window*. I sink onto the blanket beside two brown paper sacks. Damon opens one and offers it to me—popcorn.

I'm staring at him in awe. "You did all this?"

"Well, I had a little help from a few agents. They got it set up while we were driving over here."

"Exploiting your power?"

"Got to get something out of it. The benefits aren't that great."

"I just . . ." I shrug. "I don't even know what to say."

"Good. We'll have quiet for the movie. I've never seen this one."

"You haven't? Oh, man." I chomp on a handful of popcorn. "You're in for a serious treat."

By the time Damon drives me back to my apartment, I'm euphoric. It was absolutely creepy cool watching the thriller out in the open night. And Damon held my hand during the second half of the film.

When I step off the bike, he turns both legs out but remains seated, right at my eye level. "Thank you," I say, holding out the helmet. "This was seriously . . . the best night."

He places his hands over mine on the helmet, keeping it between us. "So I didn't exaggerate my skills?"

"Absolutely not. You are king of dates."

"Well." He shrugs. "It's easy to do nice things for you."

My pulse is beginning to race. I can't stop smiling. On impulse I say, "Come to church with me tomorrow."

His brow lowers. "What?"

"Well, I'm going, and you have to stick close anyway, right? Why not just sit next to me?"

Damon sets the helmet aside. "Look, Jack. Tonight was great, but don't use it to make me into something I'm not. My opinion hasn't changed."

My mood dips slightly, but I press on, "I know. I just thought—"

He catches my hand. "I don't want to give you any misunderstanding. I like you, I admit that. You—" He chuckles. "You snuck up on me. But how I feel about the gospel is permanent."

"You don't know that." There's a sudden lump in my throat. "You . . . you could—"

"What? Change?" His eyes are sad. "Jack, I like you. I think maybe you like me. Does the rest of it really matter?"

I can't even meet his gaze as I say, "It matters to me."

He blows out his breath. "Well." When I look up, he's swinging his leg back over the bike. "I'm sorry. I think maybe this was a mistake."

"Mistake?"

"I'm not going to change. I shouldn't have expected that you could."

Something cold is clutching at my stomach. "What're you saying?"

"I'm saying I'll see you later." With a roar the engine kicks to life, and a moment later he's driving off around the corner.

Then gone.

23

STUPID, STUPID, STUPID.

Why did I have to be such a roaring *idiot*?

The rest of last night and all morning remorse clings to me. It hangs over everything—pestering me and making it impossible to sleep, fumbling my fingers when I try to do simple things like curl my hair and put on my shoes. It was all going so well, and then I opened my big, fat mouth.

Bridget is saving me a seat in sacrament meeting, and when I glide in next to her just as the opening hymn is ending, she pounces. "How was it? You didn't text me! Where did he take you? Details!"

I just give a tiny, tiny shake of my head. Her face falls, and she goes silent. She places a comforting hand on my back. I lean into her for a sort of side hug that sustains me through the meeting.

With the uncanny timing that makes me feel like the Lord has a serious sense of humor, the last speaker is talking about faith and conversion. "The key," he's saying, "is to decide what you believe and then never waver from it. Because you'll have plenty of opportunities to waver. And you can't make the decision when you're in the trial of your faith. You must make it long before, or it'll be far too easy to give in."

I've never had to wonder. The ability to live how I know is right is something that's always been easy for me. Not that I haven't had my trials. But I've never doubted, not really. When I see others struggle with knowing the truth, with knowing if the gospel is real, I'm sad for them. But I've never been one of them.

Yet here is an opportunity to waver. There's a guy I like a lot—more than any other guy I've known. This guy shows me more caring than any guy before him, but he doesn't believe. Could I live with that? Could I be one of those women who goes to church alone every Sunday because the man she loves doesn't believe?

Getting ahead of myself. It's over before it ever really began. And maybe that's better. I could never choose between a man and the Lord. For me, that choice was made long ago, and any guy will lose.

Still, regret hovers over me all day. I consider calling Mom to beg off family dinner, but if I stay home I'll just mope, so I force myself into the car. The black SUV follows at a discreet distance—as though reminding me it's still here. I've seen a few of the familiar suit guys hanging around today, but Damon's clearly letting others handle the protective detail right now.

Everyone has already arrived by the time I get to my parents' house, and after a round of hugs and a pointed comment from Muriel about how young people no longer observe the rules of punctuality, the doorbell rings.

I take the opportunity to jump up with a quick, "I got it." When I trudge to the door and pull it open, I'm rattled. Damon's standing on the doorstep.

"*Damon?*" I step out onto the porch and close the door behind me. "What are you doing here? This is my parents' house!"

"We have a situation—"

"You can't expect me to keep this a secret when the FBI shows up *on the doorstep*!"

"I'm sorry. I wouldn't have bothered you, but you weren't answering my texts."

"I turned off my phone." I hug my arms. "What do you want?"

"Luke Gardener e-mailed you earlier. He invited you to tunnel singing tonight and has been waiting for a reply."

"Okay, fine. I'll e-mail him. There's still several hours—"

"He asked you to meet him early—an hour and a half from now. It would be a good chance to talk."

"Fine. Then I'll hurry through dinner and call you as soon as I'm done."

I'm hustling him off the porch when the door opens and my mom steps out.

"Jacklyn, is everything all right?" She eyes Damon with surprise. "Who's your friend?"

I turn and gape at Damon, my mouth working soundlessly. After a mute moment, he brushes past me and offers his hand to Mom. "I'm Damon Wade. Such a pleasure to meet you, Mrs. Wyatt."

"And you." She giggles, holding on to his hand. "How do you know Jacklyn?"

I'm concocting a wild story about a blown tire and a loose cougar when Damon answers, "I'm her boyfriend."

"Boyfriend!" Mom exclaims.

"*Boyfriend?*" I ask.

"Boyfriend," Damon confirms, all smiles. "So sorry to meet you in this informal way. I was running late, and Jack was just bringing me in."

"No apology necessary," Mom says, sounding rather faint. "Come in, come in!" She takes his hand and drags him inside. Over his shoulder he gives me a look like, *Just go with it.*

The screen door squeaks closed behind them, and I stand for several seconds in total shock. Then I dash frantically to follow.

Mom has already dragged Damon into the living room and is patiently waiting for the group's attention like they're on stage. "Everyone," she says. Heads pivot toward them. "This is Damon." She sounds a little choked up as she adds, "Jacklyn's *boyfriend.*"

There are several beats of total silence in which eyebrows slowly crank skyward and all gazes turn to Damon like a well-timed routine.

Then Dad, peeking over his newspaper, says, "About time!" and the room erupts.

Little Anna launches herself at Damon and locks around his knees, nearly bowling him over. "Are you and Jack going to get married?" she asks loudly.

"Anna!" I chastise. But now everyone is swarming around him. I hear Aunt Muriel cry, "Darling boy!" and deposit noisy, red-stained kisses on both his cheeks. Jeremy is pumping his hand, already asking if he fly-fishes, and the kids are searching his pockets for candy.

"Guys, can we just . . . dial it back?" I ask feebly, but no one hears me. As one big laughing, pawing, kissing, hand-shaking mass, they bear him into the dining room.

Except Jen and Delia, who instantly grab me and pull me into the little den alcove.

"Jack, who is this guy?" Jen asks, voice lowered.

"We've never even heard of him," Delia adds, glancing toward the dining room.

"He, uh, it's very new," I stammer. "Honestly, I didn't really know where we stood until . . . now."

"Well, I think he's made it pretty clear." Jen laughs. "He just willingly sat down to dinner with the sharks."

"Yeah. Good work, Jack." Delia loops her arm through mine to lead the way to the table. "He's dreamy."

Dreamy Damon is already seated at the far side of the table, sandwiched between Mom and Aunt Muriel. I feel a lurch of panic for him, but as I enter he gives me the broadest smile I've ever seen on him. Seeing all this teeth at once is alarming.

"Here, Jack," Mom directs traffic, "you sit directly across so you and Damon can look at each other."

Giving a strangled laugh I collapse in my seat. Damon gazes at me, unabashed, and even has the audacity to wink. Oh, if only he were wearing an earpiece right now.

Dad offers a blessing on the food, and then there's a general hubbub of dishes being passed and glasses filled. For a moment I think, *Maybe it won't be a big deal. Maybe we'll just eat like it's normal—*

"So, Damon," Mom begins.

Or maybe not.

"Tell us about yourself. How did you and Jack meet?"

He glances at me, and for a wild moment I wonder what lie he'll tell. Still holding my gaze, he answers, "At a wedding reception." He smiles at Mom. "She stepped on me."

A general snigger circulates the table.

"Not that reception last Saturday. Jack!" she scolds me. "You said there weren't any young men there!"

"Well." I'm sloppily piling mashed potatoes on my plate. "I didn't think there was any chance after I stepped on him."

"She gets clumsiness from her father's side," Muriel interjects.

"I didn't think she was clumsy," Damon argues easily. "I thought she was beautiful."

I stare at him, pausing only a moment before hurriedly spooning more potatoes.

"I'd spotted her earlier eating two pieces of cake." Another general laugh. "And I thought, 'Any girl that pretty with an appetite is my kind of girl.'"

"That's our Jack," Jen agrees.

"Gluttony," Muriel tsks. She spots my plate and exclaims, "Good heavens, Jack! Do you plan on saving any for the rest of us?"

I look down at my plate now piled comically high with mashed potatoes. "Oh, sorry." I scoop most of them back into the serving bowl and pass it to Delia.

Mom looks beyond tickled. "Then I take it you weren't put off by her stepping on you?"

"Not at all. It's refreshing to meet a girl who walks around actually being herself."

"It's refreshing to meet a guy who finds that refreshing," Jen says, handing him the gravy.

Under the bright light of Mom's interrogative techniques, I learn more about Damon in the next hour than I've gleaned in all our time together. His parents are divorced, and he was raised by his mom in American Fork. His younger sister is named Sabrina. His voice is unusually gentle when he says her name. She attends BYU, which is why he moved back to Utah after graduating from a university on the East Coast—to be closer to her. He loves bicycling and was forced into trumpet lessons until he was sixteen.

"And what do you do for a living?"

I'm loading seconds onto my plate, but at this question I look up, ignoring the tilted gravy boat in my hand.

"Jack!" Delia whispers fiercely, grabbing my wrist. I've drowned everything on my plate and spilled onto the lace tablecloth. We both dab at it with our napkins.

"I'm in law enforcement," Damon says, and everyone's heads snap up.

"Like a police officer?" Jen asks.

"Cops and robbers!" Anna cries, crooking her finger like a gun. "Pew, pew!"

"Extremely hazardous work," Muriel says. "Not terribly stable if you plan on having a family."

"Muriel," Jen warns.

"I'm more of a liaison between law enforcement agencies," Damon clarifies. "I oversee different factions working together."

"It sounds terribly important," Mom gushes. "How wonderful for you to do such important work!"

"It's more boring than it sounds," Damon says, and I choke on gravy. A few people glance at me with concern, but I cough it into my napkin while Delia pounds on my back.

"Do you mind him having such an unstable career, Jack?" Muriel asks.

I rein in my annoyance. "Actually, I think he's really brave."

"Hear, hear," Delia agrees.

"It's amazing that he's making a difference when so many people have jobs that mean nothing." I look pointedly at Muriel. "Florists, for example."

Jen snorts, and Delia swats her arm.

"You two are such a cute couple," Mom says. "Damon, what's your favorite thing about Jacklyn?"

"Mom," I moan.

"What? It's a fair question."

Damon nods as though considering, and I'm gripped with a sick feeling. What if he can't think of anything good to say? He stops nodding, decided. "Her faith."

"Faith?" Muriel snorts.

"Her faith." Damon looks right at me. "Even when I barely knew her, she was buoyant with this assurance that everything will work out because she has God." He gives a gentle smile. "She's inspiring."

I stare back at him, utterly robbed of words. In the silence, our eye contact crackles with connection.

"Faith is so important," Mom agrees, breaking the spell. I tear my gaze away. "I've always been so concerned about Jacklyn finding a man strong in the gospel."

Uh-oh.

"If you live in downtown Salt Lake, you might be in the same ward as my cousin Peggy. What ward do you attend?'

Double uh-oh.

"Mom, this gravy is really good," I say loudly.

"I'm not sure, ma'am," Damon replies as if I haven't spoken.

"It seems spicier today." I shovel a second spoonful of gravy into my mouth, then appeal to Delia. "Don't you think it's spicier today?"

"Why aren't you sure?" Mom asks.

Should I fake a heart attack or something? Or maybe try to throw up on the table? Why can't I vomit on demand?

Damon proceeds like he has no idea I'm dying. "Because I haven't been to church in a while."

All sound in the room stops: not a fork scraping a plate, not a jabbering kid, not a creak of the table or a shift of a chair. It's so soundless that I honestly start to wonder if I've gone deaf.

Then Muriel clears her throat. "Well. Isn't that just . . . interesting?"

"Muriel," Jen says again.

"That's *Aunt* Muriel to you, young lady," she snaps. "That's the problem with your generation: no respect." Her eyes shift to Damon. "And no dedication, it seems."

"It's not a matter of dedication," Damon says. "I'm working through some things."

"Which is what people say when they get lazy." Muriel turns to him squarely. "You think you can just pick and choose when you'll be committed?"

I find myself interjecting, "We're encouraged to find out for ourselves what we really believe."

"How? By questioning everything? That's not what true members do."

"Not everyone's perfect," I say loudly. "Who are you to judge who is a true member or not? Maybe a *true* member shouldn't be so judgmental!"

Again, it's utterly silent. Muriel looks shocked. Her stenciled eyebrows have disappeared into her beehive.

I drop my gaze to the table, ashamed, and push my chair back. "Excuse me," I say, avoiding all eye contact as I hurry out of the dining room to the front door.

On the lawn I bury my burning face in my hands and fight the overwhelming impulse to cry.

Soon the screen door squeaks and Damon comes out of the house with my purse. "Here," he says, offering me the handle.

"What was *that?*" I demand, snatching the bag.

"What?"

"All *that*—in there! Why would you pretend to be my boyfriend?"

He slides his hands into his pockets. "I was trying to help."

I'm pacing furiously. "And all the complimenting me?"

"It was sincere."

"And having to throw it in that you're not active?"

"I didn't want to lie to your family."

"Why not?" I stop pacing to confront him. "I do. I've had to lie to them about all this crap we're doing. And by the way, saying you're my boyfriend *is* lying to them."

He watches me a moment. "What exactly are you so angry about?"

"You've just made my parents worry about the spiritual status of a nonexistent boyfriend in my life. You've complicated my relationships *and* set them up for disappointment. They think I've finally found someone, and then you'll never come back."

"I just wanted to help."

"Well, stop helping!" I stalk past him toward the house but stop short, trying to get my emotions under control. Delia comes to the door with a Tupperware in her hand.

"Here." She places it in my hands. "Dessert. Don't worry about Mom. She's more mortified by Muriel than anything."

"Thank you," I say, overcome with gratitude that I don't have to go back inside. "I'll call you."

She pulls me into a hug and whispers, "Despite the awkwardness, I like him."

Tears sting my eyes again as I murmur back, "Me too." Waving with the Tupperware, I add, "Thanks," and head down the stairs. Damon follows me along the walk, hand on my back.

Once we're out of sight, I shrug off his touch, walking briskly toward my car. "You really should've been an actor. You've definitely got the chops."

"Wait. I need you."

I stop. "What?"

He looks taken aback. "I need you to come with me. To meet Luke."

"Right." It takes me a moment to recover, and I stumble a bit as I change direction toward the SUV. He tries to open my door, and we grapple a bit with the handle, jointly wrestling it open. I plop down on the seat and hug the Tupperware to my chest, saying, "If you think I'm sharing this, you're insane."

Luke has scheduled to meet early on the grassy hill next to the tunnel where the young single adults meet for tunnel singing. I've only been a few times, but I find the hill easily enough after I'm dropped off. Once Damon handed me the wire pack in the car, we were silent the entire ride, and I was only too grateful to get out.

A guy with sandy hair, a medium build, and a roundish face is standing beside a tree. A blanket is folded over one arm, and a thermos is cradled in the other.

"Luke?" I ask as I approach.

"Hey." He smiles. "You must be Jacklyn."

"Jack, please. I'd offer to shake hands, but yours look pretty full."

"Yeah." He holds up the thermos. "Pretty cheesy, but I thought maybe you'd like some cocoa. It can get chilly after dark."

"Wow," I say. "I'm impressed by the level of preparation."

Luke shrugs. "You want to sit down?"

"Sure."

A few others are already beginning to gather, lounging on the grass or moving into the tunnel for a good seat. Luke spreads the blanket, and as we sit, I try not to think of last night—Damon beside me while the movie played out against the night sky. *Doesn't matter anymore.*

Luke produces two collapsible camping cups from his jacket pocket and pours steaming cocoa into them.

"Again, impressed," I say. Without thinking I add, "Seems like maybe you've done this before."

Luke looks surprised and then laughs. "Is it that obvious?"

I shrug, smiling. "The blanket, the spiritual setting. I can imagine this kind of thing really works for LDS girls."

"I swear, I'm not as much of a player as I must seem," Luke says. "Yeah, I've done this before, but just because I like to get down to it."

"It?"

"The real stuff. In this setting, I get a handle pretty quickly on what kind of girl I'm with."

I nod and take a sip of cocoa. It's good and rich, not watery like you'd expect a college guy to make. "I get that. Sort of like a religious interview."

"Which also makes me sound bad." He looks embarrassed. "It's not like I expect a girl to prove her spirituality or something."

"Even if you did, that might not be such a bad thing." I realize how I sound and flash a smile. "Sorry. I'm being weird. Recently had kind of a bad experience."

"Oh, yeah?" Luke leans on one knee. "You want to talk about it?"

Distinctly aware of those listening on the other end of the wire, I vacillate. "Just, uh, got more involved with a guy than I meant to. Someone who doesn't believe the same things I do."

"Ahh. Gotcha. I think we've all been there at some point."

"Yeah?" I take another drink, grateful for the comfort. "You?"

"Fell for one once. Hence my odd first-date ritual. I don't want to go there again. It's bad news for both people."

"Yeah, I guess it is." I laugh a little. "Wow. Talk about serious conversation. Usually I start with 'So what's your major?'"

"Kind of refreshing, actually," Luke says. "And I'm studying music."

"Really? Singing? Instrument?"

"Piano. Got forced into it by my mom when I was a kid. She insisted I'd thank her when I was older. She was right—as usual."

The hour preceding the singing flies by faster than expect. Luke's a really decent guy and easy to talk to. With a little fishing, I discover that he's the other one who never actually met Natalie. He e-mailed her, but she didn't respond. It sounded like he wrote her right before she went missing, and she probably didn't have a chance to answer. Or he did meet with her and is lying about it? His open, easy manner makes me think he's being honest. But then, what do I know?

As dusk falls, the congregation seated in the tunnel begins to light candles. Someone offers an opening prayer—the way we commence all events in the Mormon world—and the singing begins. Some people have hymn books or are open to the LDS music app on their phones, but most of the songs are the classics that everyone knows. "The Spirit of God," "I Know That My Redeemer Lives," "I Need Thee Every Hour." Luke has a strong, assured tenor voice that carries conviction, and it's nice to sing next to him. We blend and harmonize well together.

There's little conversation between songs, and the longer we sing, the more reverent the atmosphere becomes. Then my personal favorite: "I Believe in Christ." The night outside the tunnel seems utterly silent—like there's no sound beyond the hushed chorus of our voices. The final verse of the song concludes our singing. As we sing the last notes, there are tears on my cheeks.

Everyone disperses more hushed and humble than when they came. Luke offers to walk me to my car, but I insist that I'll be fine.

"Always walk a girl to her car," Luke presses. "Rule number one."

"Really, I'm waiting on my roommate. I'll be fine." I hand back the collapsible cup. "Thanks again for the cocoa. And for tonight. I really needed it."

"It was nice." He pauses. "Look, I'd like to see you again. If you want to."

Forgetting, temporarily, that I'm supposed to secure a second date with him, I debate. Luke is relaxed, grounded, and kind—all the things I'm constantly wishing for in a guy. If I'd met him a week ago, FBI assignment or not, I'd be jumping at the chance to go out with him again.

But now I'm wishing he were someone else.

"I'd like that," I say finally, managing a smile. "Give me a call whenever."

He gives me a hug and sets off into the night. I wander back around the corner toward where the SUV dropped me off, and after a minute Damon falls into step beside me.

"So what did I do wrong?" I ask, hugging my arms. "Didn't push hard enough?"

He doesn't look over at me. "You were fine."

Hurt wells up. "Wow. We really are back to totally disconnected, aren't we?"

He sighs. "I don't know what you expect me to do. I shouldn't have gotten as close to you as I did in the first place. My superiors are asking questions."

"Just another reason it was a mistake, I'm sure." He doesn't respond, and I walk more determinedly into the dark parking lot. "Fine. Be like this if it makes you feel better."

Damon stops. "What do you want from me, Jack? I can't be a different person. I'm not that guy back there. He seemed interested in you. I bet he can give you exactly what you want."

"How do you even know what I want?"

He laughs. "Because I know you. Like it or not, I know who you are, and I know that you won't be happy with someone who's not sure."

"I could handle not sure," I counter. "We all get a little confused sometimes. What I can't handle is someone blatantly rebelling against something just because they've decided they don't have time for it in their life."

"That's not why." His voice is steely. "You don't know anything about it."

"Then what is it, Damon?" I demand. "What? What's your problem with the gospel?"

"The gospel and the Church are two different things. I can believe the gospel without believing everything in the Church."

"What kind of line is that?" I roll my eyes. "They're the same thing."

"No." He paces away and then storms back, dragging his fingers through his hair in exasperation. "You are so naïve. You live in this perfect little bubble where everything's black and white, and you never question anything. But the world isn't like that—some of us see the gray."

"The whole world is gray," I shoot back. "They've blurred the lines on purpose. They want everything to look gray so they can justify any behavior they want. But it isn't like that. You have to give *yourself* boundaries. Otherwise, where do you ever draw the line?"

He nods, his jaw taut. "Well, I'm sorry some of us have a harder time with faith than you."

"Faith is a choice, just like anything. You choose to have it, and you work at it, the same way you have to work a case. And it doesn't always come through right away, but that's the point. It wouldn't be faith otherwise."

"That's fine for you. I don't need it." He turns and stalks toward his car.

"That's so ridiculous." I follow him. "Telling yourself you don't need the Lord is the biggest lie there is. Why are you setting yourself up to fail?"

He turns. "I don't need to be in a church full of hypocrites to know I believe in God."

"Hypocrites?"

"Yes, hypocrites. Like your sweet Aunt Muriel, who does everything she should—goes to her meetings, fulfills her callings, and makes it her business to hurt other people."

"People aren't perfect."

"Perfect?" he snorts. He's watching me, and there's something dark working in his face. "You remember I told you I have a sister? Sabrina. In high school she went to a dance with a good LDS boy that my parents knew. They thought the world of him." His voice breaks on the next words. "He attacked her. She called me in the middle of the night, and I had to go pick her up. He'd just left my little sister on the side of the road." He inhales sharply, and I see tears on his face. "She's the sweetest kid. Never done a thing wrong in her life. And that animal just—" He breaks off and turns away. "How can a church be true with people like that in it?"

"Damon." I step forward and cautiously touch his shoulder. "I'm so sorry, I . . ." I brush at my burning eyes with the back of my hand. "I didn't know."

He's silent several moments, breathing unevenly. "She's never been the same. I mean, we've tried to put her back together, but . . ."

I have a sudden realization. "That's why you moved back home."

"They arrested the kid. It even went to trial, but it was her word against his." He sniffs. "And he was an Eagle Scout."

Tears spill onto my cheeks. "I'm so sorry."

"I've kept an eye on him. He never got into trouble again. He's in advertising, successful. Getting married. And there are still days my sister can't get out of bed."

"Has she gotten any help?"

"Of course. But it doesn't matter. She'll never be whole again." He laughs bitterly. "And you know what? She still goes to church every week."

"She needs it, I'm sure."

"It kills me to watch her go. Hearing her talk about how grateful she is for the gospel."

"It's because she knows."

"Knows what?"

"That the gospel is perfect, but the people aren't. They're just people—some good, some bad. There's real evil in people sometimes, even people who are supposed to be good."

Damon pulls away. "Don't preach to me, Jack. If Sabrina can't convince me, you sure can't. You're as naïve as she is."

"You should be ashamed of yourself," I say, appalled. "How can you mock your sister for the thing that's been her sanity?"

"What do you know about it? What problems have you ever had in your life?"

"Excuse me?"

"You talk about faith and forgiveness like you know something about it—like you know anything about hardship."

I laugh. "You think my life's been perfect?"

"No, you've clearly had it rough." His voice is scathing. "You didn't go on as many dates as you wanted, and you didn't get the attention of that guy you liked. You've settled into a life of mediocrity, and you're afraid you'll never actually achieve your dreams. Poor you."

"You think loneliness isn't hard?"

"Compared to what others go through? I'd take your Saturday nights in front of the TV."

Eyes burning, I take a few steps back. "I once knew a guy. Called me all the time, texted me even when he was on dates. He was always saying that he missed me." I pause. "One night he as much admitted that he loved me—who I am. But his family expected him to bring home a real looker like all his brothers did. And I didn't deserve his being ashamed of me."

Damon slides his hands into his pockets and says nothing.

"You think that's easy?" I continue. "Having every single guy your whole life tell you, in one way or another, that you're simply not good enough?"

His voice is softer when he speaks again. "No one's ever going to be able to convince you otherwise if you don't believe it."

"I guess that fixes it then."

"You talk about choosing, but you have to choose to like yourself. Otherwise—"

"I'm just a hypocrite like the rest?" I finish. He doesn't answer, doesn't contradict me, and I nod. "Then I guess that's more evidence for you, isn't it? I'm just like everyone else."

Now I'm the one that starts to turn away. But I face him again, hugging myself. "It's funny that you think you're original to call me naïve. Whenever people say that, it's like they think I'm so naïve I won't even grasp the insult. What's funny is that they think believing in something makes me weak. Faith is just for children or idiots, right? It might look to you like I'm blindly walking along, going to church, following those standards because it's all I know. Yes, I was raised in this. But I didn't just accept it. I *chose* it because I *feel* it." I'm crying but force myself on. "I know it's the truth. And it's not about other people. If it was, I wouldn't still be around. You can't build your testimony on other people or let them take it. It's about me and God. And He has never let me down."

Damon is still silent, so I hurry to the car. By the time I slide into the backseat, I'm breathing hard, my pulse throbbing in my throat. Through blurred vision, I see Damon slowly approach and get in on the driver's side.

I make it all the way home and am running up the stairs before I start to weep.

24

A DEAFENING SOUND HURLS ME from sleep. Before I've even registered the insistent pounding, I'm sitting up in bed, scrabbling for my phone. Then I realize it's someone knocking on the door, and I throw the covers aside, fumbling for a robe.

My clothes from last night are strewn in my path, and I trip on a high heel. Puffy from crying, my eyes are sensitive to the morning light as I find my way to the front door. "Who is it?" I call.

"It's Samuel."

Disengaging the chain and dead bolt, I pull open the door and look blearily out at him. "Is something wrong?"

"I'm afraid so. I've been asked to bring you with me."

"Where?"

"To the field office, ma'am. Agent Clemens wants to meet with you."

Great. I'm probably in trouble for going out with Damon. A rule against fraternizing with agents or something. Well, if they want to fire me, fine. I don't care anymore.

"What about my classes?"

"I believe Agent Wade already spoke with your professors and has gotten you an extension on your exams. One week."

Just hearing the name Wade makes me ache. At least he had the decency to do that for me. "Fine. I'll just get dressed."

"Thank you, ma'am."

It must be serious because Samuel hovers by the front door while I dress and put my face in order. Even with a substantial amount of makeup, it's obvious I cried half the night. As I'm pulling my hair into a ponytail, there's another knock on the door. Samuel opens it, and two more blank-faced agents wait on the threshold. All three escort me down to the car and ride with us into Salt Lake.

I don't talk on the drive. One of the agents gets on the phone and says cryptic things like, "And that's been confirmed? We'll be certain to tighten the parameters." But otherwise the ride is silent. The FBI certainly is a chatty lot.

Back to the field office. Back up the elevator. Back down the gray corridor past all those people in suits and into the briefing room. When we enter, Agent Clemens is conferring with three more men in suits. They look up as we enter, and I see that one of them is Damon. He holds my gaze, his expression unreadable, and I finally look away to take the seat Samuel offers.

"Thank you for coming," Clemens says. She and Damon join us at the table while the other two close the door and stand guard on either side. "Let me get right to the point. You're here because we want you to go into protective custody."

I glance at Damon, but he's not smiling.

"Is this a joke?"

"On the contrary, it's very serious. Another girl disappeared this morning."

My gut heaves. "Who? How?"

"Her name is Caroline Lambert. She's a student at BYU. Again, there were no signs of struggle. Her car, phone, and wallet were all at her apartment. She's just gone. And she's a member of *Eter-knit-ty*."

"That could be a coincidence."

"She's been on dates with two of the suspects. Maybe more."

"Maybe?"

"She posted her phone number in her profile. The site discourages that, but some people still do it. We're working on getting her phone records, but for the moment all we know is she received e-mails from a few people including Thomas Smythe and Skyler Lancaster."

"I haven't met Skyler yet."

"No and you won't. As of this morning you're going to a secure location."

I laugh. "You can't be serious. Like the Witness Protection Program?"

"No, nothing permanent. We just need to keep you somewhere until we finish this."

"And how do you plan on doing that?"

"We're bringing them all in for questioning, and we're obtaining warrants to search their homes and vehicles." She's already looking at a file in her hand, mentally dismissing me. "Something should turn up."

"What happened to getting this guy without spooking him?"

"That was before, when we weren't sure what this was. With this second victim, it's officially under the jurisdiction of the FBI and becomes a real investigation."

"So before, looking for Natalie was just a hobby?"

Her eyes narrow. "This isn't playtime anymore."

"Who was playing?" I demand. "I was serious then; I'm serious now. You need to let me finish this."

"You did fine, but we can no longer be casual about this investigation. This man is escalating. You weren't getting us anywhere, and now it's time to go after him."

"Then what are the chances for Natalie? Or this other girl?"

"We can't think only of them when there's a predator out there. We have to catch him before he can do more harm."

"And you think you can by interrogation? What judge is going to give you search warrants when you've only got circumstantial stuff?"

Clemens leans forward like she's addressing a child. "We question them and gain leads that get us the warrant. That's how it works. That's police work."

"And how long will that take? It could be weeks."

"You've been on the job a week now. Have you had more success?"

"We've eliminated people, yeah. Besides, if the guy is escalating, then aren't I a likely candidate for the next victim?"

Clemens folds her arms. "Would you like to be? Would you like to use yourself as bait?"

"If that's what it takes. It'd be faster than your way."

"You're not up to something like this. Your recent behavior has made that quite clear."

On impulse I glance at Damon, who's averting his gaze. "Look," I say. "You said you're trying to get phone records. How long will that take?"

"A few hours at most."

"And the search warrant—how soon can you get one for anybody on the list?"

She sighs, impatient. "Depending on what we find in the phone records, it could be a few more hours after that."

"So the better part of the day, if you even get it. This last guy on the list—Skyler whatever—let me go and meet him. At least then you'd have a sample of each person to help get what you need."

"Thank you, but we no longer require your assistance. Agent Terigan will see you to a secure facility." She stands to leave.

I jump up. "You can't put me in protective custody unless I agree."

"You'd rather risk it on your own?"

"I'd rather finish what you asked me to do. Maybe this Skyler is the guy. Maybe this meeting could be the one that gets you the answer."

"With respect, I've heard the recordings, and I doubt you have the skill to crack a kidnapper on a single date."

Beginning to feel desperate, I say, "At least let me *try*. You need the time to get your stuff anyway. What harm could it do?"

"The delay could let the kidnapper get away."

"It wouldn't slow you down any more than you'll already be waiting. Just give me twenty-four hours. Then tomorrow I'll go wherever, and you can do what you want."

Her face is hard. "I don't make deals."

"Even when it won't cost you anything? Come on. All it could do is help, and if it doesn't, then nothing is lost."

She blows out a sharp breath. "You're right that I can't force you into custody, but if you turn away the protection of the FBI, then we have no more obligations toward you. I'll pull your protective watch, and you can do what you like. But don't interfere with this investigation or you'll find yourself in a whole new kind of custody." She leaves, taking the two agents with her.

"Well, that went well," I mutter.

Samuel leans forward. "Go into custody. You've done all you can. If he's escalating—"

"Then pulling me out is the wrong thing to do! Right now he's moving faster, which means he'll get sloppy. This would be the time to catch him tripping up."

"Or you could end up like those other girls."

Though it pains me, I appeal to Damon, "Do you think this is the smart choice?"

"I thought our investigation would yield more than it has."

"It still can. Who does it hurt if I try?"

"It could hurt you."

I shrug. "Well, I knew that all along, didn't I?" I shoulder my purse. "Look, I'm going to meet Skyler. If you want to come, fine. If not, I'll do it by myself."

"Don't be reckless, Jack," Damon says.

"Then don't force me to be reckless," I snap. "There's no reason to keep me from at least trying one more time. Can you think of a reason?"

"It's dangerous."

"Yeah? What else you got?" I stride out the door, and Damon quickly catches up.

He begins, "If you're trying to prove something—"

"It's not about that; it's about those girls. I could end this."

"You think Skyler must be it because he's last on the list? You think he'll just magically admit it to you?"

"No, but I think a lot can be done in a day, and I'm going for it."

He's following me. "I don't like the look in your eye."

We've reached the elevator, and I step inside. "Then you better come along to be sure I don't get killed."

Damon thrusts his hands through his hair. "You're infuriating."

"You should know that by now."

Getting a date with Skyler is far too easy. I e-mail him again and insist it must be tonight. In a blink it's six o'clock and I'm sitting at Chili's, waiting. I massage my temples. A headache has wormed its way in behind my right eye and roosted there, pulsing. I fish in my purse but never have medicine when I need it.

"You okay?" The voice in my ear makes me jump, and I glance over at Damon a few booths away. He's studying a menu, but his words are clearly meant for me.

"Fine, thanks," I say tightly. It's strange to be so formal. I'd gotten used to having him constantly at my elbow. Now he's acting like a stranger again.

"You look like you have a headache," he persists.

"I said I'm fine."

"I can get you something—"

"I'm fine, Damon," I snap, heedless of who might hear me. "Either care about me or don't. Pick one."

He seems to have forgotten this is being recorded. "You think I don't care about you?"

"I think you care when it's convenient for you."

"Well, thanks for the credit."

"Anytime."

"Are you Jacklyn?"

Startled, I look up. A wide-set guy with a doughy face and sad eyes is at the table, looking at me.

And I was just talking to myself.

"Yes, hi," I stammer. "You must be Skyler."

"I am." He hesitates and hovers. "Is this a . . . bad time?"

"No. No, no, no. I was just . . . rehearsing lines for a . . . play."

"Oh." After a moment he settles onto the chair but still doesn't look too sure about this. He's dressed in a shirt, tie, and suit jacket, and he's tugging nervously at his lapels. He dressed up for our date.

Instantly I feel bad for my mangy jeans and T-shirt. This stupid shirt even has Snoopy on it. So far I'm making a great impression.

"What play?" he asks.

"Play?" I repeat, confused.

"The play you were rehearsing for."

"Oh, that play! It's, uh, it's called . . ." *Wow.* There is not a single word in my brain . . . "Raiders of the Lost . . . Ark."

His brow furrows. "Like the Indiana Jones movie?"

Crap. I used Indiana Jones with a guy. If I'd said a Jane Austen title, I probably would've been safe. "Yes, um. And no. This play is what the movie was based on."

"Really?" He looks interested. "I didn't know the movie was based on a play."

"Oh, yes, yes." I try to nod like I know what I'm talking about. "It's a . . . French play by . . . Jacques Cousteau. But it's more serious than the movie. It deals primarily with romantic deconstruction of ark anthologies in postmodern day."

He squints. But if he suspects all I've done is string together a bunch of words from my literary criticism class, he doesn't mention it. All he says is, "Sounds interesting."

"I'm sorry about my clothes," I say, partly to change the subject. "I came straight from the . . ." Again, my mind is blank, so I make a garbled sound and take a sip of my water. That may have passed for a word . . .

"Oh, you're fine." He fiddles with his cuffs. "It's really just nice that you agreed to come."

"Why wouldn't I?"

"You know. I haven't had the best luck with girls."

"Really?" The waiter stops by for our drink orders, and when he's gone I press, "Why do you think that is? That you haven't had much luck with girls, I mean."

"I don't know. I mean, I make an effort. I ask girls out all the time, and when we go I really try to show them a good time by being sensitive and respectful. But it never seems to make any difference." He swirls the ice around in his water, looking morose.

"You seem a bit down," I observe. "Something bothering you?"

"I'm sorry. I guess I really shouldn't have come out tonight. I wasn't really feeling up to it."

His honesty prompts me to agree, "Me either. I'm kind of a mess at the moment."

He gives a sad smile. "Then we're great company for each other, huh?"

"Guess so. What's got you down? The girl thing?"

Skyler leans forward, candid. "Tell me, do you know what it's like to try and try, but every girl treats you like you're not good enough?"

My eyes are wide. "Totally."

"Really?"

"Yeah! I mean, not with girls but still. My entire dating life has been about inadequacy."

"Yes, mine too!" His face lights up. "It's like you're just programmed to fail no matter what you do."

"Absolutely!" I sigh. "Dating sucks."

"Yeah."

We both subside and sip our water.

Then I slam mine down. "You know what, Skyler? I think we deserve a break."

"What do you mean?"

"I'm depressed; you're depressed. We're on this date neither of us feels up to being on. What do you say we just eat fatty foods? I'll order what I actually want to eat instead of the tiny amount you're expecting me to order. You feel free to burp or whatever it is you hold in the whole time on dates. We'll just drown our sorrows in calories and gripe about dating."

He looks uncertain, like I might be trying to trick him. "Are you serious?"

"Yeah. Better than faking small talk for two hours and going home to binge there. Let's embrace the sadness."

He sets his jaw. "All right, let's do it!"

25

OKAY, MAYBE WE DIDN'T NEED double appetizers. Or bottled root beer and fruity smoothies. Or an order of steak, hamburgers, and chicken strips apiece. By the time we're halfway through the entrees, I'm stuffed to the gills and our pity party is in full swing.

"So tell me, Skyler," I say, taking another enormous bite of bacon burger. "What's the thing you hate most about girls?"

He considers a moment. "How contradictory they are. Every girl I know goes on and on about how all she wants is a sweet, considerate guy. Then I *am* that guy, but all she does is cry on my shoulder about the jerks she dates and tells me she wishes every guy could be as sweet and understanding as me!" He's a bit breathless as he finishes and slurps on his straw. "It's completely backwards."

"Totally," I agree. "And the worst thing is I've done all that! Except my best guy friends weren't at all interested in me."

"Really?"

"Yeah. You know, guys do it too. They say they can't stand the catty girls out there, but somehow the catty girls never stay home on a Saturday night."

"So true."

"I had this roommate when I was a freshman. Mean, *mean* girl. She was writing a missionary, but she constantly went out on dates. Apparently she treated them like crap, basically just used them for free food. And she wasn't even subtle about being mean, you know?" I'm stabbing at the fried onion strings with my fork. "But did she keep getting asked out? Yes! And did I, even though I was nice and not just using a guy as a meal ticket? No!"

"Backwards!" Skyler agrees heartily, slamming a hand on the table.

"Totally! It's like the nicer you are, the more you get stepped on."

"Yeah." Skyler is nursing his smoothie and dwindles into a sad expression. "Maybe I should just stop being nice. Maybe if I were a jerk, girls would finally notice me."

"Oh no, you don't want to do that."

"Why not?"

"Believe it or not, girls really *do* want the considerate guy. Most of them just take a while to realize it. But eventually they come around. And when that happens, you'll be there."

"But how long do I have to wait?" His large eyes are glistening. "How long? A guy can only wait so long."

Understanding is dawning. "What's her name?" I ask.

"Who?"

"The girl you've been waiting around for."

He sighs heavily. "Lexi. We've been friends for years."

"Close friends?"

"Best friends! She calls me every day; we text all the time. I took her on her first date when she turned sixteen. And when her jerk senior boyfriend stood her up for prom, I stepped in. It was the perfect night. She's the perfect girl."

Gently I prod, "And she doesn't feel the same way about you?"

"Who knows?" He shrugs. "She tells me every day that she loves me, but it's never been more than hanging out. She runs around dating all these guys who don't deserve her, then comes crying to me for comfort."

"Girls are the worst!" I say heartily. And I honestly mean it. Looking at Skyler's heartbroken face right now, I'm not real proud of being female.

"I wish she could just wake up and realize that I'm right here, you know?" He appeals to me, his expression desperate. "All these years I've been *right here.*"

"That's the problem. People never appreciate what they always have."

"You have this problem too?"

I snort. "Oh yeah. I'm the girl who's always waiting around."

Skyler offers me a french fry. "Are you waiting for someone now?"

"Kind of." Forgetting who's on the other end of my earpiece, I find myself launching into it. "It's just—there's this guy, right? At first I didn't even like him. He was so serious and severe and acted like he thought I was an idiot. But then it kind of shifted, and underneath he's like sweet and funny and actually seems to think that I'm worth something. Which is pretty new, honestly."

"Then what's the problem?"

"I don't know." To my horror, I feel the tears I've been keeping at bay burning in my eyes. "We just . . . don't believe in the same things."

"Religiously?"

"Yeah. I think he does believe what I do, deep down. But he's too hurt to see it." I feel a gasp bubble in my throat and escape with a gurgle. "I wasn't even supposed to care about this dumb guy, and now I can't stop thinking about him. But I can't be with the only man who actually cares about me."

Skyler offers me a paper napkin, and I dab hopelessly at my cheeks as the tears start to come. "It's okay," he says weakly.

"No, it's not." I'm really crying now. "I can't be with him because we don't want the same things." Sob. "And you can't be with Lexi because she's too blind to see what she has." Sob. "They're both blind." Sob. I point back and forth between the two of us. "We're so hopeless—" I crash into stuttery sobs, and suddenly Skyler's crying too. I sling an arm around his neck, and we hug awkwardly around the corner of the table, crying together.

After several moments the waiter cautiously approaches the table. "Everything okay here?"

"No, it's not!" I yelp, pulling away from Skyler. "Dating sucks! Everyone is stupid!"

"That's . . . true," the waiter concedes.

I look at his name tag and ask, "Have you ever been in love, Brad?"

He looks taken aback. "Uh, once. I guess."

"And did it work out?" I blow my nose loudly into a napkin.

"Well"—he shrugs—"not, really."

"Why not?" Skyler asks.

"Uh . . ." Brad laughs awkwardly. "I really shouldn't—"

"Brad." I motion around the table. "This is a safe space. You can tell us."

"Share your pain," Skyler agrees.

Brad laughs again, looking edgy. But finally he says, "She, uh, she got married."

"To someone else?" I gasp.

"Yeah. I was on a mission—"

"Oh my gosh. She pulled the Dear John with you? Skyler, she Dear Johned Brad!" I cry.

Skyler gives another sob. "That's so sad!"

"And have you gotten over it?" I ask.

"Well, I'm working on it." Brad nods slowly. "It's only been a couple months."

"And still you have a hole in your heart." I'm crying again. "We all have holes in our hearts!"

Skyler starts to weep again, and even Brad is looking pretty miserable. A manager in a pantsuit and name tag approaches the table, and I'm sure she's going to tell us to stop crying or leave. But she just raises her voice above the noise. "Miss Wyatt?"

"Yes?"

"You have a phone call."

"Okay." I put a hand on Skyler's and Brad's shoulders and squeeze sympathetically before getting up to follow the manager.

As we reach the hostess desk, someone touches my arm, and I turn straight into Damon's face.

Suddenly I'm realizing everything he heard.

"If you want to yell at me, just save it." I blow my nose into the napkin again. "I'm not in the mood."

"No, Jack. It's not that." His expression is strange—worried. "We need to go."

"Go where?"

"The hospital." He hesitates. "It's your dad."

26

I FLY THROUGH THE EMERGENCY room doors, already searching wildly for my family. When I don't see them, I rush to the desk, cutting past the people waiting in line. "Excuse me. I'm looking for my dad—"

"Ma'am, you'll have to wait in line."

"They said he was brought here in an ambulance," I persist, hardly able to get the words out. "They said he was having chest pains?"

"Ma'am, I'm sorry. You'll have to wait—"

"Jack?"

I turn and see Delia standing in the hallway, her face shell-shocked.

"Lia!" I rush to her and throw my arms around her, then pull back and demand, "What happened? Where is he?"

"He's in surgery." Her voice is brittle. "They said it was a heart attack."

"Oh no." I clamp both hands over my mouth, tears streaming down my face.

"They got him in there fast, but they said we won't know anything for a while."

I can't respond. I'm afraid if I open my mouth, the inhuman wailing in my mind will come pealing out. Only then do I feel hands on my shoulders and remember that Damon's here. Suddenly I'm grateful that he is.

"Everyone's in this other waiting room," Delia says. "I'll take you."

We follow her down a blank white hallway with bright light bouncing off the pale linoleum floors. The whole corridor is blinding. After a few turns, we emerge into a smaller waiting room with drab carpet and plain plastic chairs. My family is clustered in one corner. Jen is beside Mom, holding her hand. Delia's kids are gathered on the floor, halfheartedly playing toys with their dad.

As we enter, Jen stands, keeping Mom's hand in hers. "Mom!" I cry, falling to my knees in front of my mother and hugging her lap.

"It's all right, sweetheart," she says, stroking my hair. "He'll be fine."

"Shouldn't I be saying that to you?" I ask, taking her free hand. "Are you okay?"

"As much as I can be." She gives a weak smile.

"What happened?"

"We were at home, working in the garden. He just grabbed his chest and kind of bent over."

"Oh my gosh." I clamp my hands to my mouth again, aware of Delia and Jen crying softly.

"I called 911, and the ambulance came. They said it's good they got to him as fast as they did, but they called it a 'significant event.'"

"Did they say anything else?" I ask.

"Not much. Just that we'll know more after surgery." She squeezes my hand, but I see the fear in her face. "I called Bishop Forester from the ambulance, and he got here right after we did. He and Brother Jessup gave Dad a priesthood blessing. In the blessing they said he would come through surgery and find healing." She nods emphatically. "So it'll be fine."

"Of course it will." I smooth back her short hair, suddenly feeling like she's the child and I'm the mother. She looks so small. "Did Bishop leave?"

Mom nods. "He had to go give another blessing, but he said he'd come back in a while."

"Do we know how long he'll be in surgery?" Damon asks. Everyone does a small double take, like they hadn't noticed he was here.

"They're not sure," Mom says. "Probably two hours."

"Do you need anything?" I ask.

"Maybe a water?" Damon suggests. "Or a hot chocolate?"

"Oh, I'm fine," Mom says. "I need to stay here."

"I'll get you something," Damon insists and turns to go back up the corridor.

There are plenty of seats, but I stay on the floor, leaning against Mom's knees. Delia checks on her kids, changes a diaper, and then comes to sit next to me, grasping my hand.

Damon returns with a hot chocolate and a bottled water for Mom. "Something warm should help," he says, offering the cocoa.

"Thank you, Damon," she says, taking it gratefully.

"Of course." He touches her shoulder. "I'm so very sorry."

Damon, too, sits on the floor across from me, leaning back against a plastic chair. For a while we make stilted attempts at conversation but eventually fall silent. A single television hangs on the wall playing some sort of game show, and I watch without seeing anything. The blurred conversation and audience cheering are the only sounds in the small room.

The carpet is a blend of bland browns and grays, and the walls, though evenly painted, give off a sort of neglect. This waiting room is for families anticipating loved ones coming out of surgery. You'd think they could make it a bit more cheerful.

Eventually I get up, unable to sit still any longer, and pace the length of the room. Even the kids are subdued in their games. The minutes stretch into an hour and beyond. Time seems to have no meaning here.

It's a limbo of extremes. Whatever is at the end of this waiting time, it will change our lives. Trying to imagine the two possible scenarios, either total elation or complete loss, I pace faster and gnaw on my thumbnail.

We all drift about the room to new positions. Some leave briefly to go to the bathroom, to stretch their legs, and then to resettle in new spots. Only Mom stays constant in her plastic chair, hands folded in her lap. Jen coaxes some of the cocoa and water into her, but she's afraid to drink too much and need to go to the restroom. She won't do anything that would take her from this spot for even a second. That could be the second when the news comes.

At some point, Damon comes to sit in a chair beside me. "Hey," he says, his voice gentle.

I glance over at him, and it's like we're making contact for the first time since that awful moment in the parking lot. "Hey," I respond.

"How are you doing?"

"Okay, I guess." I run both hands through my hair. "Besides the fact that I'm going nuts."

He nods. "I checked with a nurse a few minutes ago. She said it'll probably be another half hour."

My stomach swoops and churns. "All right."

"Do you need anything?"

"No." I grimace. "Although I wish I hadn't eaten so much."

"Yes." He gives a tiny smile. "You were quite a sight to behold."

"I bet." I sigh. "Look, about the things I said back there—"

"Don't worry about it," he insists. "It's not important."

I nod, and suddenly there are tears on my cheeks again. Fiercely I try to bite them back, but terror is bubbling in my chest. "It's so weird. He's in there. Who knows what . . ." I wipe at my face. "And all I can think about is how I never finished his Christmas present last year. It was this picture-book thing with memories of the two of us. I only got half of it done. And now—" I give a strangled little noise and cover my mouth.

Damon slides his arm around me and guides me to his shoulder, cradling the back of my head with his other hand. It's such a complete embrace that I curl into it, crying quietly into his neck. For several minutes I weep there, my shoulders shaking, and he just holds me. When I finally pull away, he strokes my back.

"Sorry," I manage, wiping my nose on my jacket.

"Don't be." He's looking at me, eyes sad, and brushes the bangs out of my face.

"I'm glad you're here," I whisper.

"Me too." He pulls me close again, and I think I feel him press a kiss into my hair.

"Sister Wyatt." Bishop Forester is standing in the doorway and strides into the room, crossing to Mom.

She stands and shakes his hand, looking relieved. "Thank you for coming back, Bishop."

"Of course." He smiles, looking weary. It's nearly eleven p.m., and he's still out and about in his suit, visiting, giving blessings, counseling, and comforting. I marvel at the role of bishops and how much they do. It must be the most exhausting job.

"Have you heard anything?"

"Not yet. He should be out of surgery soon."

"And what can I do to help?"

Mom hesitates and then asks, "Could you maybe lead us in a prayer?"

"Absolutely."

We cluster around Mom and kneel. For a moment I wonder if Damon will excuse himself, but he kneels beside me and takes my hand. When everyone is silent, the bishop begins.

"Our Father in Heaven," he says, his voice reverent, "we come before Thee this evening in supplication for our dear Brother Wyatt. We ask Thee to please protect him."

Jen gives a little sob, and I find her shoulder and clench it with my free hand.

"Keep him safe during the surgery," the bishop continues. "Strengthen and inspire the doctors and nurses working on him, and bless that all can go according to plan. Bless him with healing and comfort, both physical and spiritual, so he can return to his full health and strength." He pauses. "Please, Father, also bless the Wyatt family at this time. Comfort them, speak peace to their souls, and let them know that all will be well. Please fortify their faith and let our faith work together. We know, Father, that all things are possible with Thee. And we ask Thee to feel our faith now and know of our gratitude. We are grateful for Brother Wyatt and for Thy comfort. We love Thee, Father, and we thank Thee in the name of Thy Son and our beloved Brother, even Jesus Christ, Amen."

"Amen," we say together. As the prayer ends, Damon squeezes my hand and keeps it in his.

It's another hour before a nurse comes around the corner. We all jump to our feet, and Mom rushes forward, demanding, "Well? What's happened?"

The nurse smiles. "The surgery went well. He's stable."

There's a collective gasp of relief, and everyone starts hugging. Daisy cries, "Yay!" drawing a round of laughter coupled with elated tears.

"Then he'll be all right?" Mom persists.

"Things are looking good. Of course, we'll need to watch him, especially because there's still a risk of infection. But we have every reason to think that he'll be just fine."

Mom wrings every assurance she can from the nurse before letting her go. I throw my arms around my mother and hug her tight, feeling her finally give way to the fear she's been holding in. She cries only a few tears, then pulls back and says, "I'm just so grateful he's okay."

"Me too," I agree, still crying. But I feel so light, so relieved.

"The Lord has taken such good care of us."

Rhonda, the nurse on duty, estimates it'll be hours before Dad's conscious and suggests we all come back to see him tomorrow. Eventually Delia, Jen, and their families drift home. But Mom refuses to go, and we finally convince her to at least get something to eat while Dad's still asleep.

At two in the morning, we're in the hospital cafeteria finishing cold sandwiches. Just me, Mom, and Damon. Despite everything that's happened to me lately, this still ranks pretty high on the surreal scale.

When we return to the nurse's station, Rhonda, smiling, tells us Dad's awake but should only see people one at a time. "And then only for a minute or two," she insists as Mom scurries down the hallway. "We don't want to tire him out."

Mom emerges a few minutes later, beaming. "He's great," she says. "Not completely coherent, but he's feeling good. You can go in, Jack."

"Are you sure?" I balk. "He just got out of surgery—"

"He'll be fine to see you." Rhonda nods. "But I want you out of there quick."

Leaving Mom with Damon, I enter Dad's room. Seeing my sturdy father there in the bed, attached to so many tubes and monitors and looking so pale, wrenches my heart. There's an oxygen mask over his nose, but his breathing is shallow. Never has he seemed so frail.

His eyes are closed, but as I warily approach the bed, they flutter open and a weak smile touches his lips. "Hey, princess," he says, his voice paper-thin.

"Hi, Daddy." I want so badly to embrace him, but for fear of tugging out a tube, I just lightly touch the back of one hand. The tears have started afresh, and I wipe at my nose. "I'm so glad you're okay."

"Me too." He wheezes a bit. "I've got to see the Super Bowl before I go."

I give a startled laugh but cut it off when it threatens to become a sob. "You hang in, okay? Don't go anywhere. Please."

He blinks long, like it takes great effort to open his eyes again. "Promise. Don't worry. Even if I had to go, I wouldn't worry. You're all going to be fine."

"Not me," I argue. "I still need you. You know what a mess I am."

"No." There's that ghost of a smile again. "You're going to be just fine. Especially now."

"Now?"

"Now that you've . . . found that boy."

"Oh." The last thing I want is to disappoint him in this moment, but it feels worse to perpetuate the lie. "Well, that's not really working out. We don't agree on things."

"What things?"

"Spiritual things, you know? I don't think we want the same things, so it's better to end it."

"Sweetheart." His eyes close, and for a moment I think he's gone to sleep. But then they open again. "Any two people . . . who are trying to be righteous . . . are meant for each other." His breathing deepens, and now I'm sure he's asleep.

I just gaze down at him for several seconds, drinking in the sight of him, thanking the Lord for sparing him. Then I leave him to rest.

"Are you sure you don't need anything else?" I ask Mom as I gather my stuff to leave.

"I'm fine," Mom insists. "Jen said she'll bring me some clothes and things in the morning, so I can just stay here."

"I can stay with you, Mom. I don't want you to be here all alone."

"I need to call your brothers with an update. Then I'll probably be able to shut my eyes for a little while. Besides, I won't be alone." She gives a jubilant smile. "I'll be with your father."

It's close to two forty-five when Damon drives me back to my apartment and walks me up to my door.

"Thanks," I say, suddenly feeling awkward again. "For everything. I know you were just being nice, but everyone appreciated you being there."

"I wanted to be there," he says quietly, hands in his pockets. "I wasn't just being nice."

I nod, unsure how to respond, and unlock the door. I want to say how grateful I am, how right it felt to have him there. How, when I was most afraid, he was the one I wanted to turn to. I've already come to depend on him that way.

But last night's conversation hangs between us. Nothing's changed. Except that I want him more. And still can't have him.

"Thanks again." I open the door and start to go in.

"Jack," he says, reaching out a hand to stop me.

Heart pounding, I turn back. "Yes?"

His expression is vaguely mournful. "Can I do something without you reading too much into it?"

Suspicious, I respond, "I can't make any guarantees."

He gives a tiny smile. "I'll take my chances." He steps in, and before I can even register what's happening, he's kissing me.

It's soft, gentle, one hand cupping my cheek. There's nothing demanding or even passionate about it. It's just sweet, like a gift. And despite how much I ache, it soothes me. I realize that's exactly what it is—a gift of comfort. Nothing more. But I'm still glad.

When he pulls back, he presses his forehead briefly to mine, then turns away and says over his shoulder, "Get some sleep."

I stare after him a moment before stepping inside.

Alone, my relief is briefly eclipsed by the terror I felt in that waiting room. It's okay now, but it could so easily have gone the other way. As I put on pajamas, tears of gratitude, relief, exhaustion, and grief pour down my cheeks in silence. For several minutes I stand at the foot of my bed, lost. Then I fall to my knees.

"Father," I whisper aloud, interlocking my fingers and closing my eyes. "I thank Thee for protecting Dad. I'm so grateful . . ." The tears intensify, though I'm not sure which man I'm crying about. "I've always been so sure, Father," I murmur. "I've always known exactly what I believe. Please don't let my faith waver now when I need it most."

I must have fallen asleep kneeling there at the end of my bed.

The next thing I know, someone's screaming. There's shouting outside my door.

More voices join in, a door bangs, and several pairs of feet pound down the hall. I struggle to pick myself up from my slump on the carpet and trip toward the door, my contacts glued to my irises and a terrible crick in my neck.

As I throw open the door, I'm staring down the barrel of a gun.

27

"GET BACK!" DAMON CRIES, THROWING his body in front of mine and swinging his gun around.

"What's happening?" I shout. A mere three feet away two agents are taking a man to the ground, slamming him into the concrete.

Everyone's shouting, and they're cuffing him. They wrench him up to his knees, and I go cold with shock.

"Skyler?" I gasp. "What're you doing here?" Then I holler at the agents, "What are you doing to him?"

"He placed this on the doorstep," one of the agents says, holding out a folded paper.

Damon edges forward—gun still pointed at Skyler—to retrieve the paper and hand it to me. I can't believe it.

Spliced magazine letters spell: *I could be the end of waiting.*

"Skyler, it's you?" I ask.

He's crying openly, his face awash with terror. "What's me? I don't understand what's going on!"

Damon thrusts the paper in his face. "Why did you put this on her doorstep?"

"I just wanted to leave her a note."

"And Natalie? Did you leave a note for her too?"

Skyler's eyes widen. "Yes. I sent her one. How did you know about that?"

"Where is she?" Damon moves toward him and aims his gun at Skyler's temple. "Where is Natalie?"

"I don't know! I don't know!" Skyler wails. "I don't know what you're talking about! Jack," he appeals to me, "what's happening?"

Damon slips the gun into the holster under his jacket. "Bring him in."

28

"I'm telling you it's not him," I insist.

"Jack, give it up." Damon is striding up the hall at the field office with another agent at his side as I trail behind. "The note he left for you matches the one he sent Natalie. E-mails confirm that she went out with him the weekend before she disappeared. He was obviously fixated on her, and last night he fixated on you. You would've been next."

"He didn't even *mention* Natalie," I persist. "All he could talk about was that Lexi girl. If he kidnapped someone, wouldn't it be the girl he's been obsessed with for years?"

"Maybe. And maybe he did. We're trying to locate Lexi right now. It's possible she's missing too. Or it's possible he couldn't risk taking Lexi when it was well known they were connected. Natalie might've been a safer way to act out his aggression."

"Aggression?" I snort. "Have you seen that guy? He's a big teddy bear."

Damon glances back at me, annoyed. "Weren't you the one who went on about how killers are often the most innocent-looking guys?"

"No, I said that killers are often charming. By that calculation, *you* have a better chance of being the kidnapper than Skyler."

"Glad to know you find me charming. But the evidence points to him."

"Evidence-shmevidence," I scoff. "He sent a note to both of us. You know any sane district attorney would throw that out. That's assuming guilt because someone has access to paper and magazines."

"You've watched too much *Law and Order*. This kind of note indicates an unhealthy fixation with the victim. That's exactly the kind of thing the DA wants."

"But it's not enough, right?"

"No. Which is why we've got him in interrogation." Damon stops in front of a door. The other agent takes a stack of papers from him and continues into the room. When I try to follow, Damon blocks the door with his arm. "You're not coming in."

I laugh. "You know me well enough by now to predict my next words are *fat chance!*"

"Technically, the investigation was off yesterday morning when you refused to go into protective custody."

"And isn't it a good thing I did? Because of me, you caught the guy."

He cocks his head. "So you *do* think Skyler's guilty?"

"No, I—shut up! The point is the investigation is ongoing because I have moxie."

"Moxie?"

"Yes, moxie. And I deserve to be in there and hear what happens."

"Clemens didn't even want you brought here today. In her mind, we've got Skyler, case closed. The rest is just paperwork."

"But you don't have Skyler yet. Not buttoned-up. Maybe it's not him. Maybe he's a red herring. Maybe the investigation is still on and what he says in there could be helpful to me too."

"Helpful to you? You're not even an asset anymore."

"Well, I'm being a wildcard. I have moxie—sometimes we do that."

His mouth twitches, and for a moment it's like the old Damon trying not to laugh at me. "If I let you in there, will you stop talking about moxie?"

"Absolutely."

"And will you stand in the corner and be silent?"

"It'll be like I've gone mute."

He rolls his eyes and opens the door. "I seriously doubt that."

The room beyond is a small, rectangular space on the other side of the same interrogation room they put me in when they first brought me here. So this is where they were standing. Ignoring me.

Several suited individuals including Agent Clemens are clustered in front of the glass, murmuring to each other. Their voices are hushed and the lighting muted as though they're afraid they'll be heard or seen on this side. They're so enthralled with the scene beyond the window they don't even notice when we slip to the back of the room.

Two agents I don't recognize are questioning Skyler. In the short time between being cuffed at my front door and now, he already seems to have been broken. He's slumped in his chair, his handcuffs chained to a bar at the edge of the table, his shoulders shaking as he cries quietly.

"We know you took Natalie out." One of the interrogators is circling him. "We know you sent her a letter."

"Yes, I did," Skyler agrees feebly. "I sent her a letter."

"Why did you do that?"

He sniffles. "In her e-mail she said she was looking for adventure. Then we went out, and she was so sweet. She seemed lonely. I'm lonely too, and I thought . . . I thought maybe we could be something together. So I sent her that note to say that maybe adventure had found her. I didn't mean anything bad by it."

"Why did you cut the letters out of magazines?" The interrogator slams a copy of the letter down on the table, and Skyler jumps.

"I—I wanted to keep it anonymous, like she had a secret admirer. I thought that would make her happy. I wanted to cheer her up but not come on too strong before I got to know her better."

"And when did you see her again?"

"I didn't. I called her a few times, but she never called back. I thought she wasn't interested, like everyone else."

"And that made you mad, didn't it?" the other one asks.

"No."

"That made you furious."

"No!"

"Mad enough to go to her house and teach her a lesson."

"*No!*" Skyler cries. "I didn't even know anything had happened to her. I just thought she didn't like me."

"And that's what pushed you over the edge, right?" The agent sits, leaning toward Skyler. "She wasn't just one more girl who didn't like you. She was the last straw. Your whole life you've been rejected by woman after woman, and finally it got to be too much. With Natalie it was just too much."

Skyler looks ill. "What is it you think I did? I didn't do anything."

"Didn't you?"

"No! I didn't do anything to Natalie! I would never hurt her or anyone."

"And after you took her, you felt better for a little while. But eventually you started hurting again. And then there was Caroline. And then Jack."

Tears are on Skyler's cheeks. "Jack was nice to me."

"Maybe that's why," the first agent puts in. "Maybe you thought Jack would be different. Is that why you took her that note?"

"Yes. No—well, yes. But not like you think!" he stammers. "When Jack wrote me, she said the same thing about adventure. I thought maybe it was a sign—like a second chance. So I sent her the first note. Then we met, and I thought maybe she was different than other girls. She understood about being hurt, and she seemed to really care about me. I thought maybe she'd be different, so I took her that note. But I wasn't going to hurt her."

A woman near the window speaks low. "He's definitely on the edge. He's been conditioned by rejection. If it got bad enough to cause a mental break, he could've been capable."

"No, he couldn't!" I blurt. "That guy wouldn't hurt a fly!"

Every face revolves toward me.

So much for staying in the corner and not saying a word.

Clemens rears on Damon. "What is she doing here?"

"Observing silently," he responds, smiling tightly.

"Miss Wyatt, your services, though appreciated, are no longer needed." Clemens steps toward me, and I curb the desire to retreat. "We needed contact with you to spur some sort of action in our assailant, and it did. Job well done. Agent Wade will see that you're compensated."

"Look, I know it's not my place," I begin.

"You're right," she agrees. "It isn't."

"But I think you've got the wrong guy. It's just too easy."

"Too easy?"

"If Skyler really did take Natalie, he would have to know that someone out there was looking for her and that his note would've been found. If he knew all that, why would he risk getting caught by hand-delivering a matching note to me?"

Clemens folds her arms. "Unhinged criminals are not always logical. That's how they get caught."

"Unhinged? Is that what your criminal psychologist called him?"

"Yes." The woman closest to the mirror, the one who'd called Skyler "capable," steps forward. Her attractive face is set sternly. "I'm Doctor Ginger. I've been analyzing your recordings."

"And you honestly think Skyler is the most likely candidate?" I press. "There are a lot of lonely people out there—including me. But I've never kidnapped anyone."

"Miss Wyatt, there are many different types of disturbed personalities that do this kind of thing," the doctor says. "Whoever we're dealing with, it's someone who's gone far past loneliness."

"Then it doesn't necessarily have to be him. If there are different types, maybe it's one of the other guys. My money's on Pervy McGrabby."

Doc Ginger looks over her glasses at me. "Pervy McGrabby?"

"You know—Tommy whatsit. Because he's a pervert?" At her blank look I rush on, "Doesn't matter. The point is, just being lonely and sending someone a note isn't evidence that he's guilty."

"We'll find the evidence soon enough," Clemens says, striding toward me and taking my arm to steer me out the door. "Now, if you'll please leave us. We need to get back to doing just that."

"Please, you can't lock him up when you're not sure—"

"Thank you, Miss Wyatt," Clemens says loudly, hustling me into the hall. "We'll take it from here."

The door slams in my face. After a moment I lean my forehead against it, defeated.

"Rough day?" Samuel's standing at the head of the corridor, his expression sympathetic.

"Not my best." I sigh.

He motions with his head, and I follow him around the corner to a small break room. A single table is flanked by a vending machine on one side and a coffee counter on the other. Without a word Samuel pours himself a cup and brings me another.

"I don't drink coffee," I say, suddenly weary.

"I know." He smiles. "It's water."

"Thanks." I sip at it even though I don't want it. Acid is roiling in my stomach, and the toll of the last few days settles over me. Everything hurts. After a while I mutter, "They've got the wrong guy."

Samuel drinks his coffee. Eventually he says, "Wrong is a relative term at this point. Once we're here it's just a matter of time."

"So they don't even care if he's actually guilty? They'll just railroad him into a confession? I totally saw this on *Special Victims Unit.*"

He gives a throaty chuckle. "You really don't care, do you?"

"About what?"

"What other people think of you. You just say what you think, what you feel. You're unapologetically you. It's what Damon likes about you so much."

I fidget. "Damon is . . . complicated."

Samuel makes a noncommittal noise and recedes into silence.

He waits with me, though I'm not sure exactly what we're waiting for. The outcome, I guess. As time drags on, I send a text to Mom for an update. Dad's doing well, she tells me. Still heavily drugged but has spoken some, and the doctors are optimistic. Visiting hours will open up later in the day.

Eventually the pain in my wrist swells, indicating the medication is wearing off. I trawl in my purse for change and buy a bag of chips and a soda from the vending machine to take the pills. The medication is supposed to be taken with food, but the snack is oily and leaden in my mouth.

When this whole thing started, I claimed to understand the stakes, but now that I'm in it, it's not just Natalie. It's the other girl and Skyler. This cool spy bit is really just the work of taking other people's lives into your hands, lives you have no right to be responsible for.

The sleepless night draws my head down to the table, and sometime later Samuel shakes me awake. "Here they come."

I stay just out of sight as Clemens and her group stream up the hall, looking pleased. Damon straggles behind and doesn't seem at all surprised when I intercept him.

"Damon, please. You've got to do something to help this guy. I'm telling you, he's—"

Damon interrupts me, "He confessed."

"He—what?" I stammer. "Are you serious?"

"It took a while." Damon looks equally weary as he slips his hands into his pockets. "But he admitted to taking Natalie from her apartment."

"Then where is she?"

"We still don't know. Right after the confession he clammed up. Dr. Ginger says he's suffered some kind of emotional break. They're still working on him, so I'm sure he'll tell us eventually."

"Sure. Rip off his fingernails one by one and I'm sure he'll make something up just to make it stop."

"He *confessed.*"

"And no one who's innocent ever confesses? If he was driven to an emotional break, he might have confessed just so you'd leave him alone."

Samuel quietly excuses himself, and Damon kneads the back of his neck, looking pained. When he speaks again, his voice is low and tired. "What do you expect, Jack? At this point there's nothing else I can do for the guy."

"You could find the one who's actually guilty."

"Why are you so convinced he didn't do it?"

I stomp my foot childishly. "Why are you so convinced that he did?"

"You mean other than the evidence? You've been going to bat all day for him, and I want to know why."

My mouth works wordlessly, and finally I sigh. "Because he reminds me of my brother Rex. Super lonely and big-hearted and just in need of protection. I guess I can't see Skyler doing this because Rex never would. I know it's not a very solid argument."

Damon softens a little. "I'm not really one to talk."

"Why's that?"

After a moment he responds, "Even the state police didn't think there was anything behind Natalie's disappearance. The reason I was convinced there was a case when no one else would touch it is—"

"She reminded you of Sabrina," I finish. He just nods. "And you were right. You were right to push it."

He doesn't meet my gaze when he says, "It hasn't turned out like I thought."

"Miss Wyatt."

Doc Ginger has come up the hall with another agent. "I meant to say before that I've enjoyed listening to your recordings."

"Oh yeah?" I laugh. "You see a disturbed individual in me, maybe?"

"No. But I'd say you and Agent Wade share a common emotional dysfunction."

I glance at Damon, concerned, and ask, "What, exactly?"

She smiles. "Denial. Would you excuse me?" She and her companion continue up the hall.

We're silent at her departure, not even making eye contact.

"Well." He pauses. "Let me walk you to the car."

"Didn't think I still had a ride."

"Technically your protective detail is over, but we can at least get you home."

"Oh, how kind of you," I quip. But the anger has left me again. Suddenly I'm just very tired.

Wordlessly, he escorts me to the elevator, and then we're in the parking garage. The walk seemed instantaneous—too fast. Part of me wants to find a way to drag this out, but it's inevitable. I have to be a grown-up and go home.

Damon holds open the back door for me. I pause just long enough to fake a smile and say, "Thanks."

As I move to get in, he touches my shoulder. "Jack, I . . ." He gives a tiny shake of his head and holds out his hand. "It's been a pleasure."

I look at his hand but gather my courage to peck his cheek, then slip into the car and quickly shut the door. I try not to see him watching us as the car pulls away from the curb.

Once home, I stand in the kitchen, feeling utterly lost. There's a keen sense of letdown—like I've been a character in a play, furiously inventing dialogue and rushing into action and now the curtain's closed and I don't know who I'm supposed to be anymore.

With the extension on my exams, I have a chance to actually catch up, but I sit on the couch staring at the mound of half-written papers and just can't bring myself to begin. My mind keeps going over and over the dinner with Skyler, searching for any clue he may have dropped. But all I see is a lonely guy trying to find someone. That's why I'm so convinced it can't be him. Sure, he reminds me of Rex. But even more, he reminds me too much of myself.

And if he didn't do it, the guy is still out there gunning for me.

The thought gives me a chill, but there's nothing I can do. The FBI has no reason to protect me anymore. I'm on my own.

On my own.

It makes me want to break into pathetic song.

I find myself dialing Bridget. "Hey, you okay?" she asks when she picks up.

"Not really."

"What is it?"

"It's, uh . . ." Restlessly, I drift around the room. "It's that mystery for my class I told you about. Do you remember?"

"Sure." She sounds cautious. "That's what you're upset about?"

"Yeah. The, uh, the professor told us who the culprit was, but it's just not sitting right with me. I'm convinced it's someone else and I just . . ." My voice is quivering. "I just can't figure it out."

After a silence Bridget says, "We're not talking about a school assignment, are we?"

No point in hiding it now. "Maybe not."

Another silence. Then, "Okay. Lay out the other suspects for me."

Bridget reasons it with me round and round, but we get no nearer to understanding. "There's just no way to tell," I agonize, slumped at the kitchen table. "There's no way to know who could've secretly become obsessed with her. They all seem so normal. Well, relatively."

Bridget sighs. "Maybe we're looking at this wrong."

"How so?"

"Maybe we shouldn't be asking who would want to take her, but rather who would want her out of the way."

I sit up. That's new. The whole FBI has been thinking of this as a case of fixation because the guy found her on a dating website. But if Natalie was the problem, not the goal, it changes everything.

"That's brilliant," I say. "But it rips open the suspect field. If we're thinking like that, then anyone in the world could've taken her."

"Not anyone. Just anyone who knew her, who had some problem with her. That's who the FBI should really be looking at."

"Yeah, but I don't think they're psyched to take calls from me. Thanks, Bridge. You've given me a lot to think about."

"Keep me informed, will you?" she asks. "It freaks me out to think you're on some creep's radar now."

"Maybe not. If this was all about Natalie, not the website, then I'm totally safe."

It's not until we hang up that I see the flaw in our logic. This can't just be about Natalie because as of yesterday a second girl is missing. Caroline Lambert. *Well, back to square one.*

I surf channels, but Bridget's words churn in my brain. It all began with Natalie. Who would want her out of the way?

Infuriated, I interlace my fingers and bow my head, uttering less of a prayer than a plea. *Father, give me clarity. If I can help her, please—*

Enemies are made by more than our own actions.

The thought is so strange that my head comes up. What does that even mean? Enemies are made by more than our own actions? That's exactly how you get enemies—because of what you've done. Another thought comes instantly:

Sometimes you make an enemy not because of what you've done but because of who you are. Because of the threat you pose.

The threat you pose. My brow knits together. *The threat you pose.* What sort of threat did Natalie—?

My eyes widen.

Oh . . .

I know who took her.

Instantly I'm grabbing my keys, jamming my feet into shoes, and snatching my purse. Even as I lock the door behind me, I'm dialing.

"Damon!" I cry when he picks up, as I fly down the stairs breathless.

"Jack, what's wrong?"

"I think I know who—"

Out of the corner of my eye I see something come at my head—and a figure standing in the tiny crook on the landing between flights of stairs—but I don't have time to react before it makes contact with my skull.

Then nothing.

29

OUCH.

Ooooooouch. I've got to stop sleeping with my contacts in. It gives me such a headache.

Even before my eyes open, my skull is throbbing; pain radiates from my right temple up into my eye sockets and all the way to the top of my spine. The pain is so overwhelming that for a moment I'm gripped with the need to vomit.

Blood is clotted in the lashes of my right eye, and I fight to pry it open. I can feel more blood gummed along my hairline and crusted down the side of my neck into the top of my plaid shirt.

Dang it. I liked this shirt.

Blinking into the dim light, I reel with disorientation. I'm looking at a stretch of dull red stone lined with shelves and a workbench. Tools and tins of woodworking supplies are piled on the shelves, dusted with years of grime. For a moment I wonder when Dad last cleaned out the shed. But then I realize this isn't Dad's shed. I've never seen this place before.

"Are you okay?"

I turn toward the frantic voice, and the sudden movement jolts pain through my head, forcing my eyes shut. Panting, I hiss through my teeth until the worst passes, and then force my eyes open again.

Two dirty, concerned faces are looking back at me—Natalie and another girl I don't recognize.

I swallow with difficulty and say, "I could use a Tylenol."

"You've been asleep so long," Natalie says. "I was worried—if you have a concussion, sleeping is a bad thing."

"Yeah. Probably the least of my current problems."

I'm seated on a filthy chair, hands bound behind me and feet strapped together with duct tape. Natalie and the other girl are similarly bound on chairs of their own. The ceiling is lined with wooden beams, and to the right a set of rotten-looking stairs leads up to a closed door, suggesting we're in a basement of some sort. Behind the other girl, various lawn equipment is half covered in a moldering tarp, and a single, naked bulb emits weak orange light into the tiny space. The concrete floor has a sunken drain in the center.

"Oh good," I mutter, panic converting to snarky comedy. "I've landed in the slaughterhouse. All we're missing is meat hooks hanging from the ceiling and a rack of rusty knives."

The other girl gives a sort of whimper, and I hate myself for scaring her. "I'm sorry," I add. "I get clownish when I'm terrified."

"Who are you?" Natalie asks.

"My name's Jack. I'd shake hands, but . . ." My weak laugh dies on my lips. "You're Natalie."

She blinks, surprised. Her face is smeared with dirt and her hair is matted back from her face from lack of washing, but she looks the same. "Yes. How did you know?"

"People are looking for you." I glance at the other girl. "And you must be Caroline Lambert."

She nods, her eyes luminous and terrified. Unlike Natalie, she looks fairly well-groomed, her dark hair pulled back in a ponytail. But her chin quivers. "Is someone looking for me too?"

"The FBI," I nod. "I was helping, but—"

"You're with the FBI?" Caroline exclaims. "Then we're saved!"

"No, no, sorry. I'm just a civilian, but I was helping the FBI. But then I got kicked out because they think loneliness is evidence for being a sociopath."

After a moment Natalie says, "I think you might still be groggy."

"No, I mean I figured it out. But not fast enough to tell anyone. I tried, but—"

Footsteps overhead resonate along the floor leading to the basement door. After a moment it opens, spilling light onto the stairs, and a figure descends. For a moment I have the brief satisfaction of thinking, *At least I was right.*

"Hey there, Tilly," I say. "How've you been?"

Since serving us lettuce wraps at P.F. Chang's just a few days ago, Tilly's clearly become a little unhinged. Her pretty face is sunken and ashen, her lips pocked from obsessive chewing. She hugs herself, her tiny frame trembling within a massive sweater. "I'm sorry," she says.

"You're sorry?" Caroline echoes, her voice spiking into panic. "You're going to kill us, and you're *sorry!*"

"I don't want to kill you," Tilly says quickly. "I just . . . needed you all to disappear."

"This is about Charles, isn't it?" I ask. "This whole thing has been about Charles."

Tilly looks positively mournful. Her huge, unblinking eyes speak of mania. "You don't understand."

"I think I do," I answer gently. "You've spent your whole life looking for the guy and never finding him. Maybe something happened when you were young that made you hold on to the dream of him so tightly—like it was the only happiness you were ever going to get. Then Charles comes along, and he's everything you've ever wanted. You thought you'd finally reached the place where you were safe and it was all going to work out exactly the way you imagined it."

There are fat tears on her cheeks. "We were so happy. He made me . . . forget everything bad. He told me I belonged with him." She draws in a stuttering breath. "Then he just . . . stopped. He wouldn't call me back. I drove past his house once just to see if his car was there—just to see if we could talk. He sent me a text that said 'Stop stalking me.' And that was it. But I"—she swipes at her wet cheeks, her hands shaking—"I couldn't let it go. I couldn't let him go. He was my only chance. I just couldn't give up on us. He was my only chance." She gives a sort of wild gasp, muttering over and over, "He was my only chance."

"Why would you want someone like that?" Natalie asks, her expression one of pity. "Why would you want someone who would treat you that way?"

"It's not his fault," Tilly insists. "He's just . . . too perfect. And there are too many women in the world. He wasn't ready to settle down. But I know," she takes a frantic step forward, hands out as though appealing to us, "I know that if I just give him time, he'll see that we're meant to be together. He'll remember. I just need to give him time."

"But you got scared," I prompt. "You saw him go out with Natalie."

"A med student," Tilly says, giving Natalie a look of contempt. "I'm just a waitress. How am I supposed to compete with that? I couldn't risk him getting confused."

"So you took her, made her disappear."

"You were dangerous," Tilly says softly, looking at her captive. "I had to protect him."

"And then Caroline," I say.

"He went out with her *twice*." Tilly gives a hysterical laugh. I can literally see her coming unraveled. "He brought her flowers the second time. He only ever takes girls out once, and then he sees that they're not good enough for him. He sees they're not what he wants. When it's just once, I don't worry. But this was *twice*. I knew the warning signs. I had to get her out of there."

"I never did anything to you!" Caroline cries, her face dissolving in tears. "I never hurt you!"

"You would have taken him away from me!" Tilly roars, advancing on her. "You would've destroyed everything if you had the chance. I had to stop you!"

"It's not my fault." Caroline's shoulders are shaking. "It's not my fault he asked me out. It's not my fault he picked me."

Tilly snatches a tin can of nails from a shelf and hurls it at the opposite wall. It clatters loudly, spewing nails, and Caroline shrieks and ducks her head.

"He did not *pick you*," Tilly hisses, nearly nose to nose with her. "You confused him, that's all. But he did not choose you. He chose me. *Me.*"

Caroline cries harder, and after a minute Tilly backs off. She reins herself in and rakes back her hair, murmuring, "He'll remember." It sounds like a mantra she's had for a long time. "He'll remember that it's me."

"And what's your plan?" Natalie asks. Once again, there's only compassion in her face. "You're just going to keep us here until Charles comes around?"

"If I have to," Tilly snaps.

"Tilly, think about it." Natalie's voice is gentle, like she's talking to a patient. "I've been down here for weeks now, and you bring me two meals a day. You're a waitress, right? You can't afford to keep feeding three women indefinitely."

"Dude," I say out of the corner of my mouth. "You're really not stacking the deck in favor of keeping us alive here."

"I understand why you felt you had to do it," Natalie continues. "But this isn't a permanent solution."

"Stop giving her ideas!" I hiss.

"I'll think of something," Tilly says, trembling.

I sigh. "Tilly, you're going to get caught. The FBI has been looking for Natalie ever since she disappeared. Now they're looking for Caroline, and they'll definitely be looking for me. I've been working with them on this. That's why I went out with Charles. I'm assuming you've seen me with them or you would've taken me much sooner than this."

"They were always around you," Tilly agrees, tugging compulsively at the hem of her sweater sleeves. "I didn't know why, but I couldn't get you alone."

"You tried to run me down," I prompt. "And when that didn't work, you used the name Ralph Timen to draw me out."

"But they were still with you. Always, always with you!"

"You must've known I wasn't a threat. Charles didn't even like me. He stormed out of our date."

"That's why," she says, spitting the words at me. "You made a fool of him. I couldn't let you hurt him like that."

"But the FBI heard everything," I persist. "And when they realize I'm gone, they'll go over every inch of this case again. That includes you. They'll figure out what you've done. And then you'll be much worse off. You need to turn yourself in."

Tilly giggles shrilly. "Oh, you'd like that, wouldn't you? Then you all have Charles to yourselves."

"This isn't about Charles." I lower my voice. "This is about you. This is a serious thing you've done. You've kidnapped three people. That is super against the law. If they catch you—and they will—you are going to be in some real trouble."

"Now who's not helping?" Natalie whispers.

"But if you turn yourself in, they'll go easier on you. They'll get you the help you need."

Tilly steps toward me. Her eyes are like a crazed animal, and her tongue wets her bloody lips. "I don't need any help," she breathes. "I just need you all to *go away*."

She pivots on her heel and strides up the stairs, slamming the door behind her.

"Yeah. I may have made that worse." I sigh.

"Do you really think they'll come looking for you?" Caroline asks.

"Yes, but they have nothing new to go on. They thought they had the guy in custody. My disappearance will prove it wasn't him, but they're still looking at the *guys.*"

"What guys?" Natalie asks.

"The guys you met on *Eter-knit-ty.* You know," I muse, panic beginning to surge in my veins. "I've never understood that name. Why 'knit' in the middle? Is it supposed to be some kind of catchy thing about knitting you together as people? It's just off-putting."

"You said they heard about Tilly."

"Yes, but just as a sideline. She waited on us when I was out with Charles. It was super awkward." I'm beginning to hyperventilate, and my head, already spinning from the injury, reels. "The cake really wasn't worth it."

"You've got to stay calm," Natalie says. "Panicking will only make it worse."

"How can this possibly get worse?" I demand. "We're in a kill basement with a convenient drain in the floor, and I've just made the case for bumping us off!"

"She's kept me alive all this time," Natalie says. "I don't think she wants to hurt anyone."

Still trying to keep a handle on my breathing, I say, "I'm sorry. You're the one who's been through everything. I don't know how you've lasted this long."

Natalie smiles a little. "She hasn't treated me terribly. Before Caroline came I was upstairs on a small tether that let me move around a little. She's fed me consistently and given me water. She's not cruel. Just a damaged person."

"I'm still sorry," I tell her. "I signed up with the Feds because I wanted to help find you. But I should've worked harder. I should've found a way to get you out."

Tears glisten in her eyes. "There are worse things. I appreciate that you tried."

Tried and failed.

Fighting off despair I say, "You were upstairs before. Do you have any idea where we are?"

Natalie shakes her head. "I can't tell you anything. It's small—like a storage shack. The windows are all boarded up, and my rope was too short to reach the walls. Before Caroline arrived she tied me to the chair. Then today she brought us down here."

"Had to make space because she knew I was coming," I murmur. "How long was I out?"

"A few hours."

"Then they've known for a while that I'm gone. Damon must have worried when my call ended."

"Who's Damon?"

"The agent I've been working with. If anyone can figure out what happened, he can."

"Then," Caroline looks up, "help might be coming?"

"Maybe. We just have to wait and—" I stop, my nose wrinkling. "What is that?"

They both glance around. "What?" Natalie asks. "Did you hear something?"

"No, I smell something. Do you smell that?"

"Smell what?"

"Gasoline." My heart plummets. "She's started a fire."

30

CAROLINE INSTANTLY LAUNCHES INTO A stream of hysterical rambling. "We're gonna die! We're gonna die! *We're gonna die!*"

"Carol, calm down!" Natalie shouts. But Caroline's terror is mirrored in her own face. "You don't think she'd really—"

"Yes, I do." My own breath is quickening. "She wouldn't hurt us directly, but she's desperate to make the problem go away. If she just lights it and leaves, she won't have to think of herself as responsible."

"But this is insane!" Natalie cries. Caroline's wailing now. "He's just a guy!"

"Not to her. This goes so much deeper for her."

"Tilly!" Natalie shouts toward the stairs. "Tilly, please come back! Don't do this!"

"Save your breath," I whisper. "She's probably already gone by now."

"Then what do we do?"

I hear it then—a hiss and roar like the sound of rushing water that must be fire creeping along the floor above.

"Nothing," I say. "It's too late."

Caroline bucks in her chair, panic driving her to claustrophobia. "Can't get out . . . Can't get out . . ."

"It can't be too late," Natalie says, her eyes on the low ceiling. "There's got to be a way—"

"If this place is as small as you said, it'll burn down in minutes."

"We're gonna die!" Caroline shrieks.

"She's right." There are tears on my cheeks. "She's right. Oh, Father." I squeeze my eyes shut and plead, *Father, please. Let it be quick. Please just don't let us suffer . . .*

Table saw.

My eyes fly open.

"Table saw!" Natalie and I say together.

"I'm closer." I'm already scooting my chair toward the corner. The table saw is half covered by a muddy tarp, and I lift my bound feet— *Why didn't I do more yoga?*—to clamp them around the edge. It takes a few tries, but I manage to pull it off. Then, pushing off with my heels, I scoot the chair around so my back is to the saw.

"The blade is a little higher," Natalie's telling me. "Lift your hands."

Straining to lift my arms back at an unnatural angle, I locate the jagged edge of the saw blade with my fingers and slide the tape on my wrists against it.

"Good, good," Natalie urges.

I move my hands up and down across the blade teeth, repeatedly snagging my cast. After a mere minute, my arms are aching, shoulders strained—

"Oh, gosh," Natalie breathes. "It's starting to get hot."

The tiny room is rapidly heating up. Sweat drenches my collar and pools at the small of my back. The roar and crackle of flames upstairs is growing louder, and smoke drifts down through the rafters.

Coughing, working more furiously, I saw at the tape. Hot liquid coats my palms, and I realize it's my blood. If I'm not careful, I could slit my own wrists—

The tape snaps, and I give a cry of triumph, bringing my bleeding hands around. The tape on my ankle takes another minute. We're all coughing, and it's getting hotter now, like a sauna, scorching—

"I got it!" I pull my ankles free and trip out of the chair, blundering over to Natalie.

"You're hurt," she says as I work at the tape on her wrists.

"I'm fine. We've got to hurry." It sounds like there's a river crashing across the floorboards above, and the smoke's getting so thick it's difficult to see.

Once her hands are free, I rush over to Caroline. She's sobbing louder now and doesn't respond when I try to calm her. She's struggled so much the tape has hardened into sinewy cords around her wrists and ankles. It's impossible to find the edge. Lungs burning, I fumble my way over to the tool shelves, hunt until I find the hard handle of a knife, and hurry back to her.

Tears streaming from my burning eyes, I saw at the tape around her hands. After a minute I realize Natalie is free and crouched, working at the tape on Caroline's ankles. The binding on her wrists snaps first, and I help her saw at the ankle tape. Together we cut through it and help Caroline up from the chair.

"Put your arm around my shoulders," Natalie tells her, shouting over the roar of the fire.

I can't see the stairs anymore, and it takes us several seconds to orient ourselves in the haze. Caroline seems to have lost the ability to move on her own, and I take her other arm, the three of us hobbling together toward the stairs.

My lungs are blazing, boiling; my body is wracked with coughs as we reach the staircase. The narrow passage is only wide enough for two, and I urge them ahead of me, keeping both hands on Caroline's back to steady her.

We're nearly halfway to the top when there's an almighty crack and clatter as the beams of the floor above collapse. The debris takes me down in a shower of wood, splinters, and cinders.

Pressure compresses my lungs. The wind torn from me. Something holding me down. My head black with pain and dizziness.

"Jack!"

Natalie's screaming at me from above. "Jack, are you all right?"

I try to shout back but can't regain any air. Gouging burning ash from my eyes with trembling, bloody fingers, I see what remains of the staircase high above—a torn crescent of ceiling, flames licking down the walls.

"Jack! Can you hear me?"

A fallen beam has pinned me atop the ruin of staircase. I strain at the hot wood only to blister my fingers. My legs flop feebly, but the beam is directly across my midsection and my arms simply aren't strong enough.

I'm trapped.

Mustering a scrap of breath, I wheeze out, "Go. Get outside."

"I can't leave you!" Natalie weeps.

"Go," I repeat, then I'm wrenched with coughs. "It's okay. I promise."

I hear her sobbing. Then there's nothing, and I assume they've gone. I hope they've gone.

Again I scrabble at the blistering wood, but it's hopeless. I'm not getting out of here.

It happened so fast. Wasn't I sitting in my safe little apartment a few hours ago? In a blink, it's all over.

Tears spill from my ashy eyes. Already my body has started to go numb, like I'm not quite in it anymore. There's still a vague heat, a vague pressure, but it's like I'm watching it happen to someone else.

I'm going to die here. All I can think is how sad my family's going to be. I only hope they can forgive me for being stupid enough to get in this situation.

Father, I pray. *Don't leave me now. Please stay with me.*

And suddenly I'm not coughing, not hurting, not afraid. Despite the flame crawling its way down the beams toward me, despite the smoke filling me up, I'm infused with a strange peace. I feel, oddly, like I could go to sleep. And it would be okay.

My eyes drift shut.

It's not my whole life I see there, just a small piece. That moment watching *Rear Window* out on the grass when Jimmy Stewart is hanging from the ledge. And even though I've seen it a hundred times, I was biting my lip. I looked over at Damon, and he was watching me with this look on his face I'd never seen before. Not when someone was looking at me.

It's that moment I carry with me into the darkness.

31

"Jack?"

Someone seems to be talking to me from far away, and I wonder absently who it is.

"Jack?"

My brow furrows. This is a bad time to bug me. I was about to take a nap.

"Jack!"

The familiar voice jerks me back, yanks me into my body. Coughing again, I peer through swollen eyes into the smoke, and I see a figure silhouetted against the blaze.

Then the face snaps into focus—eyes frantic, hands cradling my head.

"Are you okay?" he demands, though I can barely hear him.

"Damon?" I breathe, confused. "How did you get here?" Panic surges into me. "Why are you here? You need to get out!"

"Nope."

"I'm serious! You've got to go—please! Damon—"

"Don't waste your breath. Can you move?"

"Not so much. There's a big piece of wood on me."

He fumbles along the edges of the beam and then tells me, "Okay. When I say three, you push up, okay? Here we go. One, two, three!"

I try with my inadequate arms to shove against the beam, but I already know it isn't enough. I see him struggling, straining, but it doesn't budge.

"It won't work," I manage.

"Yes, it will. Try again. One, two, three!" He's fighting again, grunting and shaking with the effort, but the beam doesn't move. "*Come on!*" he screams, striking at the wood with his fist.

"Damon." I reach up with blackened fingers to catch his face. I manage a smile and whisper, "It's okay. It's okay."

He gazes at me a moment, his expression wrenched with despair. His eyes squeeze shut. He leans over me and presses his forehead to mine the way he did last night. We breathe, together, the scorching air.

Then he opens his eyes and says, "One more time. One more."

I don't even try to help this time. I can't. But he closes his eyes and with a ragged breath, heaves.

There are several moments as he strains, shouting through his clenched teeth.

The beam lifts off me.

I slither out, and Damon drops the rafter, shaking with the effort. Instantly I'm in his arms, cradled to his shoulder. Wrapping both arms around my waist, he says, "Come on. We have to get you out."

My eyes drift shut again. My legs have gone limp, and he hauls me toward the ruined stairs. From far away I hear shouting, so much shouting, and then something rough around my waist, lifting me like a rag doll. More arms, dragging me. Then the sweet, sweet taste of night air.

Instantly there's something solid under my back, something else slipping over my nose and mouth. Oxygen floods my lungs, expelling the smoke in a series of wet, jarring coughs.

I'm lying on a gurney, I realize. EMTs bustle over me, adjusting the oxygen, pressing probing fingers into the side of my neck. Someone is cleaning the wounds on my wrists; someone else checking my eyes with a light.

Then Damon again, perched over me, brushing the tangled hair from my face.

My fingers find his, and he squeezes tight, his gaze anchoring me to this world.

Epilogue

SOMETIME LATER I ROUSE FROM a half dream, and for a moment I flail, certain I'm still in that burning basement.

"Hey, hey." Damon is at my side, catching my frantic hands. "You're okay. You're safe now."

I settle back into the pillows, still tense. I'm on a bed in a darkened hospital room.

Every inch of me hurts. Like, *hurts*. My back aches like someone broke me in half. My lungs burn with each breath, and my throat is raw, as though a branding iron was shoved down into my stomach. My eyes throb and my head aches and my wrists pulse with pain.

"What happened?" I manage, every syllable agony.

He folds his arms on the edge of the bed, keeping my hand. "Well, you were hit on the head, kidnapped, broke free, had half a house fall on you, fell through some stairs, and were rescued from a fire."

I manage a smile. "You sure know how to show a girl a good time."

He laughs and shakes his head. "Do you know how close you came? You inhaled so much smoke—"

"Yeah, good thing you were there." I realize something. "The stairs were gone."

"Yes, they were."

"If the stairs were gone, how did you get into the basement?"

He hedges. "I . . . jumped."

I look at him squarely. "You jumped down like twenty feet into a burning inferno?"

"Seems that way."

"Why?"

Damon shrugs. "Why did Robin get into the catapult?"

I don't know how to respond to that, so I ask, "How did you even find me?"

"Charles."

"Charles?"

"Caroline's phone records showed that he called her a few times. After we got Skyler, it didn't seem to matter, but when you disappeared, we brought him in. He was pretty shocked about the whole thing, denied everything. It was really going nowhere. Then I thought to ask about the car."

"The one that tried to run me down?"

"Yes. We had already checked the make and model against the suspects and their relatives. We knew Charles didn't have a car like that, but turns out he dated someone who did."

"Tilly."

He nods. "We caught her trying to run from the fire. She's a pretty messed-up kid. Apparently her dad left when she was young, and her family life was fairly awful. Doc Ginger says it's a classic case."

"She latched onto Charles and couldn't give him up."

"Anyway, we were pretty sure it was Tilly, but we had no leads about where she'd taken you. She shares a tiny apartment with three other girls and has no family in the area. I pored over the recording of your date with Charles, and there was nothing. Then this tiny thing caught my attention."

"What's that?"

"Horses. Charles said his family had a ranch—"

"Let me guess. He took Tilly there?"

Damon nods. "Their second date."

"Home to meet the parents on the second date?" I shake my head. "No wonder she went crazy."

"Well, thanks to you she'll actually get some help now. And Skyler's been released with a big apology."

"Good. I'm glad. How're Natalie and Caroline?"

"Fine. Natalie's a little dehydrated and malnourished, but they had hardly a scratch on them from the fire. You, on the other hand," he brushes the hair out of my eyes, "are going to be in here for a while."

I groan. "The food will be terrible."

"I'll smuggle you in some Chinese."

My pulse quickens a bit, proof that I'm only mostly dead. "Oh yeah?"

"Of course. Your family came by while you were still out. The whole group was here. Even Auntie Muriel."

"Sweet of her. I'm sure she had a thing or two to say about how I wore a bandage wrong or something."

"She was pretty quiet, actually." He smiles. "I think you being a hero shut her up."

"Oh man." I laugh, and it hurts. "I'd have liked to see that."

"I told them everything, by the way. How you were helping us, how you figured it all out and found Natalie. That I wasn't really your boyfriend."

"Oh." Disappointment sweeps over me. "Well, that's good. Set the record straight."

"Mm-hmm." He pauses and then winds his fingers through mine. "But I did tell them that I was planning on asking you."

"Asking me what?"

"To let me be your boyfriend."

I bite my lip, disbelieving. "Lying to them again?"

"Nope. I wanted all the cards on the table."

"And what are all the cards?"

He blows out his breath. "I can't promise to be a different person tomorrow. Up until tonight, I didn't even think I wanted to be, but . . ."

"But what?"

Damon cracks half a smile. "But today, when I realized you'd been taken, and again tonight when I tried to move the wood . . ."

"Yes?" I prompt.

"I prayed," he says softly. "I prayed like I haven't prayed in years." The smile returns. "He listened."

I smile back. "He always does."

"So I guess what I'm asking . . ." He inches closer, gazing at me. "Will you let me try? To figure it all out?"

"Sure," I scoff. "I guess I kind of owe you a favor, since you saved my life and all."

Damon grins. "I guess you do."

"Then again, I did solve your case." I pause. "And why is that?"

After a moment he shakes his head, easing toward me. "I'm not going to say it."

"Come on," I wheedle.

His hand moves into my hair. "No."

"You can say it. I'm a good spy. It's okay, Damon. No one will hear you."

"Just stop talking," he says and kisses me.

And for once, I take his advice.

About the Author

A VETERAN OF THE UTAH dating trenches, Kari Iroz was once just another ordinary Mormon girl looking for love. She has lived these clichés and agonized through these awkward blind dates to laugh about them with you. Now a wife (he's dreamy) and mom to the two cutest girls in the world (disagree if you like, it's my bio), she writes comedy and speculative fiction. Check out her blog CrumpetsWithTheBard.com and share your own misadventures with her.